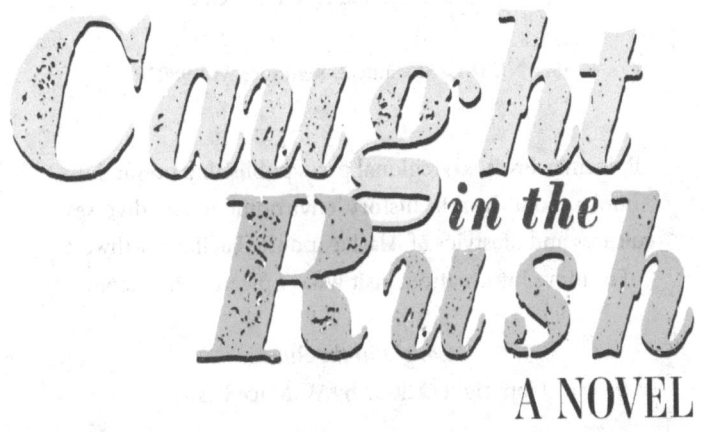

A NOVEL

A goldminer's adventure brought to life through detailed diary entries
as he travels from Seattle through the Chilkoot Pass and beyond . . .

W. MACE BRADY

Epicenter Press

Kenmore, WA

~~~Epicenter Press

6524 NE 181st St., Suite 2, Kenmore, WA 98028

Epicenter Press is a regional press publishing nonfiction books about the arts, history, environment, and diverse cultures and lifestyles of Alaska and the Pacific Northwest. For more information, visit www.EpicenterPress.com

Caught in the Rush

Cover design: Scott Book
Interior design: Melissa Vail Coffman

Library of Congress Control Number: 2022946249

ISBN: 978-1-684920-98-3 (Trade Paperback)
ISBN: 978-1-684920-99-0 (Ebook)

Produced in the United States of America

In memory of the William Mace Schooley family,
William Sr., Ann, Eva, Sam and John.

The Schooleys left their home in Nevada, Missouri,
to venture out west and settle in Seattle,
following Bill's adventures in the Klondike.

And in honor of my mother, Gladys A. (Schooley) Brady
who reproduced the diary,
researched his adventures,
retraced her father's journey
and inspired me to tell the story.

Contents

Preface

THIS NOVEL FOLLOWS THE DIARY of William Mace Schooley on his quest to reach the goldfields of the Yukon Territory. There is no evidence of any interactions between this author's characters and Soapy Smith's gang during his time in Skagway. However, the crimes the conmen of the town committed are real. Certain elements of the stories, some scenes and dialogue, locations, names and characters have been fictionalized, but the events in the story about Skagway are about real people committing real crimes, with real, disturbing consequences.

Prologue

Nevada, Missouri
1894

FOR THE PAST FEW YEARS, BILL Schooley was employed as a teacher and administrator in Missouri. He enjoyed working with young minds, developing lessons, and challenging students to strive for something they thought might be beyond their reach. But lately, he'd felt the sadness of those who had to leave school, to work on the family farms and businesses or move away in the hope that their parents could find work elsewhere.

Family gatherings around the table at home often turned to discussions about how living conditions hadn't gotten any better since the depression hit in 1893.[1] Times were tough. At first, the banks were being cautious about giving loans. Despite that, hundreds of banks and thousands of businesses were going under, the

---

1 **The Klondike Gold Rush—"The Panic of 1896"** To understand the grip the Klondike Gold Rush had on the American psyche, one must understand the economic conditions of the time. The United States had been gripped in a deep deflationary depression since 1893. Hundreds of banks had failed. Unemployment was over 14%. The stock market had collapsed. Thousands of businesses had gone under. By 1895, the US government was running out of gold to back the dollar, causing even more people to redeem their greenbacks for gold. Gainesville Coins. 120 years ago: the Klondike Gold Rush.

stock market had collapsed, jobs were scarce, and the value of the dollar was declining.

Following one of the Schooley's family dinners, a heated discussion took place about what the future might hold for those trying to get ahead. Bill's father had casually commented, "It might be easier to find gold out there in the ground somewhere than find any kind of a good job around here."

Talk like that was becoming common, and that thought definitely stuck with Bill and his friends. There had been more and more news about places like Montana, California and Alaska and what they had to offer, such as copper, silver and gold. Even Bill and his close friends, Lafe and Frank Coleman, had discussions about just that, the mining of gold, or some other ore. Gold seemed to be the most popular topic since it was directly tied to the value of the dollar.

As it became more difficult to feed a large family, like the Coleman's, Lafe and Frank more often talked about taking on the adventure of finding gold in Alaska. Why Alaska?

While there was talk about the potential of finding gold there, people weren't heading that direction there in the large numbers as they were in Montana and California. Maybe, just maybe, they'd have more luck out in that frontier than where the crowds have already gathered. As the three of them talked more, they became serious about the idea of taking on the challenge, experiencing some adventure, and at the same time, being independent of their families. Bill's considerations included leaving a low paying teacher's position.

"So, it's been decided then?" William Sr. said.

"Yes. Lafe and Frank's parents are all for it," Bill said. "It shouldn't be so bad now that the railroads have expanded all the way to Seattle, Washington. And I've got enough money from my two years teaching to get started with."

"Are the Coleman's going to be able to keep the farm running without their two oldest?"

Bill said, "Those younger than Lafe and Frank are now old enough to do the work around the farm."

"I'll admit, you've already proven yourself capable of being on your own these last couple of years. And, you won't be alone."

"No. I won't be alone," Bill look at his mother.

"Write often. We'll miss you," Ann said.

"I'll write as often as I can. I promise."

"When will you be leaving?"

"As soon as school gets out. That's a good time for traveling, and things should be thawing out further up north by the time we get there."

True to his word, the Coleman and Schooley families gathered at the depot two days after school got out. It was a tearful sendoff for the trio.

Chapter 1: Securing the Dust

Port of Seattle, Washington
September 1, 1897

I BEGAN TO FEEL UNEASY AS I made my way down the steamer's gangplank. The boxes were too heavy to carry, and even on a cart it was cumbersome to handle. The creaking noise from the wheels seemed to resonate for all to hear as my cart struggled to handle the weight. I could feel eyes shifting my way, watching.

I was self-conscious about the situation but also felt the need to watch the watchers more closely than they were watching me. *I have a right to be concerned, but I'm not overly worried*, I told myself. While I was afraid someone might be more than just curious about what I was off loading, I knew no one would be foolish enough to try anything in the middle of the day, with so many people around. I also knew I'd feel better once I got to a secure location. I hoped the appearance of a gun hanging from my belt would be enough to deter any thief. After all, I had everything we'd worked for over the last three years with me.

Methodically, I scanned my surroundings. In my mind's eye I pictured every person, every movement, every look, and stored it all, to let my mind sort out the irregularities. This had been set in motion when I first started wheeling the cart out from the captain's private storage room. I observed the man in the wheelhouse, a couple of deck-hands coiling ropes, the ship's steward, and three other lingering passengers. An older gentleman and his wife were thanking the ship's steward for his assistance, and a man was smoking his pipe along the ship's railing.

My eyes followed the descending walkway and scanned the small crowd of people at the base of the ramp. Some were passengers who had just disembarked. Others were deck hands, luggage handlers, and dockworkers. A few passengers looked back to take a final glance at the steamer, before turning to carry their bags into town or seek out a local horse-drawn buggy to move their goods. A businessman and his wife both smiled and gave me a knowing nod. I nodded in return. The harmonica player, who had provided entertainment to help pass the time on the long trip, looked my direction but then turned and joined a fiddler who had accompanied him onboard. As they moved away I sought out other curious eyes.

I knew some of the passersby along the shore would wonder about anyone arriving from the north. The nation's interest peaked two months earlier, on July 14th, with the arrival of the steamer *Excelsior* in San Francisco. Then again three days later when the steamer *Portland* docked in Seattle. As a result, onlookers were common at the arrival of any ship from Alaska. It was estimated that the *Excelsior* had off-loaded half a million dollars-worth of gold. The steamer *Portland* was estimated to have over a ton of gold from sixty-eight miners. This was off-loaded in front of 5,000 Seattle citizens. People had received advanced notice of its arrival from a telegram that had arrived from San Francisco following the arrival of the *Excelsior*. A reporter on board the San Francisco bound steamer had notified the Seattle newspapers of the arrival of the steamer *Portland*.

Now that the word was out, I knew I had a right to be nervous, but I tried not to show it. While some of the first fortunate miners held up their leather bags of gold with pride, I was more cautious. Too often I'd seen those less successful try to take advantage of those more fortunate than themselves. I would rather not have anyone know of my wealth.

One or two looked my way and then beyond, admiring the vessel. Their eyes didn't linger long enough to give me any cause for concern. But I still couldn't shake the bad feeling I had.

Completing my scan of the immediate area, I locked eyes with a man sitting on a crate, one that held of our personal goods offloaded earlier at the rear of a wagon and just a few paces from the bottom of the ramp. The man acknowledged me with a wave and a smile. I couldn't help but return the smile and let out a breath I hadn't realized I was holding. My partner, Frank Coleman, and I were sharing this burden together.

Frank jumped down from the back of the wagon, and together we loaded the last of our crates.

Seeing how concerned I was, Frank laughed and said, "Bill, you worry too much. What could happen here? Look at all the people around us, and we're in the middle of a big city now."

Although Frank and I had brought our gold to Seattle to secure, I felt it was more my responsibility. After all, I was two years older than Frank and felt responsible for him as well. His older brother, my other partner, wasn't with us. I was responsible for securing all of our gold.

It was obvious from the load on the buckboard that something significant was being moved. While placing the crate onboard, interest grew and more onlookers began to wander in our direction. My partner and I climbed aboard the rear of the carriage and I signaled for the driver to depart.

The driver shifted the reigns in his hands. The horses, sensing their master was ready to depart, became restless, causing people in front to part.

A man in the crowd, deciding to amuse himself, yelled out,

"Got gold there, do ya?" he said with a laugh. His witty comment just made me more anxious.

Frank and I both smiled as if laughing at a mildly funny joke, then signaled for the driver to get the wagon moving.

The driver shook the reins, and the wagon slowly left the pier and made its way toward Seattle's busy streets. I could see my partner look excitedly toward the big city. I commented, "It shouldn't take us too long. Once we finish at the bank, we can get settled in."

"I want to do more than just get settled in," Frank exclaimed with a grin.

All I could do was shake my head.

"Remember the last time we were here? We were too busy preparing to go north to see all of it, and now there's even more here to see. It's really grown,"

"It sure has," I had to admit. "We'll get to it soon enough though." All I wanted to do was secure the dust, get a good meal, warm bath and comfortable bed to sleep in. I knew that Frank was interested in more than just rest. He wanted to experience the big city.

"I'm just glad we made arrangements for the wagon to be waiting for us so we can get this business out of the way."

I didn't want to spoil his excitement. Being younger than me, he hadn't had the opportunities I had of experiencing a big city.

A series of telegraphs from Juneau to Dexter Horton of the First National Bank of Seattle allowed us to have transportation waiting. We had selected this bank because we'd heard it was the longest established bank in Seattle.

"Can you imagine trying to move all this without having made prior arrangements?" I said. I was referring to the crates and luggage we had brought with us.

"I agree, Bill, this is the way to do it," Frank said.

"When we're done at the bank, I expect Mr. Horton will tell us where we can best stay, eat and what to see." Frank sat back and stared out across town, looking as carefree as I'd ever seen him. The wagon turned north, away from the pier.

Little was said after that. We just took in the scenery as the horses pulled us along the waterfront and turned east onto Washington Street.

A short time later, the buckboard completed its journey up Washington to the corner of Commercial and Washington. The first National Bank of Seattle stood out as the city's first non-wood structure. Upon arrival, Mr. Horton, accompanied by two workers, stepped out to greet us.

Introductions were made all around. Horton, after inquiring if we needed the wagon any further, instructed the driver that he was no longer needed once the crates were removed. The two helpers assisted us with unloading the boxes. Frank carrying his personal luggage, followed the two workers as they carried the first load into the bank. I stayed with Mr. Horton until the two workers returned for the final load. I then retrieved my luggage and followed the workers and Horton inside.

Inside, each of the four crates was opened to reveal multiple leather pouches of gold dust. Each had been carefully weighted prior to being transported from Sunrise, Alaska. Mr. Horton verified the accuracy of the treasure's weight. It was to be equally divided into three parts, representing the two of us who were present as well as our third partner, Frank's older brother by five years, who was still up north finalizing the sale of our last claim.

It took some time before Mr. Horton spoke. He finally said, "In three equal parts, that's 296 pounds per man, or about 888 pounds, total."

Frank and I looked at each other in amazement. I said, "Lafe will be mighty pleased, don't you think, Frank?"

"Yes, I do believe my brother will certainly be pleased," Frank said very formally, yet his giddiness was evident.

"Where are you gentlemen headed from here?" Mr. Horton asked.

"We're preparing to go home," Bill responded.

"Then you're not from here?"

"We do like it here, but don't know where we'll settle as yet," Bill said. "For now, home is in Missouri."

"Very good, sir. With all your travels, I take it you're not married then?"

"No. No time for any courting in the gold fields."

"No, I suppose not . . . but," Mr. Horton smiled and added, "if word gets out about your success, I do believe you'll have plenty of interest."

To that, we laughed. "Still got too much to do to even think about that," Frank said.

Horton handed his newest clients copies of the receipts. Frank took his brother's as well as his own, "If there's anything I can help you with, just let me know."

"Well, you could direct us to the telegraph office," I said. "We need to let Lafe know that our gold is secure."

"Sure can. It's not far from here."

"Anything else you need from us?" I asked.

"Not a thing. You've signed everything and it's been witnessed, so there's nothing else you need to do here."

All three stood, and Dexter Horton walked Frank and me out the front door. From there, he pointed out a couple of hotels he'd recommended, the telegraph office as well as a few other city attractions nearby. Horton shook hands with us, and we said our goodbyes.

Frank and I continued to stand on the walkway and take in September's late afternoon sun. We both commented on how refreshing it was to have the warmth of the sun mixed with the cool breeze that was blowing in off the sound.

"I think once we send Lafe a telegram we can check into the Seattle Hotel, have a hot meal, hot bath and relaxing evening," I said.

"We could send a telegram to our parents while we're there, too," Frank suggested.

"I thought about that," I replied, "but some information I don't want to send by telegraph. It's too public. Besides, we don't know when we'll be able to leave here yet."

"Good point. Sending a letter is probably a better idea," Frank admitted.

"Going back home again sounds grand," I said. "As soon as we get settled into the hotel, I'll write home. I'd love to see my folk's faces when they read how we've done."

"After I get cleaned up a bit, I'd just as soon walk around town. Care to join me?" Frank asked.

"Be glad to," I said. "It shouldn't take me long. A walk about town might do both of us some good after being confined to that steamer for so long."

We both picked up our luggage and headed for the hotel Horton recommended.

Heading North

"One morning a gale was blowing. We were laying close up to the wind, and the first table was trying to eat. The hatches were closed down and the ship was tossing around at a terrible rate. I was still in my bed, when suddenly she gave a terrific lurch. The big range turned upside down and set the ship on fire, but the floor was so wet it could not burn fast."

—Letter to Mrs. W.M. Schooley,
from Juneau's Circle City Hotel, dated November 7th, 1897

Chapter 2: The Return

Seattle, Washington
September 8, 1897

FOLLOWING A WEEK OF RELAXATION, adjusting to city life, and touring Seattle as well as a few outlying sites, Frank and I felt well rested from the ordeals of mining in Alaska and traveling. We still talked of returning home and what we might do once Lafe joined us. How we'd travel together to reunite with our families. But we were still almost 2,000 miles away with a great deal to jointly discuss before committing to the long journey. The three of us had already agreed that whatever we did, we'd do together. A few stipulations were predetermined in this decision-making process. We'd have to decide if the time was right to make such a trip. This, at times, made me feel conflicted.

If we did determine that it was time to return home, it would take a few weeks by train. Assuming the connections were timely and available, across a land where settlers collide with the unknowns of the wild west. That was a lot to think about.

It was midday. The sky was as blue as it ever was, and could be admired as long as the winds off the sound kept the burning coal smoke from all the businesses from settling over the booming town. Coal was still the most cost-efficient means to heat homes and businesses. Seattle, as a result of being the new 'Gateway to the Klondike' was now the largest and fastest growing city in the Pacific Northwest.

I sat atop a stack of boxes, just outside Seattle's Cooper and Levy Outfitters store, taking in my surroundings. I enjoyed watching people as they made their way about town and admired how much the city had changed since we last passed through three years earlier. I was trying to process the comment my partner had just made.

"We're not going home."

I gazed toward the electric trolley that Frank had exited moments earlier. It had begun to make its way east on Yesler Way, heading toward the Seattle Hotel.

"You mean, we're going back north," I said. He was not at all surprised with my conclusion. I continued to look toward the trolley as it followed the rails, before making its climb up the long hill once known as Mill Street.

"You didn't buy any tickets, did you?" Frank said. I knew he was wondering if I had decided to return home on my own. Frank knew that I had visited the Northern Pacific Railroad ticket office, just next door, while he was at the telegraph office. Frank's brother had promised to keep us apprised of progress at Sunrise regarding the sale of our last claim before joining us.

"No, of course not." I said, "I just checked the schedule and connections back to Missouri. Besides, I wouldn't have bought any tickets this far in advance unless we knew when your brother was joining us." I removed my hat and ran a hand through my thick brown hair. My hopes about returning home had grown, but I wasn't about to share that with Frank.

"Good," Frank said. He was obviously relieved.

My eyes were still fixed on the trolley. "Evidently, you heard from him, right?"

"Right."

"Did he sell the last claim?" I asked.

"I'm not sure."

"Not sure?" I looked over to my partner. "What do you mean, not sure?"

"He said he got a bond for it from a man from Seattle. What's that mean?"

"That means he got a certificate promising payment. In other words, it's as good as sold," I stated.

"I hope the man is good for it," Frank said.

"I would certainly hope so. Even a handshake is important to honor up there. Your word means a lot around here too."

Frank thought for a moment, "Yeah, that's true."

"Is he coming down?" I asked.

"No," Frank said. He then added, "None of them are."

"So, let me guess," I said, "that means Lafe's expecting us to come back up."

"Yes." Frank reached into his inner jacket pocket and began unfolding the telegram before continuing. "He says they're all going. The whole lot."

"Well, I guess that changes things doesn't it." Just like that, *thoughts of returning home flashed through my mind then vanished.* I thought about what my father had said, *leave with no regrets before you return. It's a long way back home.*

"Yup. Just like we all agreed. If they go, we all go," Frank said.

"Strength in numbers." I concurred. I remembered how we discussed the fact that we stood a better chance of success over all those others who thought it was a get-rich-quick opportunity. *We're better experienced. If there is more gold there, we have a better chance of getting to it.*

"It's better that way."

"Definitely."

"You don't sound so sure," Frank said.

"Oh, I'm sure alright. It's just that . . . Ma should be receiving my letter soon, telling her that we'll be coming home."

"Oh, yeah, right."

Your word is your honor.

I could still remember the first of many times I heard my father say that. He was standing outside the hardware store. I stood at his side and watched as he shook another man's hand regarding building him a fence.

"It shows you're trustworthy. Hold to your word and you'll find others will respect you. When I give my handshake or say I'm going to do something it's a contract. It's binding. You can count on it," my father emphasized.

"I guess I best send her another letter right away," I offered weakly.

"Yeah, but you might want to wait until we book our passage north.

Then at least we can tell her when and where we'll be. They wouldn't be expecting us anytime soon anyway," Frank said.

"Where and when is Lafe expecting us to join him?"

"Juneau, at the Franklin Hotel. He said it is not far up to Front Street from where we off load. Once Lafe arrives, he'll start keeping the desk clerk informed about his whereabouts or leave a note if he isn't there."

"Is he sure we can get a room there?"

"Here, you can read for yourself." Frank handed me the telegram and said, "He said he'd take a boat to Juneau then go up to look around Skagway before returning to Juneau. Looks like he's expecting to have plenty of time to spare before we get there."

I scanned the telegraph. "I see that the others will be taking the land route south. That'll take 'em awhile."

"I suppose if we're going back up we'd best start looking at resupplying." Frank looked back at the store behind them. "Seems we've met at the right spot. Let's go in and price their goods. Then we can start looking at how we can store and ship everything when we head north."

I climbed down from our vantage point and stretched my five-and-a-half-foot frame, looked around and said, "We very well could have missed each other completely if I hadn't perched myself at the top of this stack."

Frank scanned the supplies that were piled along the sidewalk and nodded. They were blocking any view of the street from the walkway. The stack of boxes and bags almost extended the whole length of the street.

We walked around the piles of goods and made our way to the store's entrance. It was jammed with those who were also here to gather supplies for their move north, where they too had dreams of making their fortune.

The store was well stocked. Most of the businesses that had been devastated during the 1889 fire, which covered 29 blocks and affected over 5,000 jobs, had been rebuilt within the first year. The seven-year-old Cooper and Levy Outfitters building was an example of one of those that now met the new brick-building standards following that fire. Even the streets were now wider and no longer twisted their way about the old wooden structures that had lined the winding streets. The fire had resulted in a better city.

Frank stopped in front of the counter that held a list of items suggested for the Klondike. "This should help."

"Good. We can use this to write prices on as well," I said. "Then we can get started on finding passage to Juneau. From what the papers say and based on the looks of the outfitter stores, I can see that Seattle is quickly turning into that 'gateway' everyone's been talking about."

"It sure is," Frank agreed.

"Let's get an early start in the morning. There's a lot of waterfront to cover, to find a ship heading north," I said.

For the past week I'd been thinking of home. Although I was beginning to refocused on going back north, part of me was disappointed. *Have I accomplished all I wanted to up there?* I wondered. I had made plenty. I no longer had anything to prove—three years of successful mining had proven that.

I took a deep sigh, and tried to push the dream of returning home out of my mind. I had become accustomed to overcoming hard times in many ways. *Perhaps I could make this into an interesting, maybe even fun trip this time,* I thought. *How much more gold do I need anyway?*

PIONEER OUTFITTERS SUPPLIES

Equipment

1	Handsaw	2	Hatchets	2	Shovels	1	Whip Saw
2	Handled Axes	2	Draw Knives	1	Jack Plane	30	lbs. Nails (assorted sizes)
1	Gold Scale	2	Compasses	1	Chalk Line		Set Awls & Tools
2	Butcher Knives	2	Hunting Knives	2	Pocket Knives	1	Gold Dust Bags (buckskin)
1	Measuring Tape	1	Brace and 4 Bits	2	Money Belts	3	Medicine Case
2	Cartridge Belts	1	Caulking Iron	2	Gold Pans	2	ft. of 5/8-inch Rope
1	Wet stone	2	Prospector's Picks	2	Picks & Handles	1	Stove (Yukon)
6	Towels	2	Pairs Snow Glasses		Coffee pots	150	Granite Buckets
2	Grub Bags		Camp Kettle	2	Frying Pans	1	Granite Plates
15	lbs. Pitch	1	Galvanized Pails	2	Large Spoons	4	Granite Cups
2	Bread Pans	4	lbs. Oakum	2	Knives & Forks		
2	Scissors	20	Pack Straps		Table & Teaspoons		
	Fish Lines & Hooks						

Clothing

3 Suits, Underwear, extra heavy	2 Pairs Leopard Seal Waterproof	1 Pair Hip Boots
2 Extra heavy double-breasted Flannel Overshirts	2 Pair Overalls	2 Pair Rubber Shoes
1 Extra heavy Mackinaw Overshirt	1 Fur Cap	2 Pairs Blankets
4 Pairs All-wool Mittens	1 Pair Mackinaw Pants	1 Wool Scarf
1 Pair Leather Suspenders	1 Extra heavy all-wool double Sweater	1 Mackinaw Coat extra heavy
6 Pairs long German knit Socks	1 Suit Oil Clothing and Hat	1 Waterproof Blanket-lined Coat
1 Extra Heavy Packing Bag	1 Canvas Sleeping Bag	
2 Pairs German knit and shrunk Stockings, leather heels	1 Doz., Bandana Handkerchiefs	

Provisions

Flour	800 lbs.	Bacon	300 lbs.	Evaporated Onions	20 lbs.
Corn Meal	50 lbs.	Dried Beef	60 lbs.	Beef Extract	3 lbs.
Rolled Oats	80 lbs.	Dried Salt Pork	50 lbs.	Evaporated Apples	50 lbs.
Pilot Bread	50 lbs.	Roast Coffee	50 lbs.	Evaporated Peaches	50 lbs.
Baking Powder	20 lbs.	Tea	25 lbs.	Evaporated Apricots	50 lbs.
Yeast Cakes	6 lbs.	Condensed Milk	50 lbs.	Ginger	2 lbs.
Baking Soda	6 lbs.	Butter, hermetically sealed	40 lbs.	Jamaica Ginger	3 lbs.
Rice	100 lbs.	Salt	40 lbs.	Evaporated Vinegar	12 lbs.
Beans	200 lbs.	Ground Pepper	3 lbs.	Matches	25 lbs.
Split Peas	50 lbs.	Ground Mustard	3 lbs.	Candles, 2 boxes	
Evaporated Potatoes	50 lbs.			containing 240 candles	80 lbs.

Total Weight: 2,327 lbs.

Source: William B. Haskell, Two Years in the Klondike Gold-Fields, 1896-1898 (Fairbanks, University of Alaska Press, 1998).

Chapter 3: Passage North

Seattle Waterfront
September 10, 1897

"NO PASSAGE AVAILABLE?"
"Not for the next few weeks."

"That's the same answer we've heard at the nine other steamship companies we've visited the last couple of days," Frank commented to the young man behind the desk. Turning to me he added, "Lafe will be wondering what's happened to us."

"We can always telegraph him in Juneau. He'll understand once he knows what's going on here. There's a reason they call it a stampede," I explained.

"Everybody's in a hurry," the young man behind the counter said.

The stories of gold in the Klondike stirred people throughout the globe. It seemed that everyone was drawn to the possibility of becoming rich. Every conceivable method of transport north rapidly filled to capacity. Klondike fever had begun to spread with the stories from each returning miner. News even traveled to all corners of the globe. Soon these ships and many others would return north filled to capacity.

The Seattle Post Intelligencer reported that the mayor of Seattle, Bill D. Wood, in San Francisco for a convention when the Excelsior arrived, telegraphed his resignation and headed to Alaska without even stopping in Seattle. The fever spread across the United State quicker than any virus. Within ten days, 1,500 persons departed Seattle for the gold fields. Local merchants quickly sold out of mining supplies.[2]

"My brother's expecting us to return and meet him in Juneau by the end of next week," Frank commented.

The eyes of the young man behind the counter opened wide. "You've already been up there?"

"Yup. For the last three years. We just came down to resupply and . . ."

Frank stopped and looked over to me.

I understood Frank's hesitation. He too believed it was best not to brag about the gold, he added, "We also wanted to see if we would like to settle in Seattle when we tire of prospecting."

"Did you have any luck?" the young man asked expectantly.

"More than some . . . not as much as others," That wasn't entirely true. I saw that the young man looked disappointed. ". . . but enough to make us want to keep a hand in it."

"So, you found enough gold to live off of? The young man seemed more hopeful.

"We found our fair share."

"What's it like? Would you recommend going?"

"It's not as easy as many make it out to be," I spoke carefully, not wanting to mislead the young man who seemed intrigued by the idea of striking it rich.

"The gold's not as easy to find as you might think, and the winters aren't kind. The nights are short, and the temperatures can fall as low as 30 degrees below zero. At least where we were," I added.

2 In 1896, a year before the stampeders travelled through Seattle to the Klondike, the city's total business receipts were $300,000. Within eight months of the S.S. Portland's arrival in August 1897, Seattle businesses generated $25 million. (Klondike Gold Rush Seattle Unit, National Historical Park. US Department of the Interior).

A series of questions followed. I carefully answered as best I could.

Finally, the grateful young man thought of a way to repay our kind attention. "You know, there is one place you may find helpful in getting up there quicker," he smiled.

"Any help you could give us would be greatly appreciated," I said.

"There's a new steamship that's still being worked on down the way," he gestured toward the south. "I know it hasn't been scheduled yet."

The young man saw that we were listening intently, so he continued. "It's moored at the Moran Brothers' Shipyard, just down the street. I can call them if you'd like to see when it might be ready and where it's headed."

"That would be great. We'd appreciate it," I said.

"Give me a moment."

"Sure."

The young man turned and stepped through the door behind him, stopped just inside the room, and turned to face a box attached to the near wall.

He pulled a black listening device off its side, set it against his ear, cranked a rotating handle a few times and waited. A moment later he spoke into the mechanism protruding from the center of the box and asked to be connected to a specific number. He then waited again.

Frank and I couldn't help but listen to the young man's end of the conversation. It seemed he needed to speak loudly to be heard.

When he came back to the front desk he said, "You just helped me get some business," he smiled. "They're putting the finishing touches on the steamer and we can start booking right away. It should be ready by the end of next week. I'm sure it'll fill up quickly once word gets out. It's destined for Sitka, but you can catch a mail run to Juneau from there."

"That's great!" Frank and I exclaimed in unison.

"We expect that it'll be fully booked within the next couple of days. They'll have no problem sailing by 8:00 AM Monday. Your cabin selection can be made as soon as I get the vessel diagram."

"Where's the ship located?" Frank asked.

"It's about a mile south of here, toward the tide flats."

"Do you think they'd mind if we walked down there to take a look?" I asked.

"I don't see why not. The machine shop lies at the end of Charles Street. You can't miss it. The name of the vessel is the *Laurel*. You'll see it moored just down the pier from the machine shop with the 'Moran Brothers Shipyard' sign on it."

"We'll head down there, and we can even bring you back a diagram, if they're available," I offered. I was beginning to get excited about the prospect of seeing a new vessel and selecting our cabin.

"That would sure save me some time. I'll give them a call and let them know you're coming."

Leaving the terminal office, we started walking south along the waterfront.

The walk was a comfortable distance and only took about a twenty minutes. A slight mist filled the air, and the breeze off the Puget Sound was cool. Although the temperatures had dropped about ten degrees since our arrival in the middle of September, I noticed that the moist climate, with its overcast and mountains that blocked the winds, did not allow the temperatures to fluctuate significantly.

Drawing near the expected location, we saw the single smoke stacks on the new vessel before we found the Charles Street sign.

We turned right on Charles and spotted the Moran Brothers' sign on the side of the machine shop. Just beyond, the pier extended to where the steamer was moored.

As we approached the building, I stopped a passing workman and asked where we could find the man responsible for the steamer *Laurel*. The workman pointed in the direction of the near corner of the building, closest to the steamer and said, "You'll find the site superintendent in the corner office."

Three men were inside—one sitting behind a desk. Two others were standing side-by-side, one talking with the man at the desk. We waited patiently for a break in the conversation.

After a short time, the man at the desk asked, "Can I help you gentlemen?"

"Yes. Hopefully you just received a call about our inquiry regarding the steamer *Laurel* that's scheduled for a run up to Sitka."

"You must be the gentlemen who wanted to take a look at her."

"That's us," Frank responded.

"Well then, I'm Peter Moran," the man said. He stood, reached across the desk and shook hands with each of us. "I'd be happy to give you a tour. I've got to board her and check on a few things anyway. You'll find that seeing the actual cabin is a lot better than looking at a diagram. You realize how fortunate you are? Not everyone gets to select their own cabin on its first voyage."

Peter Moran stood and walked around his desk to take the lead. "Let's get started," he said.

Frank and I followed.

I could see the anticipation in Frank's face. He was keen on returning north. After all he hadn't left all of his family behind in Missouri, like I had. He would at least be with his brother. His connection to home was not strong, having suffered the backbreaking work of tending to a farm that no longer produced a product that was worth its salt,[3] and a father who became more depressed and withdrawn as the farm continued to fail.

When Frank's father sold a large portion of the land to make ends meet[4] the two oldest boys determined that the time was right for them to find an occupation elsewhere. The family agreed that the remaining four siblings could adequately tend to the remaining land, and that two fewer mouths to feed would make it easier for the family to manage.

---

3 **Worth one's salt:** Fig. worth (in productivity) what it costs to keep or support a person.
4 **Make (both) ends meet:** to have just enough money to pay for the things that you need.

The obvious hard truth of the matter was that the family's lack of warmth made it easier for Lafe and Frank to depart. It seemed that most of their time was spent focusing on what needed to be done around the house and how to keep the farm running rather than how anyone felt, or thought about anything. It was no surprise then that the brothers sought out other opportunities as well as a schoolmate and friend, me, to join them.

As I reflected further on my situation, I realized my emotions were more mixed about going back up. At twenty-three years old, I had already been away from my family for three years, and my family ties were strong. Although I'd lived somewhat on my own for the two years prior to my leaving Missouri, I spent much of my free time with my family, helping my father around the farm and tending to the crops whenever I could. But, I knew that teaching in nearby Enoch, Missouri, was as uncertain as the income farmers got from the sale of their crops. And with uncertainty many were vacating the region to seek jobs elsewhere. As a result, Lafe, Frank and I had all discussed the opportunities that led us to plan a joint venture that would benefit everyone.

When I shared our travel plans with my father, he sensed my reluctance to leave home and encouraged me to seek opportunities beyond what I could find locally.

"Besides, you'll always have this place to return to if you don't find a better life elsewhere," my father said.

With that I sensed that it was an appropriate time for me to venture out, especially knowing that I wouldn't be alone. Besides, I had saved money from teaching, and my younger brothers were old enough to help around the farm. At the age of twenty, the situation was ripe for me to go out on my own.

It was an obvious choice for us to venture west since we lived in the Missouri area. St. Louis was not far away and was considered the 'Gateway to the West'. We'd met many who had moved through the area on their way west. Their stories were mostly about the hope for a better life.

Reflecting back on all this, I couldn't help but reconsider why I had been so set on returning home when everyone around me was heading north.

While Peter Moran lead the way along the pier to the ship, Frank and I walked silently behind. Frank must have sensed my pensiveness. He knew me well enough to understand my lack of enthusiasm. "Well, I guess you can start writing your letter home now, unless you've got second thoughts." He was giving me the opportunity to opt out.

I gave a slight smile and said, "Yeah. I've thought about what I'm going to say. One thing my Pa said to me was about not having any regrets. If I do return home now, I'll always wonder 'what if'. I have to go back, but admit I was looking forward to being with my family again."

"So you're committed to returning?"

"Yes," I replied, "but like you suggested, I'm just not sending the letter out until I know for sure we've got a guaranteed birth on the ship and we know our actual departure date." Frank looked at me a little longer, then nodded and gave a small grin before turning away.

We arrived at the gangplank. Peter continued up the narrow ramp and Frank and I 'walked the plank'[5] together.

"I'm relieved to hear that. It wouldn't be the same without you," Frank said.

While looking about the brand-new steamship, I knew that I had committed myself to going back north. It wouldn't be easy, yet I certainly didn't realize it would be so hard.

---

5 **'Walk the plank'**: a euphemism—a mild or indirect word or expression substituted for one considered to be too harsh or blunt when referring to something unpleasant—like a method of execution practiced on special occasion by pirates, mutineers, and other rogue seafarers.

Chapter 4: Scope out Skagway

Skagway, Alaska
September 17, 1897

LAFE GAZED TOWARD SHORE, watching the seagulls circling above the end of the wharf. The birds were seeking an opportunity to grab anything they could that might be left by the fishermen who were cleaning the day's catch.

"It's full of nothin' but crooks."

The words captured Lafe's attention. He looked over to see an older, bearded gentleman standing just a few feet away, gesturing toward the town.

"I'm surprised to see so many bad apples in one bunch," the younger man, next to the older man exclaimed.

Lafe scooted closer and began listening more intently, thinking he might hear something of value.

"Well over 5,000 in population,[6] and they just keep pourin' in," the younger man continued.

Lafayette S. Coleman was anxious to scout out the area before returning to reunite with his brother and partner in Juneau. The twenty-six-year-old prospector towered above the ship's railing,

6 **Skagway population:** by 1898 Skagway booms to 8,000 to 10,000 population.

standing just short of six feet. He was as tough as any outdoorsman could be, having endured three hard and cold years in Alaska's gold fields.

The weather was cloudy, with a light drizzle, and a temperature of 46 degrees. Lafe reached into his pocket and pulled out his partner's pocket watch. For a brief moment, he admired its intricate etchings, gave its top a small twist, and viewed the time. "It's accurate. Guaranteed to not lose more than thirty seconds in a week's time," he remembered hearing his partner tell him.

The mail steamer Queen had taken longer than scheduled, the vessel filled to capacity. It didn't begin off-loading until twenty minutes following its scheduled arrival time—his timepiece showed 11:50 AM.

A few passengers held back to stand topside and watch their fellow passengers debark until the crowds dissipated. The dock and its walkway stretched more than two city blocks, so it was difficult to scope out the town from the ship's deck. Three neighboring piers north of them stretched almost as far as the one they were moored to. Lafe could see enough sand to determine that the water had receded quite a ways already, but knew the tide could still go lower, based on the length of the piers. He decided to question the men near him on the deck.

"Excuse me, sir," Lafe began. "I couldn't help but overhear you talk about Skagway as if you're familiar with it."

"You might say that," the older man smiled. "Been here long enough."

Lafe met his smile with one of his own.

"My son, Ben here, and I built our cabin here in 1892."

"My name is Lafayette Coleman. My friends call me Lafe."

"Pleased to meet ya. I'm Captain William Moore. Just call me Bill."

They shook hands.

"This here's my youngest son, Ben," the Captain said with genuine pride.

They both exchanged pleasantries and shook hands.

"Until my brother and partner join me in another week or so, I'm here to see where we can lay a claim and find the best route to get to Dawson City. They'll be coming up from Seattle with supplies."

"You and everyone else from the states," the older man exclaimed.

"Yes, I noticed that."

"Well, first off, you'll find that layin' claim here in Skagway is not the best place. Seems claim jumpers are everywhere."

"I heard you say it's full of nothing but crooks," Lafe admitted.

"Yup. You see all that land filled with tents and shacks?"

"I do."

Well, it's supposed to be mine. All 160 acres of it. My cabin's in the middle of that mess. But they don't seem to care. I was just returnin' from Juneau where I met with a lawyer about a law suit against them."

"Sorry to hear that. I wish you luck," Lafe stated, sincerely. "Where would you recommend I go?"

"First off, if you're lookin' for the shortest route, that would be Chilkoot. But it's also the steepest, too steep for packhorses. Most folks here understand that White Pass is a bit longer, but figure they can use pack animals, making it easier on them. That's why most are here. They're lookin' to take their goods in the easiest way possible without havin' to pack it themselves. But, that's just a waste of a good animal if you ask me." He went on about the horrendous conditions the animals had to endure and how costly it was to even acquire a pack animal.

Lafe shook his head. Seeing that the Captain was a caring man he continued to listen intently.

Moore continued. "If you're bringin' in supplies, this is still the best place to offload . . . even if you're goin' to Dyea. If you want to lay claim locally and lay up till the spring thaw, go to Dyea, not Skagway. It's about 10 miles further, but closer to Chilkoot Pass.

There's water access in Dyea, but it's not deep enough for a steamer like this. You can offload a barge there, but it'll cost you to move it off the beach. From what I hear, the going rate is $20 per hour if the tides out and $50 per hour if the tide's comin' in."

"Thanks, I appreciate the information. That'll make it easier for my partners and me to make a decision."

The Captain gave a tight smile, shook his head and added, "Most men here just seem to follow the crowds . . . don't take any of my advice."

The older man looked pensive then thoughtfully added, "Tell you what, when you get off the boat, go to that shed on the wharf over there," he pointed. "Ask for Mr. Hill. He's the manager of Moore's Wharf. Tell him I sent you. He'll take care of you. He also knows who the honest transporters of goods are."

"Thank you, Captain Moore. I surely appreciate it."

Ben, still looking toward the wharf, interjected, "I'll give you one more piece of advice if I might, sir."

"What's that?" Lafe queried.

"See that man over there, next to Mr. Hill's office?" He nodded in the same direction.

"I see Mr. Taft, a man I met on the ship on the way up from Juneau," replied Lafe.

"Well, if he's a friend of yours, you might want to head him off."

"What do you mean?" asked Lafe.

"He's bein' cornered by a con man."

"The man standing next to him?"

"Yeah. He's known as 'Professor' Jackson. He's one of many who are here to find a way to hoodwink you out of your money. I've gotten to know their ways over the last few months."

"He looks friendly enough," Lafe said.

"If you look close enough you'll see he has a small scar on his forehead, just over his left eye. Heard he got that in a situation that got away from him. But he's a friendly enough fellow though . . . and, he knows how to pick 'em."

"What do you mean by that?"

"Take a look at that Mr. Taft fella. He's traveling by himself. These fellas know that someone traveling by himself is more likely to appreciate getting help from someone familiar with the area."

"I see," Lafe said.

"That's right. And, Mr. Taft is dressed too nicely. That always gets their attention. Once they find you've got money, they'll make a friend of you and then take you some place where they can get it. Usually it's to their dishonest friends who have shipping companies, hotels, or gambling dens."

Lafe thought about what he could do to help Mr. Taft.

Ben's father shook his head and added, "One man even built a telegraph office. The only trouble is, there's no telegraph line. He charges $5 to send a telegram. There's no immediate way to know that no one was actually contacted at the other end until it's too late."

"Hasn't anyone complained to the authorities?" Lafe asked.

"Not that I know of."

"I think if anyone ever discovered it, they'd be too embarrassed to report it to the law . . . of course that wouldn't do you any good anyway, since the sheriff's as crooked as the rest of 'em."

"That paints a pretty clear picture. I sure appreciate it and will heed your advice," Lafe stated to his newfound friends. "Thanks again."

"My pleasure," the old man said. "I wish you good luck and good fortune."

They shook hands.

Lafe picked up his overnight bag and departed, to catch up with Mr. Taft.

Chapter 5: The Con Man

Skagway, Alaska
September 17, 1897

LAFE COULD SEE, WHILE DISEMBARKING, THAT the con man had Mr. Taft blocked near the wharf office, making like they were best friends. He kept slapping him on the shoulder and laughing loudly.

As Lafe approached, it became evident that the con man had him in his clutches. They began to turn and move together toward the town center. One of the con man's hands was resting on Taft's shoulder.

Lafe was just 20 feet from them. He yelled out, "Mr. Taft. Wait."

Taft stopped, turned, and saw who was calling, "Oh. Hi, Lafe."

"Can I have a word with you?"

The conman answered for him, "Can't now, we're heading into town." He began to edge Taft back down the pier.

"Why don't you join us for a drink. We were just heading for the saloon," Taft added.

"Sure, you're welcome to join us if you like," the con man said, hesitantly.

Lafe pointed toward the wharf's office and said, "I want to introduce you to someone."

"Oh, sure. Mr. Jackson, will you excuse me?" Mr. Taft took a step toward Lafe.

"Sure, I'll just wait for you here."

Lafe explained, "We're going to be a while. You best go ahead."

Taft looked puzzled but said, "Go ahead, I'll catch up with you."

Lafe detected a scowl from the con man but quickly turned his back on him and led Taft toward the office. He opened the door and quickly stepped inside. Taft followed.

There was only one man at the counter. Lafe said, "Mr. Hill?"

"Yes, can I help you?"

"Yes, sir," Lafe said. "I was referred to you by Captain William Moore."

"Yes, he's my boss. What can I do for you?"

"He said I could get information from you about transporting goods off the ship and moving them to Dyea. He said you might recommend someone. Someone reputable."

"I sure can. Do you need to move it now?"

"No, not now, perhaps within the next few week or so though."

"Sure thing. If you give me a specific date, I can have a man or two ready for you. If not, I can at least write your name down and make sure you jump to the front of the line, especially if you're a friend of Captain Moore's." Mr. Hill grabbed a piece of paper and slid it across the counter.

"Great. Mr. Taft, I understand you may have supplies that need moving as well, if I remember our earlier conversations correctly."

"Sure, that may be helpful. The name is William Howard Taft."

"Mr. Hill, I wanted Mr. Taft here to meet you as well, since I understand honesty, at times, may be hard to come by in this town."

"You must have had quite a talk with Captain Moore, I see," Mr. Hill replied.

"Yes, I did."

Mr. Taft looked at Lafe quizzically. Lafe spoke softly, "I'll explain later."

Lafe picked up the paper, folded it, and placed it in his pocket.

They left the office. Once outside, Lafe stopped and explained to Taft what he had learned about the con man from Captain Moore.

"It looks as though I owe *you* a drink," Taft said.

Rather than make him feel uncomfortable, since he didn't know that Lafe wasn't a drinker he said, "I appreciate the offer, but we don't know which saloon he'll be in. His presence will just make things more . . . uncomfortable, if you know what I mean."

"I do. Thank you, Lafe."

"My pleasure."

They both began walking the long pier, heading toward shore.

The Kansas City Sunday Journal.

VOLUME XI., NO. 123.   SUNDAY,   KANSAS CITY, OCTOBER 17, 1897.—TWENTY PAGES   SUNDAY,   PRICE FIVE CENTS.

The Journal Prints the Full Associated Press Report Seven Days in the Week.

FOUND WEALTH IN KLONDIKE.

Three Missourians Returning From the Frozen North With $90,000 Each in Dust.

Nevada, Mo., Oct. 16.—William Schooley, Frank Coleman and Late Coleman, who left Vernon county three years ago for the Alaskan gold fields, write from Seattle, Wash., to relatives here that they have just arrived there, and will shortly be at home. Each of them will bring with him $30,000 in gold dust and nuggets. They are all three single men, whose parents still reside in this county.

> Article (above) enlarged from boxed location below, right.

MYSTERIOUS DEATH.

HE WAS FOUND UNCONSCIOUS.

STARTLING INTERRUPTION.

BERGER MURDER CASE.

COLD WAVE AT LAST.

VERY HOT IN THE EAST.

STOCKHOLDERS SUED.

230 PEOPLE PERISH.

ONLY TWO ON BOARD SAVED.

A BRAND NEW OKLAHOMA YARN.

ENGLAND WILL SAY NO.

WANTS TO SEE A BULL FIGHT.

MOB RULE IN LONDON.

MANY DISTRICTS TERRORIZED.

IN HONOR OF MISS CISNEROS.

FEWER FEVER CASES.

SAM JONES' JUBILEE.

HART LIKELY TO BE NAMED.

FOUND WEALTH IN KLONDIKE.

THE BAIT NOT TAKEN.

ACCUSES HIM OF INSINCERITY.

The Letter

FOUND WEALTH IN THE KLONDIKE
Three Missourians Returning From the Frozen North With $90,000 Each in Dust.

William Schooley, Frank Coleman and Lafe Coleman, who left Vernon county three years ago for the Alaskan gold fields, write from Seattle, Wash., to relatives here that they have just arrive there, and will shortly be at home. Each of them will bring with him $90,000 in gold dust and nuggets, They are all three single men, whose parents still reside in this county.

—The Kansas City Sunday Journal.

Volume XL. No. 129. October 17, 1897—Twenty pages

Chapter 6: New Arrival

Nevada, Missouri
October 2, 1897

THE MODEST TWO-STORY HOME stood just a half-mile south of the town center. A row of six chairs lined the front porch of the Schooley household. William Sr's. position was first, nearest the door, followed by his wife, Ann's rocker, then Eva's chair, the oldest of the children. The next space, was also vacant, to await the oldest son, William Jr's. return. The last two seats were for the twins, Sam and John.

The twins' had just settled in their chairs, ready to take advantage of the afternoon's natural light and review their class lessons. Sam opened his math book. Looking over at his brother, John said, "I think mine is up in my room."

Although they had finished high school, their father had encouraged them to remain at home while they continued their education. He even offered to pay them for their continued chores around the farm.

John stood to leave, but stopped when he saw a young man trotting his horse up the street. The man slowed when he saw the house's occupants on the porch and pulled to a stop just outside the fence.

"Excused me for the interruption," the man said. "Could you tell me if I'm heading the right direction to reach the center of the town of Nevada?"

John answered, "You're headed the right direction alright. Looking for any place in particular?"

Sam stood and joined his brother.

"A place to stay, hopefully."

Sam took a step off the porch and began walking toward the fence. John followed suit. Noticing the dust on his clothing and haggard look, Sam said, "You look like you've been riding for a while."

"Too long actually." The man stood in his stirrups and said, "Just need to stretch my legs a spell." He began to dismount and said, "Do you mind?"

"Not at all. You're welcome to tie up here for a time if you like," Sam said, gesturing toward the hitching post just outside the gate.

"Thank you." The stranger lashed the reigns to the post, took off his hat and walked over to the fence to introduce himself, "My name is Teodora Bohannon. My friends call me Ted."

They shook hands all around and Sam said, "Nice to meet you Ted. Welcome to Nevada, Missouri."

"Thank you."

"What brings you to these parts?" John asked.

"I had to move here to keep my job with the railroad."

"Interesting, I didn't know they did things like that," Sam stated.

"A surprise to me, too. I feel fortunate, especially considering how the railroad is still letting people go most everywhere else. I guess they've had an increase in rail activity here for some reason."

"Probably because of the New Weltmer Institute for Healing," John offered.

"Seems their success rate is becoming well known," Sam admitted.

"What will you be doing?" John asked.

"I'll be the new assistant depot agent," Ted said. "I think they'd rather send me here than train a new hire."

"Makes sense," John offered. He and Sam both nodded.

"Just need to find a place to stay now."

John responded, "I know just the place. There's a boarding house halfway between Main Street and the depot. The Jenkins's family owns it. Mrs. Jenkins is a widow and lets her rooms out to people."

"Ted, if you'd like to rest a bit before heading into town, you're more than welcome to sit on the porch for a spell," Sam offered. Sam saw John smile and nod as well.

"Nice of you to offer. Getting out of this saddle for a spell would be nice."

Ted, with an obvious stiff gait, made his way through the gate and followed Sam and John to the porch.

Sam offered his chair to the visitor, who stiffly lowered himself onto the seat, dusted off his hat, and rested it on his lap.

John took the chair next to Ted, and Sam remained standing, leaning against a post.

It took little time for them to hear the highlights of Ted's history and chat about the town's businesses. The twins also gave Ted an overview of the residents of Nevada.

They had begun to talk of more trivial matters when John, realized he still hadn't gotten his math book.

He stood to excuse himself, "I just need to get my class materials. I'll be right back."

Ted also stood and said, "This is probably as good a time as any for me to get moving into town, but I sure appreciate the hospitality." John shook Ted's hand and wished him well as he entered the house.

Sam turned to say something to Ted, but saw him staring back toward the fence.

Sam looked in the same direction and saw his older sister walking toward the porch. Her gait was slow, her head lowered. She was self-absorbed, oblivious to her surroundings. Obviously, something was bothering her.

"Something the matter, sis?"

With hardly a glance, Eva said, "Just had a bad day is all," and took a couple more steps toward the front door. She tried to make it sound like a simple statement of fact, but the red eyes caused Sam enough concern to step closer and inquire further. He blocked her from entering the house.

Eva started to step around Sam but stopped when she noticed the stranger standing on the porch behind her brother.

The visitor smiled at Eva.

"Hello," Ted said.

Embarrassed for not noticing the newcomer, Eva turned her head slightly and moved to place her brother between herself and the stranger. She gently wiped her eyes and brushed her cheeks, to make herself more presentable.

Sam said, "Ted, this is my sister, Eva. Eva, this is Ted."

Eva shyly looked around Sam and said, "Pleased to meet you." She showed a quick, tight smile then blurted out, "Sorry, just got some news about a man who's been calling on me." Eva blushed and turned back to her brother.

"Hope the news is not too bad, Eva," Ted responded, looking quite sincere and not wanting to inquire further about a personal matter. Ted noticed her striking blue eyes and a faint track of freckles that crossed her cheeks and nose. "*Pretty*," he thought.

Eva sheepishly lowered her head, feeling uncomfortable about being in the presence of a stranger, but she did appreciate his gentle manner.

"Eva, Ted has just come to town and is looking for a place to stay. He works for the railroad."

Sam noticed Eva jerk her head back slightly and look over at her brother. Sam could sense her uneasiness and knew she wanted to enter the house. Eva did mind her manners though and offered her hand to the visitor.

Ted took it and held it longer than normal before releasing it. That's when Eva noticed his kind eyes.

"I was just leaving, but I do hope we meet again." Ted turned to Sam and added, "I appreciate you letting me know about the town. Thank you."

Sam responded, "I'm sure we'll see each other around, Ted. Hope you don't have any problems getting settled in."

Ted smiled and said, "I'm sure I'll be just fine. Thank you, again." He turned and walked to his horse, mounted, tipped his hat, and rode off.

Sam and Eva watched him depart.

Sam noticed Eva's ambivalence about going into the house and asked, "What's got you looking so unhappy?"

Eva retraced her thoughts. "Nothing in particular," she said, softly, "other than I now know why Stanley Barclay has stopped calling on me."

Being a younger brother, Sam didn't expect his sister to confide in him, especially over something so personal, so he chose to listen quietly and let Eva decide if she wanted to continue. To his surprise she did.

"He's seeing Alice Newton."

Sam could see that Eva was clearly both hurt and angry.

"You're sure?"

"Yes, Alice's friend, Susan, told me," Eva said. Eva opened her mouth again, as if to add something, but stopped. Instead, she turned and walked into the house.

"Eva," Sam called out.

Eva stopped at the base of the stairs that led to her bedroom.

Sam stepped up next to her. "I never said anything before about Stanley because I figured you'd see him as I do sooner or later. He's not right for you, Eva."

Eva's neck stiffened. "You think because he's so popular that I don't deserve him?" Eva asked.

Sam, seeing that Eva was upset by his comment, quickly said,

"No. Quite the opposite." Sam tried to clarify, "He's just not right for you. Sure, he can be charming, and he is good looking and popular in some groups. But, from what I've heard, Stanley can't be trusted."

"I find that hard to believe," Eva said firmly.

"Believe what you want, Eva, but before Bill and the Coleman's left, Lafe told me that Stanley was just a blowhard."

"Why would he say that?"

"Did you know he wanted to go with them?"

"Originally, yes, but he told me he changed his mind."

"That might be his story, but they didn't want him to go. Lafe said, he's was always scheming and Bill didn't trust him. He said that more than a few times, Stanley would get his friends to invest in something with him, only to lose their investment."

"That wouldn't be his fault," Eva said. "I know that investments can sometimes be risky."

"Generally, that would be true, but he'd told them it was a sure thing, and that their profits were guaranteed."

"Nothing's guaranteed."

"You and I may know that, but people swayed by Stanley are more gullible."

"So, you're saying that he can't be trusted because he takes advantage of others?"

"That's right," Sam said.

Eva thought about that for a moment and said, "Well I guess it's not a problem now anyway, since I'm not seeing him any longer." Sam could see that Eva's eyes had tears in them as she turned and started to climb the stairs. "I'm not sure what I'm going to do now," she added.

Sam started to turn, stopped and then yelled up the stairs, "You know sis, I think you caught Ted's eye."

Chapter 7: Letter Home

Nevada, Missouri
Monday, October 11, 1897

WILLIAM SCHOOLEY CASUALLY WATCHED as his wife, Ann, opened their son's letter and began to read. He soon noticed a change in her posture. She seemed to stiffen. Her eyes widened and focused more intently. Then she paled and slouched back into her chair, pushing a stray lock of her auburn hair behind an ear.

"Is everything alright with Bill?" William asked.

Ann stood and handed her husband the letter. "We've got to gather everyone. *Now.*"

William reached for the letter while Ann scurried off to get the family.

Upon completing his review of the letter, he sat back in his chair and smiled. He carefully folded and placed it back in the envelope and onto the chair his wife had just vacated.

It was a good hour before dinnertime when Ann called her family to the living room. She made it clear that they were having an early reading of Bill's letter. She ignored any inquiries as to why *now.* This was out of the norm, for it had been the tradition over the last three years for the family to sit around the fireplace following the evening meal whenever they received news of her son's latest exploits.

It had been three years since her eldest son, Bill Schooley, left his teaching job in Enoch, Missouri, to take on a venture with two family friends. From the look on Ann's face, they all knew that this news was important, so they hastened to gather around the fireplace. She waited, not so patiently, as the twins, Sam and John, and then Eva, settled into their places alongside her husband. Sam went quiet as he noticed a slight tremor in his mother's hands while she carefully pulled the letter from the envelope for the second time that day.

As an introduction Ann simply said, "You'll quickly see why your Pa and I want to share Bill's letter with you earlier than usual." Then she began reading.

It didn't take long before they all looked dumbfounded, in awe of Bill's great fortune.

When Ann finished reading, she carefully folded the letter, placed it on her lap and rested her folded hands on top before quietly looking about the room with a slight smile. It was a puzzle, how she was able to suppress her feelings of excitement, concern, and anxiousness, to sit and observe everyone else's reaction after she delivered the shocking news.

At first the family remained silent. Then, following a long pause, everyone seemed to start talking at once. Questions began to spill out in rapid succession.

Sam was the first to speak out. "Big brother's rich!"

"What's he going do with all that money?" John asked.

"He must have some sort of plans for when he returns," Sam began again.

"When is he coming home?" Eva asked.

"What's he going do when he comes home?" Sam exclaimed.

It was Pa, in his typically calm manner that got everyone's attention after hearing the battery of questions. He held up his hands, palms out and gestured calmly for the others to hear him. "Only time will bring answers," he began. "And, don't try and draw any conclusions. We'll find out soon enough when Bill gets home. He's making his own decisions now, and I imagine he'll have changed a bit since he left home, too."

"I can't but wonder when he might be home," Eva said.

"Who knows? And even when he does decide to return, there's a lot to think about, a lot of it is timing. The train's been running fairly regular since it was completed in '93, at least until snow hits the Rockies. I'm sure there's a lot of other things to consider besides that, too."

"Yeah, he's got to figure out how he's going to carry all that gold too." It was Sam who was thinking out loud now.

"He may not even be bringing it with him," their father clarified. "It may be too dangerous to try and carry all that back home. He may just leave it, or part of it, in a bank back there."

"I always thought he was looking forward to the adventure more than he was aiming to get rich," Pa mused. "I never thought he'd actually strike it rich prospecting out west."

"I hope he's finished with his adventures," Eva commented. "It'll be nice having him home again."

Ann could only smile and nod at her daughter's statement. She knew Eva missed him more, being as close as they were.

"Can't imagine what he'll be doing with all his wealth once he gets back here," Sam stated.

Through the evening meal everyone spent more time discussing what this all meant than actually eating. The evening passed, and once all the discussions were exhausted, father had the last word. "He'll be home soon enough. Given time, we'll see what he'll decide."

Even after everyone bedded down for the night, they all lay awake, energized by the possibilities. All thoughts were about the eldest son's good fortune and how they looked forward to his return.

Little did they realize that it would be some time before they'd see him again and what a ruckus his news would create.

Chapter 8: Sharing The News

Nevada, Missouri
Thursday, October 14, 1897

AFTER ADMIRING THE FABRIC'S PATTERN, Mrs. Schooley looked across the store to find the salesclerk. She saw that the lady was busy at the register with her back turned. Two other gentlemen were standing nearby. One was the mercantile[7] store's owner, who Mrs. Schooley knew to also be the town's mayor. The other gentleman she didn't know.

Ann approached the clerk and waited patiently for her to finish what she was attending to.

The clerk turned, recognized her and said, "Mrs. Schooley. How are you?"

"Fine, thank you."

"I understand you heard from your son, Bill, last week."

"Yes, I did. How did you know?"

"A friend of my son heard your family talking outside church, just after the service. News travels fast here you know."

Mrs. Schooley did know that. She pictured their family conversation, off to the side of the church and remembered thinking they

_____
7 **Mercantile:** a general store.

were out of earshot of any eavesdroppers during their talk about family matters.

News travels fast here.

She remembered a time when the boys were still in school and Sam had gotten into a skirmish with a school bully, who felt the need to establish his position in the schoolyard. When John stepped up to assist his brother, the bully changed his tune but not before landing a punch that resulted in Sam receiving a cut lip.

Mrs. Schooley knew the boys would be concerned about breaking the news to her and their father. Their father had been clear about how fighting was an immature way of responding to a problem. Before they had even left school, she'd learned of the incident from a neighbor who had taken her son into school late that morning.

The neighbor explained that her son had taken longer to complete his chores around the farm, but she insisted he complete them before going to school. The boy's mother had delivered her son by buggy so he wouldn't miss any more time from class than necessary.

On her way home she had stopped to chat when she saw Mrs. Schooley hanging laundry in her yard. What became clear during their conversation was that, "John had stepped in only after Sam had been hit by an unprovoked punch."

By the time the boys had arrived home, Mr. and Mrs. Schooley knew how stern and forgiving they would be.

The store clerk's question brought her thoughts back to the present, "Is it true what I heard about Bill?"

"I don't know. What is it you've heard?" Mrs. Schooley asked.

"I heard that your son has been travelling around the Pacific Northwest Territory and is bringing home thousands of dollars in gold."

The room seemed to go quiet. The two men next to them stopped talking and turned to listen.

Mrs. Schooley blushed. "Did you get this from your son's friend, too?" she asked incredulously.

"No. A couple of friends came in the store and were talking about it just the other day. Seems that news has spread."

"So I understand," Mrs. Schooley said. "My daughter and sons have told me of a few of the rumors that have made their way back to them, but until now I didn't know how they got started. "Some of the stories we've heard have some truth to them, but as time has gone on, these stories have become exaggerated."

"So he's found some gold but he's not rich?" the clerk said.

"Oh they've all done rather well," Mrs. Schooley confessed. "I'm just saying that I wish the people telling the stories would stop adding false information."

The clerk said, "Sorry, I didn't mean to pass on rumors, I was just . . ."

"That's alright, you were just trying to confirm what you heard. I understand," Mrs. Schooley said.

The storeowner stepped forward.

"Sorry, Mrs. Schooley, I couldn't help but overhear your conversation. Perhaps I can be of assistance.

"How might that be?" Mrs. Schooley asked.

The mayor looked to the gentleman standing next to him. "Well, at least Bernie here might be able to help."

The gentleman next to the mayor said, "If you're the mother of Bill Schooley, who I've heard so much about lately, perhaps I can help."

Mrs. Schooley looked at the gentleman quizzically.

"Sorry, Mrs. Schooley. Let me introduce myself. My name is Bernie Adler. I work with the Kansas City Journal. I too have heard the rumors about your son's good fortune and travels. Actually I came here to talk with the mayor and ask if there was any truth about what I'd heard and to find out any other news about the town."

"Mr. Adler, much of what you just heard from her," she nodded toward the store clerk, "is not correct. He's not traveling all around. He's not in the Northwest Territory. I don't know what the value of the gold he found is worth. The gold he wrote about is not just his. He has two friends with him who are also from here."

The man smiled. "It seems that the least I could do is to help set the record straight by placing an article in the paper, with your permission of course."

Mrs. Schooley looked from the news reporter to the mayor.

"It might help," the mayor said in earnest. "It could help stop the rumors."

"You do have a point," she admitted, "when my husband returns, I'll talk with him first. He's down the street at the hardware store with my other two sons."

"I'll wait here," the reporter said. "I wouldn't want to miss this opportunity."

Mrs. Schooley rejoined her daughter a few aisles away and shared the conversation she had just had. They then went back to examining the various fabrics.

After a while, Mr. Schooley entered the store. The twins waited outside by the wagon. The mayor greeted William when he arrived and led him to where his wife and daughter were.

Mrs. Schooley looked up, smiled and said, "I want to show you some fabric I got, but before I do, you should know that the mayor here has suggested we discuss a proposition."

"Oh?" William said.

"I'll excuse myself for now," the mayor said. "I'll just be over by the counter if you'd like to talk with us when you're through."

"Us?" William asked.

The mayor pointed to Mr. Adler who was standing near the counter's register and clarified his position with the Kansas City Journal. "I'll just excuse myself for now," the mayor said and walked away.

William looked to his wife. She shared the conversation about the rumors and the offer to put an article in the paper. She finished with, "The mayor has suggested that this article might help squelch the rumors about Bill and his gold."

Mr. and Mrs. Schooley discussed what this article might mean while Eva listened. All three then walked toward the two gentlemen at the counter.

Seeing William approach, the mayor introduced Mr. Adler to Mr. Schooley and Eva. William and Bernie Adler shook hands. Mr. Schooley said, "We'll allow you to write the article, but you have to understand, we don't want to speculate on anything other than what he wrote in his letter."

"I understand," Mr. Adler said.

William turned to his wife then back to Mr. Adler, "My wife received the letter, so she should be the one to tell you what it said."

Mrs. Schooley told the reporter, "We don't really have much information for you to print, since Bill didn't go into any detail."

"That's fine," Mr. Adler pulled out a note pad and pen from his jacket. "I'll just keep the article focused on the basic information you give me."

"First of all," Mrs. Schooley began, "I don't know the value of gold the three of them found. I only know that he and his partners did well based on how much the gold weighed."

"That's fine, we'll figure that out later. Tell me about his partners also. Are they from these parts as well?"

She told him about the Coleman brothers and then began to state the facts from Bill's letter.

The reporter's last question, he admitted, was for the interest of the readers, "Can you tell me if any of them are married?"

Mr. and Mrs. Schooley looked at each other and chuckled. She said, "No. They're all single."

Mr. Adler finished with, "Is there anything else you can think of that I could include?"

"Not that I can remember," she looked over at her husband, and he shook his head.

"I'd like to thank you for your time," Mr. Adler said.

The mayor walked Adler to the door while the Schooleys purchased their goods and left.

During family's trip home, they discussed the article and hoped it would put an end to all the speculation about Bill.

Chapter 9: Stormy Seas

Northwest of Ketchikan, Alaska
October 25, 1897

I LAY ON MY BACK, CLUTCHING THE SIDES OF MY BUNK. The steamer pitched again. Slowly, I opened my bleary eyes. I had been napping off and on throughout the night, never reaching a deep sleep. Ever since leaving the protection of Vancouver Island, gale winds had constantly blown off the ocean, carrying enough force to keep the steamer's passengers constantly off balance.

Since that time, I'd seen little of the other passengers. Everyone had spent most of their time hunkered down, enduring the rough seas as best they could. The winds whipped and gusted and blew. Everything was cold and damp. Seven days earlier I had been in Seattle. We were long overdue to arrive in Sitka, and many wondered if we'd make it at all.

A dim light made its way into the cabin's inner sanctum but not enough to read by. The stormy skies were making for another bleak day. It was early morning, and like the previous day no activities would be expected. The crew had announced to the passengers that even walking the outer decks would not be allowed until further notice. *That was obvious*, I thought. Outside, the winds continued to howl, tossing the steamer about like a toy played with by a two-year-old. I was only seven days into my return trip, this time to Juneau, Alaska, and the challenges of the journey were already becoming evident.

I rubbed my eyes and looked across to the adjoining bunk to view my partner. I saw that the bulge hadn't moved. At first glance I thought it looked to be Frank's older brother, Lafe. Frank was beginning to fill out, but he was still lanky in comparison. It wouldn't be more than a few years before Frank would match the bulk of his older brother. Frank was sound asleep. It seems that he could find comfort in any situation. He had proven that many times over during our years together.

The 84-ton, double-stack schooner broke through a wave, barely exposing the newly painted name on its bow. The steamship Laurel made slow headway as it battled the southerly headwinds and stormy weather just 100 miles north and west of Ketchikan. Waves passed over the hatches with each passing swell. Everything was new about her, but the winds and waves were loosening her riggings, and a crack had begun to spread along her bowsprit.[8] Outside, she was still holding, inside was another story.

Considering all that I'd endured in the Alaska wilderness, I couldn't help but wonder, is this how it would end? Out at sea, enveloped by the ice-cold waters of the Pacific. I was amazed that the steamer was still holding together. I was now twenty-three years old, not yet in the prime of my life, younger than most the miners I'd been working with. I still found little need to shave. The few freckles that once lined either side of my nose were no longer evident due to the outdoor winds that constantly turned my cheeks red. My one hundred-and-sixty-five-pound frame had become lean and strong, first from working the family farm, then from the chores of separating gold from the earth. I normally felt confidence about my abilities, when on land. But now I felt helpless, knowing that no amount of toughness could overcome the rough seas.

8 **Bowsprit:** a large spar projecting forward from the stem of the ship.

I sat up and turned to hang my legs off the edge of my bunk. I still had my pants and shirt on and was groggy from being tossed about throughout the night. I reached for a box that I had stored at the foot of my bed, opened it, and inspected my new boots. It was labeled, Coleman's of Seattle. I started to slip one of the boots onto my foot but stopped when the ship rolled again. Trying to steady myself, I grasped the bunk's sideboard and then eyed the lumpy bundle in the bunk across the cabin. My roommate still hadn't moved.

"Frank, you awake?"

No answer.

I shook my head in wonderment, and climbed out of my bunk. Once my boots were securely tied, I stood, put on my vest, and automatically reached into the vest pocket for my watch. Then I realized it was with the belongings I left with Lafe in Alaska. I missed it. It was more than just time it told, it connected me to my family. It had been a gift from my parents when I left home. I knew I had to get moving, to keep myself busy. I'd been thinking about too many sentimental things as I lay idle. I needed to find something to distract me.

The dining hall was the only other place I could go. The only option to staying in the cabin. I exited our room and started to make my way to the mess hall, one deck above. It wasn't easy. I still felt bleary, and the ship continued to toss. My cabin was adjacent to the steps that led to the upstairs passage. With a firm grip on the handrail, I carefully made my way topside.

Once above, it was just a few more steps to the forward door that allowed entry through the aft-end of the dining hall. Gripping the edge of the door firmly, I steadied myself at the mess's entry, and glanced toward the outer exit doors. I saw that they were tightly secured. I then redirected my attention to the aft entry of the dining area.

I saw a clock on dining room wall. It said 6:10 AM. Although the room was big enough to seat all sixty-five passengers, I didn't expect to see any of them there—the dining hall wasn't scheduled to be open for another twenty minutes. To my surprise, a few of the tables were occupied. Evidently, I wasn't the only one having difficulty sleeping. The cook must have looked kindly on those who needed somewhere to go, other than the confines of their cabin.

No one showed any interest in me as I entered. They were too focused on eating their morning meal and safeguarding it from sliding off the table. Most found a way to hold their coffee mug with the same arm that guarded their plate. The other free hand was used to scoop a portion of either the scrambled eggs or mush off their plate and quickly slip it in their mouth while trying to avoid stabbing themselves. Grappling with the bacon seemed to be the easiest task. Most just ate a strip at a time using their fingers. No one looked up. Their fatigue was evident.

As I scanned the sea-weary discontents in front of me, the first mate entered from across the room and hollered for everyone's attention. "We have to 'heave to,'" he bellowed. "You know what that means, just like we done before. You can figure if it's not tied down, it'll be broke or worse. As soon as ya stop usin it, stow it."

One of the passengers commented back loudly, "You think we don't know that by now? It's been seven days since we left Seattle. More than half our time aboard we've been putting up with these storms. We know the routine."

"Maybe, but it's my job ta let ya know anyways."

"What you can let us know is how many more days 'til we settle into Sitka?" another man asked.

"We're almost halfway there, but how long it'll take us depends on the weather. We figure about ten more days to Sitka at the rate we're going."

I didn't move from my stable location. Outside, I could hear the gale winds blowing stronger. The salt water was pelting the glass panes. I started to take a step forward when suddenly the ship gave a terrific lurch. I grabbed the doorway again.

In unison, everyone grabbed on to something to steady themselves then jerked their heads up, to look toward a yelp heard from the back galley. A loud clatter followed.

"FIRE . . . FIRE IN THE GALLEY!"

Chapter 10: Fire in the Galley

Northwest of Ketchikan, Alaska

ONE OF THE STEWARDS RAN INTO THE MESS HALL. "The big orange has fallen over. It's upside down!"

Nobody moved right away. Everyone was still holding fast from the unexpected lurch of the ship.

Another rattle of noise was heard. I watched the steward grab hold of the counter as cooking utensils scattered. A few entered the mess area. The steward stumbled back into the galley, as smoke began pouring out.

The first mate, still on site, immediately took charge. He began to give orders to everyone within earshot, beginning with two crewmembers sitting at a back table. "You two." He pointed behind from where he stood. "Pull the hose coiled by the forward door."

The two crewmembers, obviously trained in this activity, moved past the first mate, ready to take action.

The first mate then looked across the room, pointed my direction and yelled, "There's another fire hose by that door."

"We've got it," I yelled. On impulse, I slapped a big man on his shoulder who sat at the table nearest me and said, "You and your friend," referring to the man next to him, "give me a hand." They both hesitated and looked at the food that lay before them. "Forget about that for now. Come on!"

I reached out to the rack, grabbed the nozzle and began to pull. The other two followed suit, helping to extend the hose from its coiled position. I headed for the galley.

The first mate yelled out again. "The rest of you, listen. You can either go back to your cabins and wait further word, or stay and help man the hoses, but if ya ain't helpin', you best get outta here."

The stampede was on.

Not knowing where to go, most scampered out to spread the word or just return to their cabins. A few downed their coffee or gathered some food before departing.

The first mate redirected his attention toward both fire hose teams, "Don't open the valve 'til you're sure you've got enough people to man the hose." He hollered. The crewmen working the other hose were struggling to untangle it from around a table. The first mate joined in to assist.

The only one not focused on the hoses was the steward, who was intent on collecting the utensils. He was unaware of the blaze that was creeping his direction, along the serving counter. A flame caught the tail of his serving jacket.

I recognized the steward's predicament. I looked back to the big man's friend, who was still extending the coil near the valve, and saw that more immediate action was warranted than what we could offer with the hose. I dropped the nozzle and directed the big man, "Hold it, I'll be right back." Once I saw him acknowledge me, I ran to the galley sink, grabbed a dishtowel, and dunked it into the sink that was half filled with soapy water.

Unaware of his situation, the steward was bent behind the narrow serving isle when I landed on him.

I pressed the soaked dishtowel to his backside.

The steward didn't know what hit him until he tried to roll over. He looked up to see a stranger slapping at his backside with a wet rag and felt the heat simultaneously. He now knew his jacket had been ablaze. Once doused, I grasped the steward's hand, pulled him to his feet, and directed him to sit for a moment at the table near the exit.

Joining the big man's companion, I retrieved the end of the hose and looked back as the big man tended the valve. I gave him the high sign to open the valve.

The surge of water was almost immediate. My attention was directed back to the situation at hand. The range had fallen forward and was resting on the molding that surrounded the burners. The door to the firebox lay open. Cinders had spread across the deck setting the varnished wood afire. It had already covered much of the kitchen floor and had spread along the deck to the dining area. The wall that bordered the back of the range and divided the kitchen as well as the dining area was now ablaze. It was beginning to reach the ceiling.

I quickly started spraying the wall. I knew we'd lose control of the fire if we allowed it to climb to the ceiling.

I had to brace myself between the kitchen's entry and a neighboring table to keep my balance—the boat continued to lurch about.

Moments later the crewmen's fire hose joined ours. They began focusing their efforts toward the far entry to the kitchen.

With the two firehose teams working in unison, we were able to get the fire under control in less than fifteen minutes. But we were not done, yet. We had to spend more time searching out and dousing smoldering hot spots.

With the drenching of the galley and most of the dining area, I knew the cleanup and repairs would take much longer.

Once the water was shut off, we disconnected the fire hose to drain the water before gathering them up. During this time more crewmembers arrived—those who had been trying to sleep while off duty. They took over coiling the hose I'd been working with and returned it to its rack. Not until then did we have a chance to take a well-needed break.

I made my way over to the first table and sat. Looking about the dining hall I took in the scene. Our eating area was a mess. There was water everywhere. Crewmembers had begun to right the range and set it back in place as well as collect the battered utensils that were scattered about the galley. This included the many dishes that had been abandoned on the eating tables and knocked to the floor. I listened as they viewed the spectacle before them.

One man shivered at another's comment about how quickly the flames had spread as a result of the flammable polish used on the varnished wood. Everyone seemed to be amazed that the inferno hadn't spread faster, seeing that there was wood everywhere.

It wasn't until a few minutes later that I became aware of how cold and damp I felt. As the adrenaline wore off, I realized I was shivering. Everything I had on was soaked. I looked at my boots. They didn't look so new anymore.

A tray of food slid across the table and came to rest in front of me. I looked up and saw the steward smiling at me. "The bacon's a bit crisp and the bread's somewhat soggy, but it's edible. I don't think we'll be serving much food anytime soon. I gave you some extra ham with the eggs, too, to tide you over. There's enough here for your roommate as well."

"That's mighty nice of you." I responded.

"It's the least I can do. I appreciate what you did," the steward said sincerely. "I have to get back to helping with the cleanup, but again, thank you."

"You're welcome," I smiled. The steward was obviously pleased with being able to reciprocate in some way.

"Good job." I turned to meet the voice from behind me. It was the big man I'd recognized during the fire's onslaught.

"May I join you?" the man asked.

"Seems to be plenty of room," I gestured to the empty spaces around the table. He took the one across from me.

"You're a man of action, I see."

Exhausted, I could only muster up a weak smile before saying, "Appreciate your help."

"Like everyone else onboard, are you heading up to mine gold?"

"Hope to."

"I figured you as a miner. You look like a man who sees what he needs to do and plunges ahead to get it done. I respect a man like that. And I suspect the steward appreciates it too."

I looked over to where the steward was still cleaning up.

"Sorry. I need to mind my manners. My Name is John Clancy. I'm a businessman. I'm heading up to Skagway."

"I'm Bill Schooley," I responded. I looked at my sooty hands.

"That's alright." He looked down at himself, "I look pretty dirty and ragged myself," but still offered his hand. We shook.

"What's your business up north?" I asked.

"Mainly saloons, in Seattle and Skagway," Clancy said. "Where are you headed?"

"On my way to Juneau," I said.

"Might be seeing you around then. I'm going through there, too," Clancy added. "Here, let me give you my business card." He retrieved one from his pocket as he stood and placed it on the table in front of me. "If you ever make it to Skagway, look me up. I'll buy you a drink."

"I'll keep that in mind," I said. "But, seeing that I don't drink liquor, I'll have to pass on the offer."

"Then I can at least offer a sarsaparilla,"[9] Clancy said with a smile. "From what I understand, any more delay in our actions and this ship would likely have been destroyed. Thanks to you, we got it extinguished before it could spread. I'm afraid most of us just froze and didn't know what to do . . . You, on the other hand, took immediate action."

"The fact is, we all got it done," I said.

"Thanks just the same," Clancy said. "I'll leave you to finish your meal."

---

9 **Sarsaparilla:** a preparation of the dried rhizomes of various plants, especially smilax, used to flavor some drinks and medicines and formerly as a tonic.

I palmed the man's business card and slipped it into my pocket as Clancy turned and left.

After finishing my breakfast and resting for a spell, I returned to my cabin. Just after I closed the cabin door, I could hear Frank begin to stir.

"Hey," Frank said. "I smell bacon."

"Oh, so that's what it takes to wake you up, bacon?"

"I suppose," Frank smiled.

"Yup, been up for a while. Couldn't sleep, so I went to the dining hall."

Frank rubbed his eyes and looked out into the dim light. "Whatcha got there?" he asked.

"Brought you something to eat."

"That's nice. But I could have gone to the chow hall."

"Not really."

"What do you mean?"

"They won't be serving anytime soon . . . at least today."

"Why's that?"

"Had a bit of a fire."

With that, Frank sat up. "I thought I smelled smoke." Getting a better look at me he added, "You look terrible."

"Well, that's what happens when you wrestle with a fire hose."

"Why would ya wanna do that?"

"Somebody's got to make sure nothing interferes with our journey to the Klondike."

"The fire was that bad, huh?"

"Coulda gotten away from us," I said. Frank didn't say anything. I handed him a plate full of food.

"Thanks."

"You might want to make it last for a while."

He started gobbling it down, looked up and said, "If it's one lesson I learned while we were working our claims in Sunrise, it's to eat what I can and when I can. We may not know when the next meal's coming."

"Well, I guess that's true today," I said, as I began to rid myself of my wet garb, and lay them out to dry.

By the time I'd undressed, Frank had devoured the rest of his food.

I found some dry duds and began dressing again. I decided to let Frank know what I'd learned about our progress. "The first mate said we're well past the halfway point to Sitka, but the storms don't look like they'll be letting up any time soon. Hard to say how much longer it's going to take us to get there. They're predicting five more days, weather permitting."

"I'm sure Lafe will be wondering what's happened to us," Frank said. "Lafe said he'd catch a steamer coming down to Juneau the middle of last month."

Having not been privy to other telegraph messages Frank received from his brother, I asked, "Your brother knows we'll be coming up from Sitka, right?"

"Yeah. He knows there's a boat that makes a regular mail run up to Juneau from there, so you know he'll be checking it fairly regular."

"Don't know about you, but I'm anxious to get up there," I said.

"You're looking forward to mining again?" Frank asked. "I'm surprised. It wasn't that long ago you were ready to go home to Missouri."

"Actually, I'm just anxious to get off this steamer," I said. "Mining can't be any worse than being here."

Chapter 11: Calmer Waters

Off Prince of Wales Island, Alaska

TEN DAYS LATER, I AWOKE with the sun glaring in my face. Still sleepy, I was amazed at how bright it was inside the cabin. I made my way to the porthole and set my eyes on the majestic mountains of Alaska that were highlighted by a piercing blue sky. The few clouds that could be seen looked like puffs of cotton floating above. I took in the scene with admiration. The morning sun was already well above the horizon and was casting a dark shadow over the evergreens that covered the nearby eastern hillside. Evidently, I'd slept in. Soundly. Having somewhat gotten my bearings, I looked at my cabinmate's empty bunk and began readying myself to head topside to find some coffee.

When I arrived at the mess hall, Frank immediately waved at me from across the room. I waved back as I entered the crowded space. He was sitting with the same familiar faces we had been sharing a table with since the galley fire. This bunch had come together like soldiers who had survived a battle, united by a common experience. We had fought the flames in the mess hall and established a bond.

Looking at the table of new friends, my mind drifted to thoughts of friends up north who Frank and I had banded together with as we endured the trials of mining in the rugged outdoors. While that bond had developed over years of being together, I noted how our shipboard calamity had caused some of the others, like Clancy, to join with us in a similar fashion. That's how I got to know John Clancy better.

I found him to be a rather interesting fellow. He had a knowledge about a place that Frank, Lafe and I would soon be passing through. That, and his frankness about conditions there I found intriguing. Skagway would be our entry point to the Chilkoot Trail that would lead us into the Klondike, our destination. Clancy's establishment was located in the town of Skagway where he'd partnered with his brother to build a saloon.

As I approached, Frank scooted down the bench to make room for me at the end of the table, across from Clancy. Sitting next to him was a man I knew to be sharing a cabin with John. Until now I hadn't had an opportunity to talk with him since he was rarely seen outside the cabin due to being seasick throughout our time at sea. I knew him to be a potential business partner of Clancy's by the name of Jeff. John had stated that he was normally a rather outgoing man, but all I saw was a pale, slim figure who was biding his time in the dark holds of an inner cabin until he could get on solid ground.

I'd come to enjoy John, and sometimes Jeff's, company. Jeff stayed quiet most of the time we saw him, either because he didn't want to mingle or was seasick. Our routine of eating together continued from the ship-board fire to the end of our trip.

While we disembarked in Sitka, that wasn't the end of our journey. Following a two-day stay there, we transferred to the *City of Topeka*, a boat that made mail runs on a regular basis between Sitka and Juneau. At the end of our day-trip to Juneau, we parted ways, not knowing if our paths would ever cross again.

I still remember Clancy's last words to me just before debarking in Juneau. I was struck with his directness when he said, "I highly advise you to tell your traveling companions to avoid any of Skagway's saloons and anyone who wants to buy a drink." I was struck by his frankness.

When I asked Clancy why he would say such a thing he said that Skagway was a lawless town, full of people looking for ways to take a miner's money. "Much of it occurs in the saloons," he added, "There, a con man will be your best friend and buy you a drink so he can get you involved in a poker game or some other scam, just so he can get your money."

These thoughts lingered in my mind until we reached shore. Then, all I could think about was getting together with Lafe, and begin moving inland.

Dyea Claims

"We are now climated, brought our snow shoes and camping outfit, and will be better prepared than most of the men."
        —*Letter to Mrs. W. M. Schooley, November. 7, 1897*

". . . the rivers are very unlike the rivers in your country, in that they are in the mountains, are all very swift, and have worn their way down through the solid rock."
        —*Letter to brother Samuel Schooley, December 22, 1897*

Chapter 12: Trio Unite

Juneau, Alaska
Sunday, November 7, 1897

B Y THE TIME THE CITY OF TOPEKA steamer arrived in Juneau from Sitka, more than half of the nine hours of daylight had already passed. It was late in the afternoon when we got everything we brought with us off-loaded and stacked on the pier. The plan was to contact Lafe at the hotel after finding a place to store our supplies. It took a little longer than expected to find an available porter to move our stack of goods into the pier's temporary storage facility. Most were tied up helping others.

We grabbed our overnight bags and left the pier; most of the other passengers had already made their way into town. We could see that there were still a number of people milling about outside taking advantage of the remaining daylight when Frank and I left the waterfront.

We made our way up the hillside and easily found the Franklin Hotel. Its sign was prominently displayed across the wide deck that covered the front of the hotel, which overlooked the town below. Split wood was stacked along the base of the boardwalk just to the right of the wide stairs that ascended to the center of the hotel. Once we arrived at the base of the steps, I saw more kindling and log rounds piled under the walkway as well. We could feel the dampness in the air. The early-November temperature had reached its high in the upper thirties. We were expecting the night to fall below freezing.

Climbing to the top of the stairs we saw a number of men gathered in front of the hotel entrance, enough that I was concerned about whether or not there would be room for more boarders. Gold seekers could be seen everywhere. A number of men were sitting on the benches and standing along the railing that bordered the wide-planked walkway along the front of the building.

Anxiously, we made our way to the hotel's front desk. Once we discovered the inevitable—there were no rooms available, we inquired about Frank's brother. The lady at the desk said she did recall Lafe, particularly because the name was so unusual, she added, ". . . but he left over a week ago."

"Do you remember him saying where he might be going?" I asked, hopefully.

"No, sorry," the lady said. She then turned her back on us, to view the letter slots behind the counter.

Seeing that she wasn't paying attention to us and seemed too busy for any further conversation, we began to leave.

The lady then turned around and held out an envelope. "He did leave this," she exclaimed. "Are either of you Bill Schooley or Frank Coleman?"

"That's us!" we responded in unison and gave a sigh of relief.

Frank tore the envelope open as I crowded in beside him.

Frank glanced at the signature and confirmed, "It's from Lafe." He quickly read the message, smiled, and handed it me.

The lady said, "I assume this is what you were hoping for."

Frank nodded with a smile. I read the note carefully.

Frank and Bill,

I'm staying at another hotel just a couple of blocks north of where you are now. It's called the Circle City Hotel, on Third Street between Seward and Franklin. It has 80 rooms, a bar and a dining room. If they're full by the time you get here I was told we could put a couple more cots in my room until other rooms become available. It's about a ten-minute walk and easy to find. If I'm not there, I'll be back shortly. I often walk around, exploring the town and trying to talk with people who are familiar with the area. The warehouse is just off the wharf, a half block from where you are now, where you can store any excess gear you don't want to haul to the hotel. The costs here aren't too unreasonable, all things considered—I've looked around.

Lafe

I asked the lady what the most direct route would be to Third Avenue, between Seward and Franklin. The lady recognized the location, gave us directions, and told us we'd enjoy staying at the Circle City Hotel. "It's larger and brand new," she said. We both expressed our gratitude and left the hotel.

After a short discussion, we decided to return to the pier to check on the availability of porters to move our outfit by wagon to the warehouse Lafe had recommended.

Once the process of moving our goods was underway, Frank headed up to the hotel to find his brother and hopefully a room. I stayed to supervise the porters and our goods.

It was over an hour before I was able to complete the move and begin the hike up to the hotel to join my partners. During my walk, I passed a number of homes and noticed that some had "room for rent" signs posted in their front windows. Obviously, many of the locals were taking advantage of the overwhelming housing demand.

Making a little money on the side. Have to keep that in mind. Got to take advantage of the opportunity while it presents itself. My father always seems to be with me.

"Glad we bought extra supplies," I couldn't help but smile at the thought.

While I walked along the homes bordering the street, My mind drifted to thoughts of my first arrival, three years earlier, in another town further to the northwest.

Sunrise, Alaska,[10] wasn't much different then, with its muddy streets and houses that were just a step up from the rough-cut shacks outside the town. Boardwalks and planks were too few for those less inclined to muddy their leggings during the damp fall days. Back then, my arrival in Anchorage marked an earlier influx of folks seeking a better life prior to this current stampede.

I then recalled our family's discussions at home in Nevada, Missouri. It was shortly after the "silver panic," when jobs were scarce, the farm was experiencing droughts and crop prices were dropping that the Colemans and I, with the support of our families, *decided that leaving home would improve our families' home situation—fewer mouths to feed.*

We came out here to show we could make it on our own, and we did. I couldn't help but smile to myself. Initially the call to mining had been more of a dream than a reality. But we knew they had what it took—a strong will, strong backs, and a determination to succeed.

I chuckled to myself when I thought about how I was getting caught up in this new wave of prospectors. And it's all because of a guy by the name of Skookum Jim Masson who discovered gold in Bonanza Creek, south of Dawson city, in 1896. Word didn't really get out until gold from steamers landed in Seattle and San Francisco in the summer of 1897, right when the Colemans and I started heading for home.

I pondered my arrival in this town of Juneau. "Am I making a mistake not continuing my journey home? Are the pastures greener where we're headed, or were the deposits we left in Cook's Inlet as good as we'd experience?" As I thought about the miners gathered

---

10 **Sunrise, AK:** The summer of 1898 saw 8,000 prospectors on Cook Inlet. For a few weeks that summer, Sunrise City, with 800 people, was the largest city in Alaska.

on the porch of the Franklin hotel, I wondered what drove them here as well.

I found the Circle City Hotel, just as the sun began to set, and entered to find the Coleman brothers waiting for me in the lobby.

We exchanged pleasantries before moving to the comfort of the hotel's bar just to the left of the lobby. Entering, we observed a number of tenants warming themselves by the fireplace to the left and then moved to a table near the far wall to await service.

Frank filled his brother in on how it went securing the gold in Seattle. A moment later, a man approached, lit the kerosene lamp at our table and asked what we'd like to drink. We each ordered a soda and then began sharing our individual adventures.

Lafe started by telling about packing up the last of our belongings from Cook's Inlet, the success he had at closing out the last of our claims, and moving what was left of our goods to Juneau. He also related how our friends and neighbors at Sunrise, Alaska, had made the decision to join us in either Dyea or Skagway, once they completed their travels overland. "Last I saw them, they didn't know exactly when they'd be leaving Sunrise. Dutch said that if they don't run into us, he'll leave a note at the post office in Skagway, once they find a place to settle in."

The waiter returned with our drinks and took our food order. We then turned our discussion to Seattle itself. Normally quiet, Frank became enthused as he spoke of the changes. "There was an energy that could be felt in the city," he began, and elaborated how the businessmen were doing well as a result of the Klondike stampede. Our conversation then turned to our own situation, to include why we'd bought twice the rations we'd need when leaving Seattle.

"Twice the rations?" Lafe exclaimed.

"Since food and supplies are costlier up here, with the demand as high as it is, we figured we can afford to bring twice the amount needed and sell off whatever we don't need as a way to pay for other things," I explained.

"That's not such a bad idea," Lafe admitted, "as long as we're not overwhelmed with moving them. Speaking of which, I went up to Skagway before you arrived and know who can move and store our goods when we get there . . . at least temporarily. But, from what I've gathered, we don't really want to be there any longer than need be."

"Why do you say that?" I asked.

Lafe told us about his visit and what he learned from Captain Moore about the town's new residents.

"First thing in the morning we can take a look at what we've got stored down the street," I said then asked, "What's the situation on rooms here?"

"We brought in a couple of cots while we were waiting for you," Frank said.

"Cots are fine with me. It's got to be better than trying to sleep in a room that sways," I said, referring to my steamer experience. I looked over at Frank and then said to Lafe, "Frank seems to be able to sleep anywhere, any time."

Frank smiled while Lafe and I laughed. "He always could sleep through any storm," Lafe added, as the waiter brought our food order.

The rest of the meal was filled with talk about family before retiring for the evening.

Chapter 13: Inland Planning

Juneau, Alaska
November 8, 1897

WE ENTERED THE WAREHOUSE just a short distance up from the wharf. Stacked between two half walls, our goods could be seen resting snuggly. A narrow aisle divided our supplies from those of another, which lined the opposing half wall. Each stack was clearly marked with the name of its owner.

"Wow, that's a lot to move," Lafe said, walking along our stacked goods.

"It's hard to believe that the Canadians are requiring a ton of food stuffs for each person crossing into their country," Frank commented.

"Not when you consider all the tenderfeet who have been caught in the wilderness without enough food to make it through the winter," Lafe replied. "Evidently too many have tried mining in the Klondike in the winter, unprepared, and not made it out alive."

"Yeah," Frank added. "I think many figure they can stop at a saloon or a store, or even catch a fish in the local rivers when they get hungry. They don't understand how important it is to have extra food. It's not easily available here, and you never know when you might get snowed in."

"Knowing how pricy and difficult it is to get what we need here, I'm glad you bought all this in Seattle," Lafe said.

Frank and I leaned against our stack and smiled at Lafe, obviously proud of all the supplies we'd brought up with us.

"We might want to invest in something to help us pack all this in," Lafe said, smiling in return.

Frank and I instantly agreed.

"I found out some prices in Skagway, if you're interested," Lafe said.

"What did you find?" I asked as I located a box to sit on.

The Colemans each repositioned nearby crates and sat as well.

Lafe said, "First, I don't recommend a pack horse, because even though it may be cheaper—about $60 for a horse and cart, the route they have to go on is longer and too dangerous. I've heard that hundreds, maybe even thousands, of dead horses line that path."

"What do you recommend, then?" I asked.

"Even though Chilkoot Pass is much steeper, it's a great deal shorter."

"But if, like you say, it's too steep for horses, we'd have to carry all our stuff ourselves," Frank said, astounded by the thought.

"We could always get some dogs," I offered. "Sure, we'll have to walk at times, but with a sled harnessed to a dog team we can leapfrog our supplies more easily. I understand some sleds can carry as much as half a ton at a time."

I waited. I knew they were trying to do the math in their heads and compare that to the number of horses we'd need otherwise.

"Can I assume you've checked the cost of that as well, Lafe?" Frank asked.

"Yes, I have. They might go for about $100, but I think it's worth it. They'd be a lot easier to care for than horses, too." When it gets too cold out, we can pull the dogs inside our tent." Lafe laughed, "Not so easy to do with horses."

"Sounds like it's worth looking into," I said. "Need to keep our eyes open for a good team."

"Right," Lafe responded. "We should especially keep a watchful eye out for departing prospectors. I've seen some big outfits sold at a reasonable price just so the owner could get money for a ticket back home to the states."

"Sounds promising," Frank interjected.

"Just so you know, a railroad is being built through White Pass, but it won't be ready this year," Lafe added.

"When will it be ready?" Frank asked.

"Not until this time next year," Lafe responded, ". . . and by that time, tens of thousands of gold seekers will have passed through the area. All the prime claims would be taken. We can't wait that long."

"I agree. That wouldn't work for us," Frank said.

Lafe and I nodded our heads in agreement.

Lafe continued, "Hopefully, we can work a claim this side of the pass until we can determine the best time to cross over into Canada. It won't do us any good to make our way over the pass until Lindeman Lake and Lake Bennett are free of ice. They form the headwaters of the Yukon River. Once the river thaws, we can float down the Yukon into Dawson."

"Hopefully we could find enough gold on this side of the pass to at least pay for our supplies at least until the thaw, when we can cross over into Canada," I said.

"Seems like a good enough plan," Frank added. "That way we'll keep ourselves busy enough to stay warm during the cold spells. That's better than going up the mountain, trying to mine in the deep snow."

Frank and I were in complete agreement and nodded to each other.

I looked over at Lafe who sat quietly, a big grin on his face.

"What?" I asked.

"I thought you'd go along with that," he said widening his grin.

"You found a claim up the trail," I said.

Frank look at his brother in amazement, "You didn't."

"I did," Lafe said, showing a triumphant smirk.

Frank and I both laughed.

"I figured you'd agree and want to get settled right away." Lafe stood and looked at the mound of supplies. He walked to the end of our stack and then turned. "Do you have a list of what's here?" he asked.

Frank reached in his overcoat pocket, and pulled out a folded piece of paper. "We used a list the Seattle stores have for suggested supplies. I thought we might find this handy," he said proudly as he handed the list to Lafe.

Lafe looked through the list. "Looks like it's got the provisions already weighed for us, too," he said. "That'll make it easier for us to ensure we meet the requirements before crossing into Canada.

Frank added, "That's two tons of food and supplies for each of us. Some items we bought we already have but thought they needed to be replaced."

"I've already stored our equipment in Skagway that I brought with me, and the town's engineer has provided me with the survey of our plat. My timing, getting to Dyea, was fortunate. I was able to work with a number of other prospectors, to help map out a town-site. We got one of the first plats in the new town.

"For now, I think we can leave this here," Lafe said.

"Okay. When should we be heading for Skagway?" Frank asked.

"The sooner we get there the sooner we can build a cabin on our plat and move our goods there," Lafe continued. "We can pick up what we need from where I stored our supplies and have our camp set up before nightfall tomorrow."

Frank and I looked at each other and smiled. Getting back into roughing it was expected.

"So, I guess we're leaving first thing in the morning on the steamer?" Lafe said.

"Sounds good to me," I replied. "I'd like to have some time to relax and write a letter home before I turn in. Looks like we're going to be pretty busy the next few days. What time is it now?"

"That reminds me," Lafe said. He stood, reached in to his pocket, and pulled out a pocket watch. "I knew you'd be missing this." Lafe handed it to me.

"Thanks." I gave Lafe an appreciative smile. "I certainly didn't need it while we were working our claims in Sunrise." I looked at the time. "I just wish I'd taken it out of storage before Frank and I went to Seattle. Only in the city do I need to hold to times and schedules."

"Well, I guess giving it back to you now doesn't do you any good, knowing that you'll just be putting it back into storage here," Lafe said.

"No," I said, "It has a value, other than time," I added more softly. I began to inspect its markings.

"Listen, Bill," Lafe said carefully, ". . . I know it means a lot to you, being from your dad and all, so I made sure I carried it with me. I took good care of . . . it's still in perfect condition."

"I knew you would, and you're right about it meaning a lot to me . . . especially lately . . . after we started talking about going home," my voice trailed off. I was lost in thought as my fingers slowly traced the timepiece's outer edges. I carefully inspected the intricate designs that decorated the side and back cover.

Lafe stood, saying, "Well, we should head to our room and get a good night's sleep."

Frank joined his brother and looked back at me.

Thinking about home, I slowly slipped the timepiece in my pocket and joined my partners.

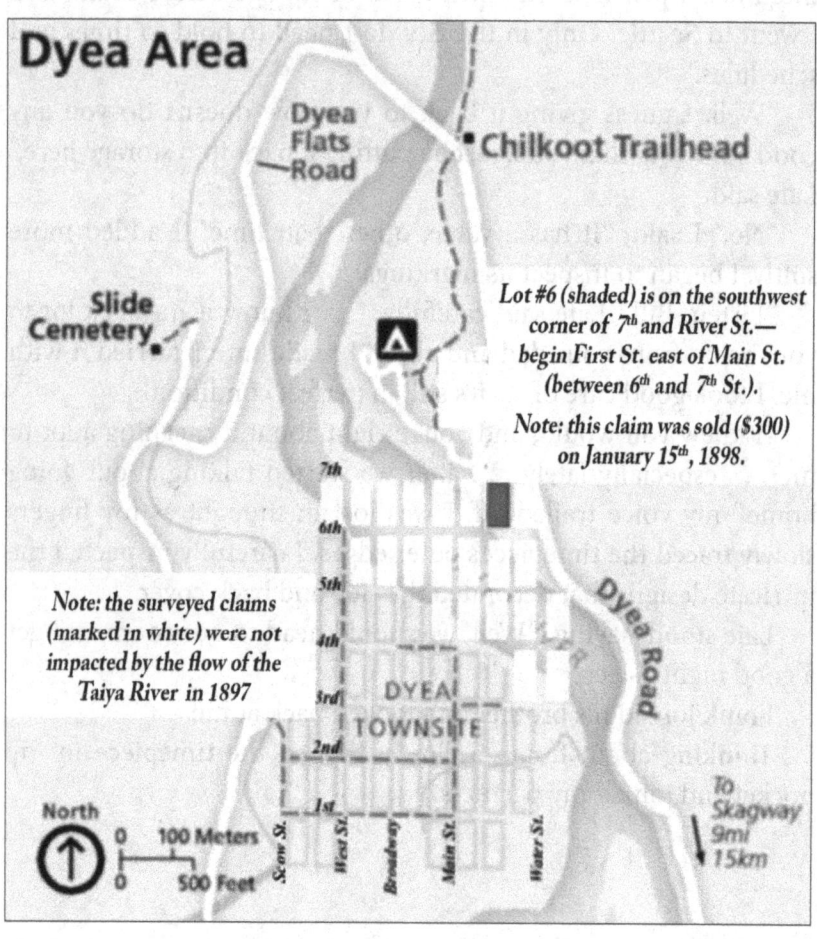

Dyea Area

Dyea Flats Road

Slide Cemetery

• Chilkoot Trailhead

Lot #6 (shaded) is on the southwest corner of 7th and River St.—begin First St. east of Main St. (between 6th and 7th St.).

Note: this claim was sold ($300) on January 15th, 1898.

Note: the surveyed claims (marked in white) were not impacted by the flow of the Taiya River in 1897

7th

6th

5th

4th

3rd

2nd

1st

DYEA TOWNSITE

Dyea Road

To Skagway 9mi 15km

North

0 — 100 Meters
0 — 500 Feet

Scow St.   West St.   Broadway   Main St.   Water St.

Chapter 14: Getting the
Lay of the Land

Skagway, Alaska
November 10, 1897

TRAVELING UP TAIYA INLET, the captain sounded the whistle as the Skagway piers came into view. The passengers congregated to view the town from the deck. The Colemans and I did the same. We made our way along the rail as far forward as the crowd allowed.

As best he could from the steamer's vantage, Lafe gave Frank and I an orientation to the town, which wasn't much, considering how far out from shore we were. The pier itself extended quite some distance over the tide flats before reaching depths that could handle a ship the size of the steamer. Lafe was able to give us a general overview of how the town was laid out and in which direction the muddy streets and trails headed. He also clarified the difference in the depth of this port as compared to Dyea, for unloading purposes, and identified which of Skagway's four piers we were headed for. As we drew closer, he pointed out Moore Wharf, where the steamer

would be tied, as well as the office where we'd find Mr. Hill, who
would eventually help with the inland transportation of our goods.

"I'm looking forward to panning, soon," Frank said.

"Better yet, I'm anxious to get our first sluice box working,"
his brother responded. "That's when the real money starts coming in."

"Everyone's got the gold fever," I mused aloud.

We all commented on how anxious and naïve we had been
when we first arrived in Sunrise.

"Getting caught up in the rush sure is contagious," I said, "No
wonder it's referred to as having gold fever." Frank and Lafe chuckled in agreement.

"I'm glad you got a claim when you did, Lafe," Frank added.

"I had the time. Figured I best take advantage of being here,
especially knowing a lot more folks would be arriving soon," Lafe
said, as the steamer slowed.

We all watched the crew secure the lines to the pier before we
disembarked and headed down the ramp. To get into town, we had
to walk the long pier before traversing through rutty wagon tracks
before reaching a planked walkway. Once away from the muddy
streets, we walked past the clothing-goods store, a general store,
and three saloons intermixed with other small shops, before noticing a small church.

"The buildings we just walked past sure give me an idea how
quickly the town had grown and what the interests of the people
are," Lafe said. "Just take a look at the ratio, and you'll discover the
church is probably not as well attended as the saloons."

Lafe led us to the warehouse, where he'd stashed our camping
equipment. In a short time, we were loaded with packs and back
on the planked walkway, heading toward the trailhead following a
quick stop at the surveyor's office.

Mr. Reid's office rested between two similar buildings, behind
a small cluster of trees, next to a muddy corridor considered to be
the main street. His office, like many of its neighbors, consisted of

unpainted boards, with one window in front to capture the light of the short winter days.

We crossed the street, walking between two horse-drawn carts loaded with gold seekers hauling their supplies inland.

A few men were milling about, outside the surveyor's building. There seemed to be a lull in the mid-morning business activities. Lafe led the way as we entered the building following a few soft knocks on the door and an immediate "come on in" from the only man inside.

He was sorting through a stack of papers, periodically glancing at what appeared to be a map spread across his desk.

"We're just passing through town and wondered if I might ask a couple of questions, if you have a minute," Lafe asked.

"Certainly. I remember you. You got one of the first plats in Dyea."

"That's right," Lafe smiled and introduced his partners, before proceeding.

"We've already got a couple of claims in Dyea, but we're interested in finding a plat further up the trail, toward Chilkoot. Could you tell us how you handle claims up that way?"

Reid smiled. "Lately, that's where most of my inquiries have been . . . up in the hills. How far up are you thinking?"

"A day's hike with a full pack from Dyea. Hopefully along the river," Lafe said.

"Let's take a look." Reid referred to the map stretched across his desk, put his finger where he knew their current claim was, and ran it along the route he knew we'd have to take. Eventually, he stopped and tapped his finger. "Nobody's laid claim to anything in this area, as yet." He indicated where the river ran, not far from the trail. "It's near Canyon City, about eight miles from the trailhead, just under 500 feet elevation. That about what you're looking for?"

Frank looked further up the trail and commented to his partners, "That looks good to me. What do you think? From there, we can leap frog to this spot," he made his comment while pointing at a marker labeled Sheep Camp, another twelve miles up the hill from Canyon City, and an elevation of about 1000 feet.

Frank and I both confirmed that we liked the plan.

I looked at the surveyor and asked, "How do we handle it now?"

"You go up there when you can, identify the locations you like, and when you return, I'll take care of the paperwork for you. I can't help you if someone else comes back here and pays me to stake a claim before you, though." Reid then clarified how far each claim was allowed to extend up the river and how wide the plat would be on either side. "To ensure neighboring claims don't overlap," he explained.

Lafe said, "That's helpful. Once we meet up with some friends and take a look around the area we'll be back. Shouldn't take more than a couple of day."

"Great. Recommend you not wait too long though. There's been a steady stream of folks coming in. And it's increasing each day."

"I understand," Lafe responded. "You'll be seeing us soon. We've got a lot to do before we can build our cabin and start mining."

We said our goodbyes and set out for the tasks ahead.

Chapter 15: Checking on the Gang

Skagway, Alaska
November 13, 1897

A FTER RETURNING FROM HIS TRIP, Mr. Smith took a few days to relax before making the rounds to his establishments and checking with his partners. Once completed, he decided to take the time to have his business associates check in with him. Concerned that some things could always go wrong in his absence, he first talked with his closest confidant.

"I want to hear all the news, good and bad. Not as a group. From each one of them individually."

"By when?"

"By the end of the day."

"All right, I'll tell 'em." Jefferson Smith's most trusted lieutenant, Van "Old Man" Triplet, turned to leave.

"Oh, and Van," Triplet stopped and turned. "Make it clear to them that I want straight talk. I'll be checking to ensure I'm not getting the watered-down version. I don't want any of them candy-coating[11] anything."

---

11 **Candy-coat** (idiom): to attempt to make something seem better or more palatable than it actually is, especially something perceived as negative or unfavorable.

The Old Man knew what he meant. "Right boss," he replied.

Being out of touch for a time didn't bother Smith, but the trip took longer than he intended. He needed to be updated on how things were going. He was always concerned about his men getting out of hand. Not all of them, just those that could be considered too violent. Some were known to be more aggressive than others.

He didn't mind aggression since they brought in customers that provided a significant income for his ventures, but he had a reputation to maintain. He didn't want any of them stirring up public resentment. He also needed to keep a balance, too. While he trusted them *not cross the line*, he also needed them to understand that he'd be there when they got in trouble with the law. He paid good money to the sheriff to keep that under control as well. He needed them, and they needed him. There was a fine line to maintain.

Smith thrived on the challenge of not holding the reigns on his men too tightly, but he had to have some control over them too, to ensure that the local community viewed him in a positive light. He knew he could avoid undesirable consequences resulting from his underhanded schemes through his generosity to improve the town. He was open about his methods, being careful not to hurt the locals, even boasting how he only took advantage of those who needed to be taught a lesson. Anyone who was naïve enough to think there was a quick and easy way to get rich best be careful. These naïve tenderfeet would quickly learn that lack of judgment when gambling beyond their means or spending their gold frivolously would soon part them from any possible riches.

Yes. I'm doing them a favor, Jefferson was convinced.

His closest lieutenants were to have personal contact with him before the day's end. Each of them had people of their own to manage, as well. They, too, wanted to report to him, to have the opportunity to brag about what they could do, prove themselves and move up in their standing in the gang. But he needed a buffer, and his lieutenants needed some level of responsibility themselves. Trusting their judgment was part of the game.

Shortly after a few of his band entered his establishment, Smith went into the washroom, looked in the mirror and adjusted his tie. His image was central to how people viewed him. After scrubbing up, he took his time adjusting his hat. He wanted his men to wait a while longer out in the Klondike Saloon. He then planned to take his time and visit one of his partners, Ira Coslett, before hearing their reports. It was good to make his deputies wait, show that he was the boss, and give them time to reflect on what they would say.

Later this same evening he would gather them all together and tell them the news he'd already told his other partner, Martin. But he would first keep Ira informed before passing on the good news to his lieutenants. He would move away from his partnership in the Klondike and the Clancy Saloons and build his own parlor.

The first two reports were as expected. "Reverend" John L. Bowers and "Slim Jim" Foster worked separately to recruit the wealthier arrivals as they left the pier. They were always helpful to the passengers off-loading from the ship, befriending them, and leading them toward the nearest saloon that might then lead to a friendly game of poker, where they'd then be separated from their money.

The first one they'd enter would be Clancy's. If that was full, they'd move up the street to one of the many others, who were either Jefferson's partners or where his men ran the games, allowing a cut to go to the owners. With the steady influx of gold seekers arriving on a regular basis, it was no surprise to hear how successful he'd been.

The next report, however, was more concerning. 'Professor Jackson' was known for increasing his followers and spreading them not only about town but up the trail as well. This in itself wasn't as great a concern as how quickly his team had grown and how that affected the professor and his men's effectiveness. There were so many that they'd fight, sometimes literally, to prove themselves.

Jackson had also shown more tension in his dealings with others, showing less patience when facing conflicts, being more aggressive in his demeanor. He began his report with his successes, as everyone typically did, and then alluded to how he and some of his cronies had been rebuffed by citizens of Dyea. It was obvious that his men wanted to challenge the threats made by the citizen of Dyea or at least bypass the town and work the area further up the trail. When Smith started asking questions, Jackson became vague in his answers. Rather than elaborate, he tried to move on to another topic.

Smith wouldn't let it pass.

Smith persisted with his questions and in a short time discovered that it had been made clear that his men were no longer welcome in the town. 'Jackson and his kind' had been threatened by the town's people. They were no longer welcome in Dyea, or anywhere near that part of the Chilkoot Trail. Once Smith understood the circumstances, he made a mental note to keep an eye on the situation.

"Had any further problems from that situation?" Smith asked.

"Nothing I can't handle," Jackson said. "We'll just work further up the trail till an opportunity presents itself."

Deciding to bring this meeting to an end, Smith said, "I can protect you within the town, but be careful up the trail. I understand they have a vigilante attitude about handling things."

With that being said, they parted ways.

Chapter 16: Growing Popularity

Nevada, Missouri
Monday, November 29, 1897

WILLIAM AND HIS DAUGHTER SAT SIDE-BY-SIDE on the buckboard as they traveled toward town. The twins rode alongside their father's side of the wagon on their own horses, with Sam
in the lead. William was taking the opportunity this Saturday to
visit the hardware store and have his sons help him fill the wagon
with supplies for the coming winter. Eva went along to gather some
foodstuffs that her mother asked for her to get while she did some
shopping of her own.

"I was hoping to get more done around the farm this past week,"
William directed toward the boys. "Other than the feed we're picking up today, the barn's in good shape. But I'd still like more wood
cut and stacked alongside the house." William looked up at the sky.
"As you can see, the weather's starting to turn."

They all felt the dampness in the air. Besides having on layers
of clothing, Eva had a wool blanket across her lap to fight the late
fall temperatures.

"We could have gotten it all done if we didn't have so many

distractions," John said.

"You mean all those people who have come by to ask about Bill?" Sam asked.

"There's not much we can do about that," Eva said.

"We could start putting them to work," Sam stated. "That would stop them from coming over."

Sam and John both chuckled.

Their father failed to see the humor. "The rumors have been put to rest, but now more people seem to know about Bill's good fortune."

Sam could see that the decision to allow the news article to be published was eating at his father.

"Until the newspaper confirmed his success, many didn't think much of the stories they'd heard about Bill," William continued. "Now that it's in print, the town's people are more excited about his ventures and want to know more."

"Yeah. But we don't know any more than what's already been printed," Sam replied.

"Right. Other than what we just learned in his follow-up letter," his father said sadly. "And that's not worth another article. That's what bothers me."

"Oh. Yeah," Sam said, softly. Wanting to steer his father toward the more positive aspects of the topic, he said, "You think that's why Eva has more callers, Pa?" he said, smiling at his sister.

Sam ignored her scowl.

"Not everyone comes by to talk about Bill," Eva retorted.

"Oh, really now. None of your visitors asked about Bill?" Sam said.

"Well, of course they asked about him. But Stanley didn't ask about him the first time he came by."

"He came more than once?" Sam had to think carefully about that for a moment. He knew Stanley to be too clever to talk about his intentions.

"So, you're seeing Stanley again?" John asked.

"He came by a few times, is all I said."

"Then you're not interested in him?" John asked.

"Even though it's none of your business, maybe I am interested," Eva said with a hint of annoyance in her voice. "He's been more attentive and proper since he's started coming by again."

"You think he's the right man for you?" John asked.

"You can judge for yourself. He's coming to dinner, tomorrow."

"Dinner? Tomorrow?" Sam said, trying to conceal his shock. "It wasn't that long ago he broke things off with you. For another girl, if I remember right."

"Evidently, he's thought better of it," she said smugly.

"You don't think of him differently after the breakup?" Sam asked.

"I'm optimistic, but taking it slow. I figure the dinner is another way of getting to know him better, you know, when he's around our family," Eva responded simply.

"Then we can all take a good look at him," Sam muttered to himself.

"Since he's come by a few times this week, Ma thought it might be nice to invite him for dinner, and I agreed."

"Well, when someone's right for you, you'll know," her father offered.

Eva smiled and nodded at her father's comment.

"You don't want to show you're too interested, though," John added.

"If the man is too forward, beware," Sam said.

"Alright, thank you everyone for your wonderful advice, but I think I can manage," Eva shook her head and laughed softly.

Arriving at their destination, Sam and John spurred ahead to tie up their horses in front of the hardware store.

William guided the wagon off to the side of the street and lashed the horses to the hitching post, next to the twins' mounts. William then looked at his daughter and said, "We shouldn't be too long. We're just going to pick up the feed, and then I'm going to look at some paint."

"I'll just wait here, if you're not going to be long," Eva said.

Eva's father said, "As soon as we get back, we can go to the general store." He then followed the boys into the hardware store.

Sam said, "Pa, we can get the feed if you want to select the paint you want."

"Good," William replied and headed to the aisle where he could find paint.

After a spell, Eva decided she was wasting valuable time just sitting in the cold. She looked down the street toward the general store then dismounted and entered the hardware store to tell her father where she would be.

Entering, she saw him reading a label while talking with another man who looked familiar. She walked over and said, "Pa."

Her father turned around, as did the young man he had been talking with. The young man said, "Hello again."

"Hello . . . ah . . ." Eva said hesitantly. "Pa . . . this is . . ."

"My friends call me Ted," he interjected, "Ted Bohannon."

William noticed his daughter's eyes brighten. "Well, nice to know the man I was talking to is not only knowledgeable about paint, but someone I should meet, as well." William smiled and offered his hand.

They shook hands as Eva looked on.

Ted looked back to Eva.

Almost self-consciously, Eva broke eye contact and said, "Ted came by the house a couple of weeks ago and visited with Sam and John. I met him briefly before he left."

"They were kind enough to give me directions when I first arrived and some information about the town. I just moved here to work with the railroad." He forced himself to look away from Eva and connect with her father.

"Then I should say welcome to the city of Nevada, Ted. I trust you've found a place to stay and have gotten settled in," Mr. Schooley said.

"Yes sir, thanks to your sons."

"Glad to hear it," Schooley replied.

William noticed that the young man looked a bit uneasy. He could see that Ted had difficulty keeping his eyes off his daughter, yet he looked uncomfortable talking to her. *Is there something between them?* he wondered.

Sam and John walked by with feed sacks over their shoulders as they headed toward the front door, to load the wagon. Sam recognized Ted and said, "Well, I'll be. Hello, Ted."

John, standing behind Sam, shifted his load to the other shoulder to see who Sam was talking to. Recognizing Ted, he greeted him as well.

"Need a hand with those?" Ted asked.

"Not with these, but we are loading another half dozen others from the back," Sam responded.

"I'll give you a hand," Ted offered.

"Great," Sam and John said in unison.

"The wagon's just out front," Sam added.

"Nice to meet you, sir," Ted said to Mr. Schooley. "Good to see you again, Eva."

"The pleasure's mine," Mr. Schooley said. He then watched Ted make a quick exit to help the twins.

Mr. Schooley was impressed with Ted. He nodded his approval, looked back at his daughter and smiled as Ted walked toward the front of the store with a sack of seed.

"Seems nice," he admitted, "but seemed in a hurry to leave, wouldn't you say."

"I wouldn't know, Pa," Eva looked puzzled.

William could see that his daughter continued to look in Ted's direction.

"What were you going to say, Eva?" her father prodded.

She hesitated as if coming out of a trance before saying, "I just came in to let you know I'm going to walk up the street."

Her father sensed her distraction, continuing to watch Ted as he exited the building.

"He wasn't one of your callers, was he?" her father asked.

"No, he wasn't," she said.

Eva tried to shake off Ted's appearance as well as her father's comment and said, "I'm going to the general store, Pa."

Chapter 17: Dinner Guest

Nevada, Missouri
Tuesday, November 30, 1897

S AM ENTERED THE PARLOR with an armful of wood. John followed with more. After Sam set his load on the hearth, he stood and saw Eva place a stack of their good dishes on the dining room table. John placed his load alongside Sam's and began to move them to a rack, off to the side of the fireplace.

"That should be enough for the evening. Can you handle that, John? I just want to talk to Eva for a minute," Sam said.

"Go ahead, this won't take me long," John replied.

Sam wasn't about to be as direct as he'd like, since he knew Eva had begun to show a fondness toward Stanley again. But he knew he had to say something to get her to question Stanley's honesty and true intentions. Since hearing that Stanley would be attending dinner with the family this evening, Sam had stayed in town long enough to see a couple of Stanley's friends and ask about him.

He didn't like what he'd heard, *"He's not the honorable person Eva thinks him to be."*

"Eva, I saw Stanley yesterday."

"Oh, where?"

"In town, at the hardware store."

"What did he have to say?" Eva asked.

"I didn't have a chance to talk with him," Sam said. "John and I had just gotten on our horses and were following Pa to the general store when I looked back and saw him entering the store."

Eva looked puzzled but she waited for Sam to continue.

"Didn't you say that Stanley had been seeing Alice before calling on you?"

"Yes. Why?"

"Ah . . . I was just wondering . . . since she was with him at the store."

Eva stayed quiet. Sam could see she was absorbing his comment. Realizing that he had probably put a damper on her spirits for an evening that was supposed to be special, he added, "It doesn't mean they're together . . . just that they were *together*."

"I'm sure you're right," Eva said softly.

"Otherwise, why would he still be coming here this evening?" Sam gave her a quick smile "I'm sure it doesn't mean anything."

They heard a knock at the door. Eva looked in the kitchen at her mother. Ann said, "Eva, you go meet him." Looking at Sam, Ann added, "Sam, finish setting the table. I'm almost done in the kitchen."

Sam watched as his mother looked at her husband, to prompt him into performing some agreed upon role. William, took his cue, carefully folded the newspaper and set it on the end table. He then motioned for John to follow him as he entered the dining room to join Sam. "Boys, I just want to remind you that our role is to try and make Stanley feel welcome."

Sam and John looked at each other. They both showed amused smiles. John said, "So, we're not supposed to tease him?"

William said, "I'll let you be the judge of what's appropriate. But, I do expect proper behavior."

"Sure thing, Pa." Sam offered. John nodded.

"Alright then, let's wait in the parlor." The boys followed him.

Eva led Stanley from the entrance hall into the parlor to greet her father and brothers. As she joined them, so too did her mother, taking off her apron.

Following formal introductions, Stanley was invited to sit with Eva's father and the twins while her mother finished placing the last few items on the dining room table. Stanley took his place on the settee, next to Eva.

William began the conversation and asked, "Stanley, I haven't seen your father for some time. Last time we talked, he was thinking about turning over the farm to you boys. I understand his leg injury may be bothering him more these days. That was quite a spill he took off the horse some years ago. How is he doing?"

"He's not taking part in any of the chores anymore, just keeping the books, now," Stanley responded.

"I suppose you boys are taking on a great deal more now?" William asked.

"My oldest brother, Joseph, is taking on most of the responsibility. Being the eldest, he'll take over the farm eventually. My other two older brothers help a great deal too, and my younger sister helps Ma as much as she can."

"Do you work the farm with your brothers?" William inquired.

"Some," Stanley said. "I take care of the horses and wagons, but I'm also the idea man of the family."

Idea man? I've got to keep my thoughts to myself, Sam thought.

"Ever since pa's accident I've been the one to take him where he needs to go on the buckboard. Since then, I've been running errands into town for him and the family."

Sam wondered if he sensed some bitterness in Stanley. He was the youngest and had become the errand boy, perhaps not being given as much responsibility working on the farm.

"Do you plan on continuing in the family farm business?" William asked.

"No. I've got bigger plans. I guess you might say that since I've been going into town as often as I do, I've had more time to think about how I can use my skills in some other way. I don't want to be tied to the land so much."

Oh, oh. Here we go, Sam thought.

The 'bigger plans' statement got Sam's attention, remembering a comment he'd heard yesterday from a past friend and investor of Stanley's. Sam was determined to watch over his big sister. If Stanley was going to try and get Eva involved in a scheme, he wasn't about to stand idly by and just let it happen. He thought about how he might bring up something during this evening's conversation that would challenge Stanley's ability to be candid.

"Tell me about your plans," Mr. Schooley said.

Sam doubted Stanley needed any prodding from his father.

"I believe I can make a great deal of money working with the new machinery that makes life on farms easier," he smiled smugly. "Once I get one more investor I'll be ready to get started."

Blowhard.

"Sounds like a grand plan," William stated.

Yes it does, Sam thought.

Stanley looked to the paper on the end table and asked, "Oh, the Journal. Is that today's or last Sunday's edition? That reminds me, maybe Bill would want to invest with me," Stanley let out a laugh that was too boisterous.

Sam thought he caught a hint of where Stanley's interests lay.

Blowhard.

Just then Ann came into the parlor and announced, "Dinner is ready. Shall we all move into the dining room?"

Everyone took a seat at the table.

After filling their plates, the conversation wandered from the weather and what they could expect through the winter, to the boys' education, health, and the like.

As they were all waiting for Ann to bring in dessert, Sam, in an upbeat manner, said, "I saw you at the hardware store yesterday and waved, but I guess you didn't see me. I was just down the street when you entered."

Stanley responded only after looking up at Sam and giving a quick glance at Eva. "Oh, sorry, I was probably deep in thought about what hardware I needed to pick up for my Pa."

Sam noticed Stanley's face flush slightly.

Yeah. You were sure thinking about the hardware, all right, Sam thought. He then detected a furtive glance from Eva. He didn't know if it was directed at Stanley or himself.

Stanley changed the topic. "Have you heard from Bill lately?"

"Not since earlier this week," Ann said.

"You must all be very proud of his success up north," Stanley said.

"Yes we are," William responded. "We're very proud of him."

"I read the article in last Sunday's newspaper. Seems they did very well, but the article didn't say much beyond that."

He's fishing for more information, Sam thought. *Blowhard and opportunist.*

"Allowing the writer from the Kansas City Sunday Journal to at least confirm the basic information was our choice I'm afraid," William said. "We didn't really want anything written up. But by the time the papers caught wind of the boys' good fortune, and asked to write about it, we thought that might help stop some of the inaccuracies we've been hearing. Even the Colemans agreed with us after we'd told them what we'd done."

Ann, returned from the kitchen carrying an apple pie and proudly said, "I have a copy of the article here if you'd like to look at it." She set the pie on the table and turned to a cabinet behind her and pulled open a drawer, reached in and pulled out the front page of the newspaper. She set it on the table in front of Stanley. An additional cutout of the article was clipped to the front page as well. Stanley picked it up and read to himself while Mrs. Schooley handed out slices of pie.

"That article sure got a lot of people's attention," Stanley began. "Did he say anything else that's not mentioned in the article?"

"Not much else," Mrs. Schooley said. "Just what the paper said."

"When do you expect they'll be here?" Stanley asked. "Wouldn't he normally be here by now if, like you said, he sent the letter to you a month ago?"

"It's hard to say when he'll be returning, now."

Ann offered the last piece of her pie, which everyone declined, before Stanley had a chance to inquire further.

Hearing a banging noise from outside, Ann said, "Sounds like the wind's picking up out of the south—that was my rocker on the porch." She looked out the window. "Getting darker each day."

"Stanley, Eva, I know the two of you would like to talk without us fussing over you. Why don't you two go out by the fireplace? We can take care of the dishes."

"Thank you, Mr. Schooley, Mrs. Schooley. The meal was delicious."

"You're welcome," they said in unison.

Mr. Schooley stood and stated to Stanley, "Let's stoke the fire so you can sit in its warmth."

Stanley stood and followed Mr. Schooley into the parlor. Eva instinctively began helping her mother and the twins clear the table.

After Eva took one trip to the kitchen, Ann said, "We can do this. Go ahead and visit with Stanley."

As Eva started to leave the kitchen, Sam walked up beside her and said, Eva, "I know you think nothing but the best in people. That's just your nature, but just so you're forewarned, if he talks about asking William to invest in something . . . well, his interests may be in the wrong area."

Thinking that was an odd statement from her brother, but not wanting to keep Stanley waiting, she gave her younger brother a tight smile. Then she stepped away to join Stanley by the fireplace. After a few steps, she turned and said, "We may have a lot to talk about, Sam, but I don't know why you think *that* would be one of them."

Sam watched her join Stanley and thought, *Yeah, you've got a lot to talk about alright. Blowhard.*

Chapter 18: Warning Signs

M R. SCHOOLEY STOKED THE FIRE with two more logs and went to help his wife in the kitchen.

Eva joined Stanley by the fireplace and watched him poke at the logs as she sat on the settee. Once he was satisfied that the air was circulating underneath for a better flame, he join her.

Eva knew that they'd be alone only as long as the rest of the family was busy in the kitchen. Then his mother would find her way into the parlor, to conveniently knit in her rocker by the window. Her father, not far away, would start reading his newspaper.

"I've been looking forward to talking with you alone all evening, I have something I'd like to share," Stanley began.

Thinking he wanted to share his feelings about her, she looked down and blushed.

"First, I want to say, I enjoyed myself and talking to your parents," Stanley said. "Tell your mother that the apple pie was especially superb."

"Thank you. I will," Eva replied.

"We didn't have a chance to talk about Bill's return."

"No we didn't, but I don't think you want to talk about Bill right now," Eva said thinking she was helping to spur him on to his real purpose.

"When do you think he's coming home?"

"Why do you want to talk about him?"

"I just wanted to offer him an opportunity."

"Stanley, is *that* what you were looking forward to talking about all evening?"

Realizing that discussing her brother was a mistake, he continued, "No . . . not about Bill directly. I really wanted you to know how excited I am about a profitable business opportunity that I know he would want to invest in."

"Oh, I see. It's all about money."

"Well . . . no, not all about money," he said guiltily. "It's about how I can afford to treat you when I am successful."

Eva began to think about Sam's comment earlier.

"An investment idea?" Eva looked perplexed. She didn't want to believe what her brother had implied.

Sam was trying to warn me.

"Yes. Remember when I mentioned about the new machinery that's now available to help make farming easier?"

"Yes . . . and that's what you wanted to talk with me about?"

"Yes. That and Bill."

"Stanley, you're talking in riddles. Why do you want to talk with me about Bill and investments?"

"I, ah . . . thought you would talk with Bill for me."

"About?" She wanted him to make his intentions perfectly clear.

"Ah . . . you know . . . about my investment opportunity. I just need to have you tell him I have a great opportunity for him to invest then I'll take it from there." Stanley said, smiling proudly.

Warning.

"Stanley . . ." she stammered, embarrassed—thinking about Sam's comment. Recovering, she said, "Stanley it wouldn't be appropriate for me to do that. First, you have a proposition for Bill, not me. If you have an offer for him, you need to talk with him, yourself."

Abruptly she stood, looked out the window at the gathering clouds and stepped out toward the foyer. "Stanley it's time for you to go."

Stanley stood, walked to Eva and followed her gaze. "I'm not worried about the weather," he said. Eva glared at him. "Eva, you're upset with me?"

Eva walked to the front door. Stanley followed.

She stopped at the door and turned. "Of course I'm not happy with you. Think about it. You've spent an evening with my family, I'm assuming because you have an interest in me. But, when you have a chance to be alone with me in the parlor,[12] all you want to do is talk about an investment opportunity for my brother."

Stanley didn't say anything.

"Now I suppose, if I were to ask you what you were talking with Alice about, while at the hardware store, you'd tell me you were making the same offer to her."

Stanley's face flushed. "Ah . . . well . . . actually, I was," he said softly. "I admit, I did talk with her about offering her father the opportunity to invest in my enterprise, to be honest with you," he stressed. "I even told you during dinner that I had an investor."

"So, Alice's father is going to invest?"

"He . . . he hasn't exactly said that he will, yet . . . but I'm sure he will."

"Stanley, you told my father that you only needed one more investor, implying that you already had an investor. And now you're saying you're counting on him. That's not the same thing as having a confirmed investor. You're not being entirely honest with me. Or my father for that matter."

Stanley stayed silent.

"Do you care about me, Stanley?"

"Of course I do."

---

12 **Parlor:** a sitting room in a private house.

"Evidently not more than some financial scheme. You have a lot to learn about what matters to a girl."

"But . . . I've been doing all this for you . . . for us . . . you know, so I can treat you the way you deserve to be treated."

"You think I'm a fool? Stanley, you're just kidding *yourself*. Don't you be a fool," She held open the front door, looked him straight in the eye and said, "Good night, Stanley."

Stanley didn't argue. He stepped through the entryway, stopped, turned and said, "Will you talk to Bill when he gets home, or at least let me know so I can talk with him?"

Exasperated, Eva sighed and said, "Well, guess what Stanley? He's *not* coming home."

"But the news article—"

"That was before we got another letter letting us know he's gone back up to Alaska."

He's not coming home.

Stanley's faced began to darken, his neck stiffened, and his jaw tightened. "You know, Eva, you're not the person I thought you were," he said indignantly.

Shocked, Eva said, "What are you talking about?"

It's a two-way street, Eva. You need to think about what I want to do and what I have to offer. If we're ever to be together, you should appreciate that I know how to be successful. Crossing me is a big mistake.

"Crossing you?!" Eva exclaimed. "I'm not crossing you."

Stanley's face darkened even further. He stood tall, pulled his chin back, as if trying to maintain his dignity, and walked out the front door. While the door was still open, he said, "Pushing me away is a big mistake, Eva."

Eva watched as Stanley walked out to his horse, mounted and rode off.

"Funny thing, Stanley. I feel more relieved now," she said to an empty foyer.

Relieved.

Eva reentered the parlor where her mother was waiting. Ann looked over and noticed her daughter's red, teary eyes. "Eva, is something wrong? What is it?"

"Oh mother, I feel like such a fool. All this time I thought Stanley was interested in me, but instead all he wanted was to use me to get to Bill and his gold."

"I'm sorry, Eva," her mother said, and stepped in to embrace her daughter.

Eva added, "At least I found out his intentions now. I suppose I should consider this a good lesson. I wish Bill were here."

"I know you do, honey. I know you do. I miss him too."

Eva said with a sigh, "I'm sure Bill is just whooping it up, while I'm here feeling miserable."

December 1897

Ignis Fatuus

"We just completed a building on one of our lots and will start the other tomorrow. We could turn our lots in now and get five dollars for every dollar invested, to say nothing of the buildings, but do not think it time yet, for the rush is hardly on."

"There is something wonderfully fascinating about this mining after one is well into it. I believe that a man will uncomplainingly endure more privations and hardships than in any other occupation. The uncertainty of the thing and the frequent examples we have of poor men being suddenly stamped as millionaires are sufficient to enable one to overcome all obstacles, or consummate all tasks however arduous they may be. The "Ignis fatuus" keeps leading us on, keeps beckoning to us to follow on to the pot of gold that hangs on the end of the rainbow, and we poor, lost, benighted creatures follow, even though we suspicion the loyalty of our leader. I, for my part, intent to follow on until I find a big stake, as they say the excitement will justify me in doing that."

—*Letter to brother Samuel Schooley, December 22, 1897*

Chapter 19: First Claim Settled

Dyea, Alaska
Friday, December 18, 1897

THIS PAST MONTH HAS BEEN A BLUR.
Having completed my work for the day at the cabin, I helped a few neighbors haul their supplies off the tide flats. I was exhausted enough now to find comfort just sitting on a crate recently brought inland off the flats.

From Dyea's waterline to two hundred yards inland, the scene could have been from a town rebuilding following a hurricane. I could see stacks of lumber, as well as other supplies and provisions piled everywhere. If not hustling to move their goods off the tide flats, many of the town's new residents were walking about, rummaging through the timbers, looking for just the right board to add to their buildings. Big buildings were going up so fast that it was impossible to keep the place adequately supplied with lumber. Yet, the miners just kept coming.

It was no wonder that those helping to pack goods from the shore could asked such exorbitant wages. Once the barges were off loaded, their owners were left to get their supplies to dry ground on their own. It was hard work when you considered how quickly you had to move the goods inland.

Most of the residents understood that twenty dollars per hour, to move supplies out of the tide flats, seemed high until the cost rose to $50 per hour with the rising of the water. It was either pay the price or watch your purchases wash away with each breaking wave. Many had learned the hard way that water over one hundred feet away would arrive within minutes on such a gentle slope. A rise of just a few inches in water height could quickly cover 50 feet of beach.

Over the past two weeks, we had worked hard to set up a structure on our plat near the back edge of town that included a portion of the river. Our first cabin was now complete, and it was big enough to sleep all three of us. Our original plan was to erect a shed on the two other sites we'd also laid claim to. But there was no longer an immediate need to build the other cabins now that we had a place to keep us warm through the night, with enough room to store our goods. Erecting a Log cabin on a piece of land was an investment, improving the value of the plat.

In all, we had located one plat and bought two others for $185, thanks to diligently checking with Reid whenever we found or heard of something promising. Working as a team allowed us to efficiently coordinate our efforts. While one or two of us staked out our claim or worked on our campsite, another would travel to Skagway to secure a deed or order lumber to build on the lot. Each evening we discussed what we would try to accomplish the next day, and establish who would complete the chores.

If we weren't working on the cabin we were off-loading lumber from the barges coming ashore at Dyea for others—at a price. We were always looking for ways to pay our way. Materials were expensive and were getting costlier with each surge of prospectors. The competition for materials was intense. We could only hope that when the time came for us to move inland, the price of our plats would increase as well.

Twenty minutes later, I was still gazing at the chaos around me when Frank approached. He brought with him a slab of cold bacon and a few biscuits that he'd cooked, after setting up our stove in our cabin. The timing of this this morsel was appreciated, knowing it would tide me over till our next meal.

"Lafe should be down here shortly," he said simply.

I nodded. We both sat, quietly resting. I watched a small band of men methodically working the masses, seeking work from those needing their goods moved.

Many of them seemed lost, overwhelmed with what was needed to even start searching for gold. This was even more evident in Skagway where I saw even more naïve gold seekers cluttering the streets. I thought about how many of them would be burning up their savings, not even knowing how to get started in the mining business. Was I becoming cold to the concerns of outsiders, becoming less sympathetic to their ineptness? I wondered. They were just taking up precious space—my space. I had a single focus, adding to our plats. *I just hope they stay out of my way,* I thought, *especially when we start moving inland.*

I continued to watch the chaos around me. A school lesson I'd taught during my short teaching career in Enoch, Missouri, came to mind.

Instinctively I said aloud, "Ignis fatuus."

"What's that mean?" Frank asked.

"It's a 'misleading illusion' that keeps leading us on. It keeps beckoning to us to follow on to the pot of gold that hangs on the end of the rainbow, where we poor, lost, creatures follow."

"And what's the cause of that deep-seated thought?"

"It's just a thought I had from a book I read some time ago. I used it for a lesson in my classroom." I knew my appetite for reading intrigued Frank. I told him once that it helped shed light on how I could view the world.

"Take a look around and tell me what you see," I challenged.

"I see a lot of folks looking to get rich."

"That's my point," I said. "They all come here—"

"Like us,"

"Yes, like us, to strike it rich, to seek that claim that exceeds all others."

"So, getting rich is just an illusion?" Frank asked.

"Could be . . . . for many of these dreamers. Many will curse the day they arrived."

"I see," Frank said.

"I think many are disillusioned by what they thought they'd find and overwhelmed by what they see. They lack perspective."

Frank silently took in my comment.

"See those men over there?" I continued. I gestured toward those I had just observed seeking work.

"I do," Frank said. We both watched them for a time.

"Do any of them look to have their own claim, or space?"

"Hard to say. They're just helping others," Frank observed.

"They may be serving others, but many of them lack their own purpose," I said.

"Fair enough. So what are you driving at?"

"I just want them to stay out of my way. Our way."

Frank looked at me, blankly. "That's not like you, Bill."

I continued, "The stampede has caused chaos—that doesn't help matters. Many are so overwhelmed with what they see once they arrive, they lose sight of what's important to be successful. There's too much going on around us, too many distractions to prevent them from staying on track with what's important. Many don't even know how to go about mining gold or how to even approach such a grand task. Some of their dreams have blocked out the reality of the situation—it's harder than they expected."

"That's very insightful, Bill. But what do their problems have to do with your concern?" Frank prompted.

"This," I exclaimed. I pulled a letter out of my pocket that I'd received earlier and thought about its contents. Much of the activity around me had me reflecting on it.

I stayed quiet for a moment, and then said, "I guess I'm just being more thoughtful because of the letter I got this morning, from my brother."

"Sam or John?"

"John."

"Oh."

"While sitting here looking out over all this, I can't help but think about this letter and wonder." I held it up, then tucked it back into my pocket.

"Wonder about what?"

"Wonder how I can best answer his question."

"Which was?"

"He's interested in joining me. Asked if I'd recommend his coming here."

"You can't give him a simple yes or no now," Frank concluded.

"Right. In some things I can. I can tell him how we mine gold, but don't know that I can advise him to join me here."

"Tell him how it was for us and what these people are now adjusting to," Frank said simply. "If you remember, it wasn't easy for us when we first arrived, but after a while we adapted. We were able to learn from those around us. We listened and sorted out what we needed to do to succeed."

"True enough," I mused out loud, "but I see the situation differently now from when we first arrived three years ago. There weren't so many of us when we first started."

"I assume that's why you're having a tough time putting it into words for Sam?"

"Right. I think I'd just as soon tell him to wait until all the deadheads get out of the way. I can assume that not all these folks here will endure whatever it takes to find gold. It'll surely wear on most. Most will be gone within a year."

"I hope that's not us," Frank decided.

Instinctively, I started to say "me too" but then thought better of it. A few weeks earlier I was excited about returning home.

Now I realize I can't even have my brother join me. I thought about how much of this predicament irritated me because it kept me from reuniting with family and how much bothered me due to the ineptness of those around me.

Either way I knew I was bothered by this whole situation.

I dismissed my thoughts and shifted back to the miners. "I know I can tell him that anyone who stays with it may find some success in time, but it is far from being a sure thing. As much as I would like to have either one of my brothers here as a partner, I know that gold is not lying about in such quantities as the steamboat companies would have you believe."

"One done, two to go."

We both turned toward the voice.

"Hello, Lafe," I said.

"Need a rest myself. Got room for another there?" he asked.

Frank and I scooted down a ways for my broad-shouldered friend.

"Cold and dampness in the air. Glad we got this cabin done," Lafe admitted.

"Shouldn't take us as long if we decide to build another structure," Frank said, "We're getting better at carpentry."

"The carpentry will be easier but not the work we have yet to do." Lafe said.

"You mean when we start moving to our latest claim up the trail," I added.

"Yup. That part is going to be more difficult," Lafe watched a few light snowflakes floated onto his coat sleeve.

"There's our motivation, to get a lot of things done sooner rather than later," I said.

"And more quickly," Lafe added. "Maybe we should consider retrieving our goods from Juneau. At least we could see how capable we are in packing a load of our goods to our cabin."

"Good idea," I said, "We can see how well we handle moving our goods without additional help."

"Might want to get our snow shoes unpacked, too," Frank said, looking up at the thickening white clouds hanging overhead. "And, if we're going to go to Juneau, maybe we can eat a few hearty meals and rest up. We're going to have some busy days ahead of us after we get back."

"So, now the fun begins," I sighed.

Chapter 20: Trouble on the Boardwalk

Skagway, Alaska
Monday, December 20, 1897

WITH LESS THAN SIX AND A HALF HOURS of daylight available this late December day, Lafe, Frank and I rose at the break of dawn and had breakfast before making our nine-mile trek into Skagway. With the cabin now finished, we decided that time was ripe to deviate from the daily grind that we'd endured over the past month. Getting more supplies was also a priority. We needed to prepare for the next phase of our journey inland, to our next claim. Some immediate provisions were needed, at least until we can access the supplies we stored in Juneau.

In Dyea's short existence, the building was going as fast as it could, but it was not expected to catch up to Skagway anytime soon. While most of the building materials in Dyea had to be beached in the mudflats, Skagway had a long pier that could handle deeper water steamers. Hence, Skagway's ability to better provide what the miners needed. In other words, we still had to periodically make trips to Skagway for some of our provisions.

While there were a multitude of stores beginning to set up

shop just blocks from our Dyea claim, we still needed to make trips to Skagway to pick up provisions that Dyea wasn't ready to offer. Other than a few pieces of additional clothing and food to eat along the way, our backpacks were essentially empty. We needed to make room for the provisions we would pick up.

We first made a short stop at Skagway's mercantile store. We gave them a list of what provisions we needed and promised to return later to pick them up. While speaking with the merchant, we also received a recommendation on where to find clothing to better fit the dropping temperatures. After getting directions to the clothing store, we left.

Returning to the planked walkway that bordered the streets of the town, we headed out. Like others around us, we were cautious about walking the planks. Frank fell in behind Lafe and I behind Frank as we made our way along the narrow boardwalk. During our walk, we discussed the eventual trip we'd need to take to Juneau, to gather up our supplies.

"I'm ready to go today," Frank said. "The sooner we get our supplies back here, the sooner we can get our goods in position up the hill before the weather really gets bad."

"Or within the next few days, before everyone else here starts moving their goods up the trail," Lafe added.

"Considering the number of trips we'll be taking with our backpacks, I'd like to get started sooner rather than later, too" I threw in. "Unless we get—"

Frank bumped into the back of his brother. Lafe had abruptly stopped, then began backing up.

Pressed in behind Frank, I glanced up to see a man bounce off Lafe's sturdy frame and drop from sight. Lafe was still stepping back when the man ran into him. Obviously, the man was either not paying attention to his surroundings, going too fast for conditions on the walkway, or both. He landed in a sitting position on one of the planks, with one boot in the street to stop his fall, spraying a mix of slush and mud onto himself.

One of his four companions who was following him placed a hand on his friend's upper arm to assist but was brusquely parried away by a quick movement of the sitting-man's shoulder.

"You all right?" Lafe asked, extending his hand to assist the man back to his feet.

Instead of accepting Lafe's hand, the bearded man jumped to his feet and began to strike a fighter's pose with his fists clenched.

Lafe put his arms out wide with his palms forward to demonstrate he had no intent to cause further harm.

"Why don't you watch where you're going?" the man responded, and then he relaxed his hands after seeing the size of his foe.

"Come on, Jackson . . . " The man's companion started to speak but evidently thought better of it and stood in silence.

Jackson looked at Lafe and said, "I know you."

"You look familiar yourself." Lafe looked at the small scar on his forehead, just above his left eye. "And the Jackson name sounds familiar, too," Lafe added.

"You came off the boat a few weeks ago. I saw you at the wharf. You interrupted a conversation I was having with a friend."

Lafe thought about that. "Most of what you're saying is true, except . . . that man wasn't your friend."

"What did you say to him anyway?"

"Look. I met the man on the steamer. I liked him. I didn't like you taking advantage of him, so I told him to avoid you."

Hearing this, the man started to lose control of his temper. He took a moment to compose himself, then said, "Now, that's not so kind."

"Oh, I'm sure you'll find others like him."

"What are you implying, mister?"

"Not much, other than you're looking for a patsy to take advantage of."

Jackson huffed, then said, "I don't like you butting in."

"Well, that makes us even. I don't like you taken advantage of other people in order to part them from their money."

Jackson looked back at the four men behind him, either to ensure they were still there or to let Lafe know he had backers. Lafe didn't know which but didn't care either.

"You're going to regret messing with me, mister," Jackson spoke loud enough for everyone to hear.

"You're not worth messing with. Now if you'll excuse me, I've got more important things to attend to."

Lafe started to brush past and move on, but the con man put his hand to his chest. "You're not going anywhere, mister."

Lafe stopped and stared down at the man's hand in disgust. "You don't want to do that," he said calmly.

Four more men approached from across the street. The lead man yelled over.

"Hey, Lafe, got a problem here?"

Lafe smiled at the group, then looked straight into Jackson's eyes. "Do we?"

Jackson glanced over his shoulder, in the direction of the new voice and lowered his hand.

Lafe said, "No. I think everything's fine here. But thanks for asking, Dutch."

"So I see," Dutch replied.

While it was common for crowds to gather during any kind of ruckus, particularly a brawl, Jackson realized that Lafe had friends here in town. Both parties watched Jackson turn back to his men and comment, "Another time, boys. Let's move on." Jackson then looked Lafe squarely in the eye and gruffly said, "You're lucky I'm feeling generous, but just know that I'll be watching for you, mister," then brushed past him with his men close behind.

I looked back as the men walked away. I recognized the show the man put on for his companions. I'd seen it too often with schoolyard bullies, especially after losing face in front of his group. *I don't think we've seen the end of this,* I thought.

I turned to catch up to Lafe and Frank.

The Colemans were talking with the four men who had shown

their willingness to intervene in Lafe's situation. I knew Dutch Dehous and Guy Bunge because they worked a claim not too far from our own in Sunrise. We'd give each other a hand when needed. Pettit and Press, who I only knew by their last names, had claims further away and had called on Dutch for advice now and again. We had done the same. Dutch was the most experienced of the lot, having worked in the area for well over five years.

I stepped up to join in on the backslapping and hand shaking. "Good to see you, Dutch." I looked at Pettit and Press, nodded and said, "Your timing was good."

"Looks like you haven't lost your knack for trouble, Lafe," Dehous laughed.

"I wasn't the one looking for it," Lafe admitted. "He asked me a question and I gave him an honest answer. The man's a crook . . . tried to rob a friend."

"What brings you here?" I asked.

"Just finished registering our claims and picking up a few supplies before heading back up," Dutch said. "Found some decent sites up the trail a piece from Dyea."

"Where are the others?" Lafe was referring to his other sidekicks.

"Miller, Lou, and Jake are out somewhere looking for wood to make sluice boxes for the claims, and Orval, Heely, and Will are just a little ways past Dyea, working on our campsite and watching over our outfits.

"What's your story, Lafe?" Dutch asked.

"Don't have much to tell . . . you mean about scar face back there?" Lafe said.

"Yeah."

"Like I said, the man's a crook . . . actually a con man, from what I got from a man by the name of Ben Moore. His dad's the one who owns the land that Skagway's on."

"Interesting. And how'd you come to know that Jackson fella?"

"I met him on my first trip down here a few weeks ago. I learned more than just about the town from Captain Moore and his son,

Ben." Lafe told them about how the town was originally Moore's land until the gold seekers took it over. "Unfortunately, I have to admit, there's too many of his type around here," Lafe added. "We were hoping to meet up with you boys before you got settled so we could make sure you avoided Skagway."

"Well that's nice to know, but it seems we already made the decision to locate up past Dyea, anyway," Dutch replied. "I just hope this trouble doesn't catch up with you."

"Oh, he's harmless enough," Lafe said, "as long as he has no cause."

"And he's not around others like himself," I added.

"Where you headed for now?" Dutch asked.

"We're going to look into buying some mackinaws,[13] then pick up some provisions we ordered at the mercantile store before heading back to our cabin in Dyea."

"Great, we'll be heading to Dyea, ourselves," Dutch said, "Good time to get caught up on how you're getting on."

The group of six made their way to the clothing store then to the mercantile store before continuing their conversation while returning to Dyea.

---

13 **Mackinaws:** a short coat or jacket made of a thick, heavy woolen cloth, typically with a plaid design.

Chapter 21: Truth Revealed

Nevada, Missouri
December 21ˢᵗ, 1897

E VA COULD FEEL THE EXCITEMENT as she stepped down from the wagon.

The park and adjoining barn were filled with the citizens of Nevada, Missouri. They were every age—gray-haired seniors, couples walking about, some with families, some without. Many carried an assortment of picnic baskets. Some of the younger ones played tag, others were skipping around, waving at friends. A young mother sat at a table rocking her baby while her husband arranged items on the table.

A few families clustered among the picnic tables to chat after they'd unloaded their goods. The tables were positioned in rows that stretched around an open area designated as a dance floor. A small band of women gathered near a quilt display. A group of young men and older boys wove in and out of the crowds, heading toward the barn.

Outside the barn, to the right of the entrance, a puppet stage was being set up. On the left were a series of worn out shirts and overalls stacked next to a pile of straw, to be used for the scare-crow contest. Beyond the barn was a corral that bordered the park. There, a few young men gathered old fence posts and barn boards that were strewn nearby, for the bonfire.

Eva and her mother made their way to the picnic tables. Both scanned the crowds and waved at others they knew, who were also here to celebrate the end of the harvest season and All-Saints Day. Over the years, since the arrival of the Irish immigrants in the early years of the 1800s, both events had been combined.

Eva and Anna reached their destination and began setting up their table.

A short time later the twins arrived.

"This is all of it," Sam said, as he and John arrived carrying a load of picnic items from the wagon.

"Just set them here," their mother said, indicating the end of the table.

"We helped Pa unhook the horses. He's taking them behind the barn now, where he's getting them water and a bag of oats."

"We can take care of setting the table if you two want to go visit your friends."

"We'll be helping out with the bon fire, Ma." That wasn't news to Mrs. Schooley or Eva. For years the young men had taken on the chore of building the fire.

The twins set off to do their duty.

Eva followed their departure until she recognized a lone fig-ure standing across the dance floor. A look of concern crossed her face.

Her mother noticed and asked, "Is something wrong, Eva?"

She paused before responding, "No, Ma. Just feel a little chilly is all."

Anna looked up at the sky. "I'm sure glad we don't have the mist we started with this morning. The bon fire should take some of the chill out of the air, if you want to go over there."

"Maybe later," Eva said.

Eva watched the twins cross the dance floor. She also watched the lone figure out of the corner of her eye. "Looks like the music will be starting soon," Eva said. Musicians were positioning their chairs for the festivities. Eva was determined not to let the lone figure's presence put a damper on[14] this festive day.

"They're probably just setting up," her mother responded. "I don't think they begin playing until dusk."

"Maybe they'll practice early," Eva was hopeful.

"Maybe."

Eva asked her mother if she'd like to walk around the grounds with her to see the various activities.

They circled the area, passing a group of children bobbing for apples before stopping to watch some men participate in the corn-husking race. Each competed to remove the husks from four ears in the fastest time. Eva scanned her surroundings to take in more of the attractions.

She considered the puppeteer storyteller and scarecrow contest on either side of the barn entry, when a familiar face caught her attention. Alice walked out of the barn, alone, looking back inside. Eva smiled, thinking it might be a good time to visit with her.

"Ma, care to see the art projects in the barn?"

"Yes," Anna said.

The two headed for the barn when Eva saw another man approach Alice from behind.

Eva didn't like what she was seeing. The same person she'd seen earlier was now standing next to Alice. When Eva first saw Stanley approach Alice she thought nothing of it until she placed her arm inside his. The handle of a basket was looped at Alice's other elbow. Eva watched as they stood by the barn entrance and talked.

Eva stopped.

"What is it?" Anna said.

"Shouldn't we be getting our jellies to the preserve exchange?"

---

14 **Put a damper on** (Idiom): to discourage, inhibit, or deter something; to make something less enjoyable, pleasant, or fun; to have a subduing or deadening effect on something.

"There's no hurry to do that now unless you want to get it out of the way." her mother said.

"Might as well," Eva responded.

They turned and headed back to their table.

As they walked, Eva peeked at the couple.

Mother and daughter collected their jars of jams, jellies and pickles to take to the swap. This provided participants an opportunity to collect a variety of food for their pantry for the winter.

Once they laid out their jars, Eva and her mother began reading the labels on the other preserves to determine whose contributions would be most interesting to try. They were being careful to select the best and not take more jars than they had brought for the exchange.

Eva heard the musicians tuning their instruments. She looked up to see if they were going to practice and spotted Alice and Stanley off in the distance. They had stopped at the far corner of the dance floor. He said a few words, and Alice removed her arm from Stanley's. He walked off toward the bonfire. Alice turned and headed in Eva's direction, alone.

Eva glanced over at her mother and tried to look busy.

Alice unfolded the cloth wrapped around her preserves as she walked to the table, oblivious to Eva's presence. She reached into her basket and pulled out a jar of pickles and placed it on the table.

Alice then glanced to her left and recognized Eva, who was looking through the preserves next to her.

"Eva! Hello," Alice said. Alice pulled out another jar from her basket and asked, "Would you like to try one of mine?"

"Oh. Thank you," Eva gave her a smile.

"Eva, I want you to know, I feel a little awkward right now, since I just arrived with Stanley."

"You shouldn't," Eva said evenly.

"Well . . . Stanley's been very forthright with me, so I know he was seeing you before he started calling on me."

"That's true," Eva replied.

"I just hope you don't mind that Stanley is calling on me now," Alice said sincerely.

"No. I don't mind at all."

"Oh, good. I just don't want any hard feelings between the two of us because he decided to break things off with you."

"Breaking things off with me?"

"Right . . . and I know that a situation like that can be hard on a person."

"I appreciate your concern Alice, but I don't care about Stanley any longer. And, he didn't break up with me . . . it was the other way around."

"You broke it off with him?" Alice looked surprised. "But he told me . . ."

"Alice, I hate to tell you this, but he's not the person you think he is." Surprised at herself for blurting out these words, Eva hesitated. She liked Alice, but couldn't stop herself. "When I found out that he was mainly interested in using me to get my brother to invest in his scheme, I got angry and told him to leave."

"He wanted your brother to invest?"

Eva noticed Alice's look of alarm.

"I'm sorry, Alice. I don't want to hurt you. I just thought you should know. He originally said he was doing all this for me . . . for us. The last thing he said before leaving was I should be thinking more about him and what he has to offer. That's when I realized he only had been thinking about himself all along."

"Right . . . yes. I'm . . . yes," she stammered, looking hurt and confused. "I'd best be going now." She took the rest of the jars from her basket, placed them on the table, and left.

Eva watched Alice retreat and thought, *I hope I did the right thing by telling her.*

Wandering off to seclude herself from those celebrating all around her, Alice found herself standing behind the barn, alone, trying to sort out what she knew to be true and what was in her heart. After carefully consideration, she brought herself out of the fog, and realized what she must do.

Tears began to flow as she felt the shame and embarrassment. Then the anger started to build.

Chapter 22: Bonfire Breakup

ALICE MARCHED UP TO STANLEY AT THE BONFIRE.
A number of heads turned as it became evident that something unpleasant was about to happen. Bystanders shied away from her target but stayed close enough to view the spectacle. Amongst this group were John and Sam. The twins kept their distance while watching the scene unfold.

Alice's voice indicated she didn't care who was listening. She struggled to gain control but said sternly, "Did you ask Eva to talk with her brother about your investment?"

Stanley looked around and sheepishly said, "Alice, this is not the place for a discussion."

"Just answer my question. Did you?"

Stanley could see that he needed to respond, or this would drag on. Alice looked determined. "Yes, but . . ."

"Is that any different than you asking my father for his money?"

"Well, yes," Stanley said quietly. He looked uncomfortable around the crowd. "I wanted to make sure I could support you in the way you deserve."

Thinking about Eva's comment, Alice's eyes went wide. "Isn't that the same way you approached her?"

"Well no . . . I mean yes. I mean . . . I care about you, Alice."

"You lied to me, Stanley."

"No I didn't."

"You said you broke it off with her."

"That . . . was a misunderstanding."

"Misunderstanding? Stanley, here's something you won't mis-understand. I don't want to see you again."

She turned and stomped off as tears filled her eyes.

Stanley stood in place, not moving a muscle. As he became aware of those around him, his embarrassment turned to anger.

He spotted Sam and lashed out. "What are you looking at?"

Sam didn't speak.

"Your sister is the cause of this."

Sam was puzzled but stood silently.

"I don't like your sister trying to make me look like a fool."

Sam couldn't restrain himself any longer.

"I don't see her here," Sam said and looked around, implying that Stanley had done a pretty good job of demonstrating his fool-ishness without help.

Stanley stepped close to Sam and gave him a shove. Since he was much older and bigger, Sam went tumbling.

Sam scrambled to his feet and tried to reciprocate only to be pushed into the unlit bonfire.

Again, he rebounded to his feet. Once on his feet, he lowered his head and shoulders and ran full force into Stanley, knocking him to the ground.

Entangled, they both struggled to their feet. Stanley pushed Sam away from him, trying to move him far enough so he could take a swing.

Freeing his left arm, while keeping Sam at a distance with his right arm, Stanley brought his left fist back to deliver a blow.

A hand reached in and grabbed Stanley's left arm, and stopped it from moving forward. The arm continued the backward motion which caused him to twist around and stagger backward.

The intruder bellowed, "Why don't you pick on someone your own size?"

Stanley scrambled to regain his balance, looked at the stranger and said, "Who are you? This is no business of yours."

"You made it my business when you started a fight with someone much smaller than you," the stranger added, "and, he happens to be a friend of mine."

Sam brushed off his clothes. John joined him.

"You all right Sam?"

"Yeah, thanks Ted," Sam smiled. "You know I almost had him."

"Right." With a knowing grin, Ted added, "Just didn't like seeing a man attacked without cause is all."

Eva had seen the commotion and was now arriving to join her brothers.

Stanley, clearly humiliated, tried to regain what was left of his composure and threw out a hollow threat, "You'll pay for this. You hear me? Your whole family . . . you'll all pay." He then left, pushing bystanders out of the way as he made his way through the crowd.

"Thank you," Eva said.

"My pleasure," Ted smiled. Ted looked back at Sam. "Mind telling me what that was all about?"

Sam gave a brief explanation, telling of Alice's public breakup with Stanley.

"That doesn't explain why he lashed out at you."

"I was convenient I guess," Sam said.

"That was my fault," Eva cut in.

Ted look at Eva, puzzled.

Eva looked at Sam, "I told Alice about how he tried to use me to get to Bill's money."

Sam said, "Now I understand."

Ted was still puzzled but chose not to ask any questions. Eva noticed his quizzical look and continued, "Stanley's the man I was seeing when I first met you. We got back together later, but then I broke it off with him, permanently." She then added, "He was more interested in getting to know my brother than me."

"Then he's not a very smart man," Ted remarked.

Eva blushed. "He spent more time trying to convince me to help him talk to my brother about a money-making scheme than talking about us."

Eva saw Ted look toward Sam and John and said, "No, not them, my other brother, Bill. He's still mining gold in Alaska. Stanley wanted me to talk with Bill about investing his money in some moneymaking idea of his. I just told Alice the truth about how I broke it off with him, not the other way around, as she was led to believe. She put the rest together on her own. Once she realized that her role was to warm her father to his investment idea . . . well, you saw the result."

"So," Ted thought back to his first visit at their house, "he was the man who had been calling on you when I came by?"

"Yes."

"That's a relief."

"A relief?" Eva asked.

Ted smiled. "You're not seeing anyone now then, right?"

"Right," Eva replied. She looked down at her hands as a blush crept up her neck and across her cheeks.

Sam looked at Ted and asked, "Are you by yourself?"

"I haven't really had the opportunity to meet anyone yet, if that's what you mean," Ted answered.

"Then why don't you join us," Sam said.

"If you don't think I'd be intruding," Ted replied, looking at Eva.

"You're welcome to join us," John remarked, "That's the least we can offer for saving Sam."

"He didn't save me," Sam clarified.

Eva laughed and said, "You're a welcome addition." She put her arm through Ted's and led him toward their picnic table, where her mother and father were waiting.

They walked past the dance floor where the musicians were warming up.

"Do you enjoy dancing?" Eva asked.

"I've been known to dance a little."

That's music to my ears, Eva thought.

Chapter 23: Checking on Jackson

Skagway, Alaska
December 28, 1897

FROM THE REFLECTION OF THE BAR'S MIRROR, Smith noticed Jackson entering his parlor. He promptly excused himself from the group of men surrounding him, crossed the room and cornered Jackson before his cohorts, who had followed him in, could join him.

Without a greeting Smith said, "Jackson. Heard about your latest exploit."

"Yes. I've been making some progress up the trail a ways," he gave Smith a proud smile.

"That's not what I'm talking about. I'm referring to your latest tussle in town the other day."

"Oh that," Jackson said.

"You're not letting your temper get the best of you, are you?"

Jackson looked at him, wondering where this was leading. "I bumped into a man in the streets. Nothing to worry about."

"Nothing to worry about," Smith repeated.

"What are you concerned about?"

"I understand you've had a 'run in' with that gentleman before."

"Who told you that?" Jackson glanced over to his friends gathered at the bar.

"It doesn't matter. Is it true? Makes me wonder how you're handling yourself up the trail too."

"I can handle myself."

"I'm sure you can. Just remember, ultimately, I'm the one who has to back you in the event you get into trouble. Do you have anything you'd like to tell me so I won't get surprised later, and find out from someone else?"

Jackson's hesitancy was evident. He knew Smith had eyes everywhere. He took a deep breath and began, "I did have a bit of a run in with that stranger earlier. I was going to bring in a man who I befriended from the steamer, until this miner interfered."

"So, you think that affected your response to him when you bumped into him later?"

Jackson thought about how embarrassed he felt, falling down in front of his men, ignored this and said, "I suppose, it could have."

"How did that turn out?"

"I didn't fight with him, if that's what you're wonderin'. I wanted to, but it would have become bigger than you'd have liked." Jackson knew what his boss was concerned about. "We both had a few men with us who would have gotten involved. But before we parted, I warned him to stay clear of me and my men."

"Not unreasonable. But now you're concerned that the word might get out that you're not someone to be . . . careful of." Smith's astute knowledge of people made it clear that this was a statement, not a question.

"That did cross my mind," Jackson thought for a moment. "Haven't had any problems since then though."

"If you come by this man again, you need to walk away."

Jackson was taken back. It wasn't like his boss to be so direct. "I don't see him as being a problem," he countered.

"You might not always hear if there's a problem," Smith added.

"You need to avoid any potential confrontations with the man. He's a seasoned local. Out-of-town greenhorns are a different story. They deserve to learn a lesson or two if they're willing to blow their money on drink, gambling or women. Understood?"

Smith watched as Jackson gave a resigned shrug of the shoulders. Smith sat back and scratched his beard, letting a moment pass. "Don't let this cloud your judgment," he warned. So far Smith felt good about his ability to smooth out any situation that might arise with his men. In fact, with each situation he worked through, he had gained confidence in his ability to calm any and all situations. But Jackson concerned him more than the others.

So far, he's avoided a confrontation.

I wonder how long trouble can be avoided with this man, Smith thought. He quickly brushed this thought aside as he considered how successful he'd been on this front.

He began considering how much slack he could grant his men.

"Now tell me about your progress up the trail."

"We've gathered a box here and a crate there. Not that much that anyone would miss."

"Tell me what your plans are."

And Jackson did just that.

Soapy's Gang

"I have been placed here among saloon men and used to find it a little hard to say no when some of the boys I knew and chummed with would say, "Come on Bill and take a drink"; but I always did, and still do take a sort of inward delight in saying, "No." You have no idea of the temptations along that line. You cannot because I did not before I went to the happy-go-lucky West. I knew a number of cases where men would make a few hundred dollars mining during the summer, and on coming to the settlement for winter quarters, would say they would not spend this but would save it. They would get along fine so long as they did it. But in the course of time they would be persuaded by some old friend to take just one drink on him. Then the game would be up. The boys would not rest until he had 'blowed himself in'."

"It is wonderful to step into the saloons and dance houses and see the amount of money changing hands over the gambling tables every night. This class of men, as a rule, are reckless and free hearted, and will do anything for a man who needs help."

—*Letter to brother John Schooley, December 30, 1897*

Chapter 24: A Better Plan

Skagway, Alaska
January 7, 1898

THIS MORNING WE GOT AN EARLY START and left Dyea at day-break. Carrying only a few extra layers of clothing in our backpacks, we headed for Skagway. There was compact snow on the trails making the trip manageable.

Until a few days earlier, we'd planned to go to Skagway today to pick up more provisions and return straight back to Dyea. But that was before we put more thought into our longer-range needs. It was time for us to consolidate all our supplies before moving them up the trail. We couldn't afford to keep our goods in the Juneau warehouse any longer. We wanted to get into Canada, like everyone else, as soon as we could—at least if we wanted to get a decent claim. And, we had to consider the changing conditions yet to come.

To travel over the summit too early would not be feasible. Traveling on Canada's side of the mountains would not be possible until after the winter thaw—the lakes and rivers would be unpass-able due to the frozen conditions. And the trip would be tedious at best. If we haul our own gear, one-backpack-trip at a time, we'd be too worn out to do anything but rest on our time off. We'd originally hoped to pan gold on a regular basis, to be able to buy what we needed as we moved inland. That wouldn't happen if we were constantly in an exhaustive state.

But we still had to consider getting to the pass in a reasonable period of time. Getting our stockpile of goods up there earlier would make it easier than when the weather conditions worsened, later. What we might normally be able to accomplish in a few days during the summer, would take us twice as long now. By mid-winter, it might take three to four times longer. The shortened daylight hours limit what we could accomplish each day. That, and the increased snow, lower temperatures and stormy. high winds would make it worse.

Lafe, Frank and I rehashed all this as we made our way along the trails. As we got closer to Skagway, we got more excited about getting underway. We would first stop by Frank Reid's survey office to advertise the sale of our Dyea claim before boarding the steamer to Juneau.

Not far from town, we heard a loud whistle off in the distance. We knew the daily ship from Juneau was arriving. Our timing was good. We had plenty of time to visit Mr. Reid at his surveyor's office.

Following the trail across the waterway and into town, we made the final turn that took us into town. Approaching the pier, we came upon a small crowd of locals who had gathered at the foot of the pier. They were obviously there to greet the passengers after they offloaded and walked the pier that stretched out beyond the mud flats.

We continued on until something caught my eye. I couldn't help but stop to watch the spectacle before me.

Chapter 25: Smith's Ride

Skagway, Alaska
January 7, 1898

THE CRUNCHING OF HOOVES BROKE THE QUIET of the snow-draped hills as a lone rider moved through town on his white stallion. While you could always find a few of the town's folks braving the cold outdoors, they didn't waste their energy visiting. Those outside, strode along quietly.

Lately, the town's people had become accustomed to seeing Mr. Smith prance by. The horse he rode was symbolic of the hero he aspired to be, one with divine powers. He was well aware of the quiet stares he received as he progressed through town. He had made a name for himself, one that demanded respect. Not that he deserved it, but he expected it.

As he traversed through the winding streets, he sat tall in the saddle, as if strutting, while making his way to the wharf for all to see. Those he knew waved as he passed by. He would return their gesture with a nod of his head and a slight tug on the brim of his hat. Periodically, his horse would trot or rear up on its hind legs. All this time, he was watching his men and beyond them, to the passengers offloading from steamers at the end of the pier.

"They're all here and ready," Smith heard one of his men yell to him.

"Now we'll see who is worthy and who is not," he responded in return.

He had taught his men the skills he honed in Colorado, before bringing a few of them with him to Alaska. Smith had started gathering an even larger following once he'd arrived. And, while he did not consider his gang a criminal organization in the strictest sense, he conducted his business with a certain flair and reputation. It didn't take him long, after he'd arrived, to have his bunco artists control the growing town of Skagway. Sure he had a bit of a setback when a few of his men were ousted from Dyea, but his group had grown. And some of his men were looking beyond the town.

For now he focused on the skills of those before him. With each offloading steamer, more men competed to become part of his group. He had dozens spread throughout the area. But to succeed to he needed more. He needed new blood, recruits who understood what it meant to work for him. Not all were here at this location. Some were waiting at the saloons and card tables. Others preying on those needing a distraction from the hard times ahead.

Mr. Smith watched as his men separated themselves from the group on shore and maneuvered their way through the crowds to greet passengers walking on the pier. Another group stayed back, to meet the passengers as they came closer to the town, knowing some would be needing assistance to find the best places to go, once they left the wharf.

On the dock, the focus was to greet those who were dressed well and gave off an air of wealth. These individuals were given careful consideration. They knew a wealthy individual might be a greater challenge, but could still be duped as well as anyone if handled properly. Some might even start with offering assistance carrying luggage while leading them to a more experienced manipulator who had the necessary finesse and skill.

Some of the more senior of Smith's bunch skillfully presented themselves in a sophisticated manner as they watched over their minions. Each, in his own way would find a patsy, depending on how well they connected with the new arrivals.

"Old man" Triplet, the one who had yelled to Smith that all the recruits were in place, played the role as a well-dressed gentleman, an easy man to approach for advice. He was lovable-looking, with a white beard. Those who truly knew him, saw him as a man with a black heart. Similar to Triplet, John Bowers played the part of a Reverend, while Jackson referred to himself as the professor.

After looking around, Smith yelled to Triplet.

"Hey, Old Man, where's the professor?"

"He's headed up the trail. Took Foster, Hopkins and a few recruits with him."

Smith pondered the ramifications of Foster and Hopkins going with Jackson. *Hopefully they don't cause too much of a problem themselves. While Jackson has the right men in case trouble finds them, these men could cause problems of their own.*

While "Slim Jim" Foster was the feisty one, he knew Hopkins to be dangerous. Smith was one of the few who knew of his ill-tempered history. He was a violence-prone veteran of San Francisco's Chinatown tong wars.

"I understand two of the new saloons in Dyea are up and running now."

"Right. Foster's hoping to reconnect with the owners and convince them that they can benefit by working with us."

Smith smiled, "How is progress further up the trail?"

"We've found a good place to stay for the night, if need be, but we're still looking for where we can stash our wares."[15]

"Okay. Let me know when Jackson returns," Smith said before riding off.

---

15 **Wares:** articles offered for sale: *traders in the street markets displayed their wares.*

Chapter 26: Scanning the Crowd

Skagway Pier, AK
January 7, 1898

S EEING A MAN ON A WHITE HORSE prancing along the shoreline like a showman, I stopped to watch the spectacle. My eyes were easily drawn to the dark figure on horseback. I couldn't see his face, since his attention was toward the off-loading newcomers, but it was evident that he wanted to show an imposing image. His collar was also pulled up on this brisk day and the brim of his hat covered his face, I couldn't help but stare and wonder who he was. He certainly stood out. He wore a black tweed suit and black fedora hat that contrasted with his surroundings. He seemed to float above the crowd, his stallion matching the color of the previous night's freshly fallen snow.

Lafe saw what I was gawking at and scanned the locals lining up along the shore. He pulled Frank and me off to the side, and we watched the passengers offload from the steamer.

"Bill. Frank. I know I've told you some of what Captain Moore shared with me, when I first arrived, but I should point out a few things that are going on in front of you, right now. You remember what I told you about that Jackson fellow, the one I ran in to here on the pier, don't you?" Seeing that we understood, he continued, "I told you about how the incoming miners built this town on Captain Moore's land, but what I didn't tell you about the other con men that you'd find here."

Looking out along the shore, Lafe said, "I want you to look carefully and see what's really going on here."

We followed Lafe's gaze and began scanning the crowd while he explained. The display before us was more than just a man showing off his steed. Lafe was sure the man on the horse was the one Captain Moore warned him about.

"What you're watching is more than likely the key to the problems in this town." Lafe then reminded us of his experience with Jackson, "That Jackson fellow, like many others here, work for the horseman. Take a closer look. Watch who he communicates with. Those will likely be the people, like Jackson, we need to avoid."

We carefully watched and were amazed at the sometimes open and more often subtle communications that were carried out with the man on the horse. There was clearly a connection between him and a number of the men scattered across the shore. I could see how the positioning of men was carefully orchestrated. Ignoring the man on horseback who was now riding away from us, heading back toward town, Frank and I took in the scene in front of us as Lafe made us more aware of what was occurring here.

"I don't see Jackson out there, yet, but I do see a couple of others that Captain Moore's son brought to my attention when I first arrived." He pointed out the two.

I also noticed how oblivious the passengers were to the setup. Some appeared confident and single-minded about where they were headed. However, others looked unsure, hesitant in their actions. This gave an air of vulnerability that I was sure the vultures were attuned to and saw as easy prey.

Whether they were seeking an unknown destination or were in awe about what lay before them, I knew there were plenty of locals

available to assist. Perhaps a good meal, a place to stay, directions
to a particular place or searching out a friendly face who might
know his way around town. Little did they know that not all of the
locals had the passengers' best interests in mind.

The anxiety in my gut was raised once again. It felt the same
as when I watched the chaos across the mud flats in Dyea when
the masses were clamoring about, not knowing what they were
doing. Now, I realized, I had the added concern of not only working around miners ill prepared for the challenges ahead, but skilled
con men who sought to take advantage of the more gullible new
arrivals.

Why do I let it bother me?

I realized that detaching myself from these distractions would
be difficult. I care about people. That's why I had originally worked
as a teacher. But I also felt helpless, seeing so many so vulnerable.

Then I remember our purpose here was to find Reid, the surveyor, and make him aware of our desire to sell our Dyea claim.

Seeing enough, we moved on.

Chapter 27: Meeting with Reid

Skagway, AK
January 7, 1898

THE SURVEYOR'S OFFICE WAS CLOSED. So the Coleman brothers and I entered what we understood to be Frank Reid's favorite drinking hole, the closest saloon to his office. We were surprised to see the place was crowded so early in the day. Looking around, I notice a few who looked familiar, mainly merchants I'd dealt with since my arrival in Skagway. The way they moved about the room and greeted each other gave me the impression they were here for some specific purpose.

Lafe, the tallest of the three of us, spotted Reid at the end of the bar, talking with the bartender. We headed that direction.

Seeing us make a beeline toward him, Reid watched us approach as he downed the last of his drink.

"Howdy. You're a bit late for our . . . little discussion," he said.

"You had a meeting?" I asked. "That's why so many folks are here?"

Reid started to say something, then thought better of it. After an uncomfortable silence, he said, "Can I assume you're aware of the problems our town has been having?

I looked to Lafe and Frank before speaking. "We're aware of the conmen running the town, if that's what you're referring to."

"I'll let you in on something you shouldn't be spreading around to the wrong people."

Seeing a look of concern, we remained silent.

"We just finished an informal meeting to discuss how to approach our problem. All these people around you, are mostly business men from this town and are concerned about the town's image. Most are starting to leave now, to get back to their businesses before the crowd from the steamer arrives. They . . . we want to bring law and order back here. We want to make it a place where people would be proud to live. But it might not be easy to make things right. We just finished a discussion about how we can remedy our situation."

"You mean Mr. Smith and his gang?" Lafe asked.

"Right."

"So . . . you can't just bring it up at a townhall meeting?"

"A lot of these folks are concerned about retaliation. Smith and his gang are the law in this town."

"So, not everyone is onboard with this?"

"Not everyone. Unfortunately. Some fear getting involved. Others like it the way it is."

Reid ordered a drink and pointed at an empty table for the bartender to deliver it to. Lafe, Frank and I also ordered our sarsaparillas before following Reid across the room.

Once we were seated, Reid gave a short rendition of how the situation in town had escalated. After our drinks arrived, we talked about the town's leadership.

"Much of it comes under the control of a man named Jefferson Smith," Reid began, "otherwise known as Soapy Smith. This nickname, which he doesn't much care for, he received in his days working in Colorado where he used a successful scam that got people to buy a bar of soap for anywhere from $1 to $5."

"You mean a bar of soap that costs about fifteen cents up here?" I said.

"That's right."

How could he persuade people to buy a bar of soap for such a high price?" Lafe asked.

"He's known to be rather charismatic and can be persuasive. During his presentation to a crowd on the street corner, he'd demonstrate how he would randomly wrap anywhere from one to a hundred dollars around a soap bar, under a plain wrapper. He'd then supposedly mix that bar with all the others he had in a box and then offer to sell the soap at a set price. The buyer was led to believe there was a chance more money could be made. I call it the "prize package soap sale swindle."

"Are you implying that nobody profited from this?" Lafe asked.

"The only winners were the people he planted in the audience."

"How do you know this to be true?" I asked.

"I use to work as a bartender for him when he first opened one of his saloons. I heard a lot and was paid well to keep my mouth shut. One of the things I was expected to do was herd the unsuspecting greenhorns with money toward the gambling tables. That's one of the reasons I eventually quit and started my own business as a surveyor. I had some experience in surveying in the army and it seems I could make a decent living that way. Actually, the idea came when a gambler left surveying equipment as collateral with me and never came back to pick it up."

"So how did someone like that become the leader of all these other crooks?" I asked.

"He's shown himself to be rather resourceful. Those who have learned their scams from him, would give him a cut from what they made, and in return he would protect them from the law."

"I can't believe there aren't enough honest people in this town to put a stop to that," Lafe said.

"You might think so, but unfortunately many of the gambling, and drinking establishments here benefit, and they provide a service that many people want. They don't prey on the locals, just those who are passing through. The greenhorn[16] gold-seekers. Using a kind of warped logic, I've heard Smith say he's doing them a favor taking their money here in the seaport, rather than them losing it in the inhospitable arctic. He believes he's being charitable."

I looked over at Lafe and Frank, knowing we'd talked about this earlier before asking, "Don't some of the locals want to correct this?" They were equally attentive to Reid's comments.

"Because of his generosity, no. Smith actually donates a great deal of money to the churches and to town causes. Even those who have lost money gambling, he treats as a charitable cause. He's been known to give them enough money to travel by boat back to where they came from."

"So, Mr. Smith is concerned about his image," I said. "How many work for him?"

"Some say over a hundred. But I think some common thugs just want to brag about being part of the gang since they're becoming so powerful. Some even say they're one of Smith's closest friends, but I know that there's only a few who actually are. The ones he most trusts are "Reverend" Bowers, W.E. "Slim-Jim" Foster, Van "Old Man" Triplett, and "Professor Jackson." They're his key lieutenants."

"So, this Jackson fellow is one of Smith's top dogs," Lafe murmured.

That explains his arrogance, I thought. "Have they demonstrated any violence?"

"Whenever there's a dispute, Smith's men converge on whoever is causing the fuss to intimidate them. This usually ends as quick as it starts when the victim sees they're outnumbered. When they find out the law won't take any action, they wisely choose not to return."

"Do they hurt anyone if they do return?"

"Smith urges his men to go easy on the violence and avoid any killing, lest it stir up public resentment," Reid said.

"What are his rules regarding those who work for him. He's got to know they're robbing people."

---

16 **Greenhorn:** a person who is new to or inexperienced at a particular activity (see tenderfoot).

"He says there may be some trickery, like in the shell game, but denies that any of his folks break the law. He says all the saloon games are on the up and up."[17]

"Nice to know," I said.

"Remember, be careful who you share this information with," Reid emphasized.

Lafe, Frank and I nodded and said we would.

"Since you didn't come in here for the meeting, why are you here?" Reid asked.

"We just came by to let you know we want to sell our Dyea claim," Frank said.

"We figure it's the right time," I added. "We've completed the cabin on the lot, and we'll be moving up the trail soon."

"We decided the best place to advertise its availability would be through the man who originally did the surveying," Lafe said.

"I appreciate the business and will let my customers know. I assume you'd like me to handle the paperwork for you as well?"

"Yes. That would be great."

Having finished our business, we left.

---

17 **On the up and up:** *open and honest, legitimate.*

Chapter 28: Negotiating the Deal

Skagway, Alaska
January 7, 1898

WE STILL HAD PLENTY OF TIME to board the ship after our talk with Reid. The ship's stewards were still assisting those who needed extra help offloading their luggage. We entered Mr. Hill's office on the pier and paid for our tickets. We were then told not to wander off too far from the pier and that we'd be notified when we could board.

While waiting, we walked along the pier and watched the last few passengers debark and make their way to shore. Many of them were accompanied by stewards pushing baggage carts. It would be a little while before the stewards and carts would return, so I decided to stroll a little further toward the shore. Lafe and Frank stayed back.

As I neared shore, I notice a man nailing a notice to a pole near the base of the pier. The post was intended for messages that would be seen by passengers from the ships as they entered Skagway. My curiosity got the best of me and I approached.

After a quick reading of its contents, I immediately turned to the man who'd posted the note.

"MISTER," I yelled, as I tore the paper from the post. He stopped walking and looked back.

I caught up to him and waved the note in my hand. "I'm interested."

"I certainly didn't expect a response this quickly," the man said.

"Bill Schooley," I said as I reached out to shake his hand.

"Richard Worthington," he responded.

"I've been talking with my partners about how to make it easier to move our supplies, Richard. I think your dog sled team might just be the answer we were looking for. Can you tell me about them?"

"They're a good healthy bunch, as you'll be able to see," he started walking along the sled to the dogs. I followed.

"Had them long?" I asked.

"I've had them for a few years, and they've been very reliable," Richard said.

Taking a cursory look as I walked along the team, I could see that they were alert and full of energy. "How much are you asking for the whole lot?

"I figure they're worth a good hundred and twenty," Worthington said.

I knew that was higher than the price Lafe estimated some weeks ago.

Hopefully I can talk him down, I thought.

But considering the arrival of snow and the goods we had to carry, a sled and team were even more valuable now. Walking on the frozen ground was better than the mud we had endured a few weeks earlier, but with the arrival of snow, travel would once again become more difficult. The little snowfall we received over the last week would be just the beginning.

Seeing my companions coming to join me, I walked back to the sled and awaited their arrival. Richard stayed at my side.

I introduced Worthington to my two partners.

Lafe looked admiringly at the sled and dog team. "Well, we've been talking about something like this for some time, Bill," he said.

I shared the asking price with Lafe and Frank, "What do you think, Lafe?"

"Pretty high, if you ask me."

Concern on his face, Richard said, "Feel free to take a good close look at the team. They're well trained, and they respond well to me. At times," he said with a chuckle, "I believe they take better care of me than I take care of them. They're very protective," he said, with a grin.

Lafe and Frank began inspecting the team and gear, while I had the opportunity to continue our conversation.

"Lafe arrived in town before we did and researched the prices for both pack horses and sled teams. That's why I asked *him* what he thought. My partners and I have been talking about finding an easier way to move our goods, I've always been hoping for an outfit like this."

"To be honest with you, I might normally consider a lower price, but I really need the money. I have to buy enough grub and supplies to last me a while, until I can pan enough gold to get back on my feet," Worthington said sadly. "I lost a great deal of money in a stupid poker game, but I'm determined to keep my claim."

Although I feared hearing about another's misfortune, I instinctively asked, "What happened?"

"My mistake was going into the saloon in the first place," Worthington admitted, "I should have known better.

"I was feeling so good about my find that I celebrated at a saloon with a drink, and I happened to mention that I was celebrating my good fortune. A man, who I had become friendly with, bought me a second drink . . . and then a third, and more. Before I realized how unsteady I was, I had accepted an invitation to play a friendly game of poker. At first, I was winning and got excited about how much more I could win. That's when I started to bet more and more. Then I started losing. In a short time I lost all my holdings."

"You lost everything?" I was stunned.

"Not only everything I had on me, but more," Richard continued.

As much as I wanted to talk him into lowering the price of the sled and team, all I could think about is how I needed to hear to the rest of his story.

"That's when my friend, the one who bought my drink," Richard continued, "offered to give me credit so I could win back what I had lost. I don't know why I took him up on the offer. I guess I wasn't thinking straight and was desperate. But after continuing to lose, I found that I owed him too much to continue."

"I'm sorry to hear of your misfortune," I said as I felt anger building inside.

"Thank you," Worthington said and hung his head, ashamed.

As much as I had earlier wanted to stay separated from the injustice going on around us, I felt that I should help this man.

"You still have your claim, though," I said, focusing Richard's attention on the one positive thing I had heard him talk about.

"I do. But now that it's getting more difficulty to pan gold in the cold weather, I wasn't able to make the last payment on my gambling debt. He's offered to buy my claim, but not for what I know it's worth."

"So you told him no," I said.

"Right. I'd just as soon go without my team than lose my claim," he took a deep breath. "I still owe a great deal more, so if I still want to work my claim, I have to sell my team."

"Before all this happened, I had made enough money to return home. I was even planning to sell my claim and go back down to Seattle to join my family, but that can't happen anytime soon," Richard admitted.

I can relate to that, I thought. *Making a sacrifice. Being away from family.*

"After you sell your team, what do you plan to do?" I asked.

"Don't rightly know. I suppose I'll just go back to my claim and start over. Selling will allow me to get by for a while, but it costs so much to live up here, I don't know how long I can stay. I've still got my tent and enough food to last me a few days. Eventually I hope to get back what I lost," Richard said.

I watched Lafe head back our way. A plan was forming.

"I have an idea," I said. "Let me talk with my partners for a moment." I stepped away to have a private chat with Lafe and Frank.

"The dogs seem healthy, and the sled's been kept in good condition," Lafe said.

I summarized what I learned from my talk with Richard and then said, "I've got an idea that might help us all."

When I finished sharing my plan, I noticed Frank's look of surprise. "You don't like my idea, Frank?" I said.

"Oh, yeah," Frank smiled. "I think it's a great idea. I'm just glad to hear your caring self has returned."

I looked blankly at him.

Frank continued. "If you remember, just a few days ago you told me you didn't want to get involved. Don't try to pretend that you don't care."

"We could use the help," I said frankly.

We all stayed quiet for a moment, considering the possibilities. Lafe broke the silence, "I like the idea, Bill."

I nodded and went to share the proposal with Richard.

Richard wholeheartedly endorsed the plan. "Just so I understand correctly," he said, "you'll pay off my full debt?"

"Right. I'll make your payments as long as you're helping us and pulling your own weight like the rest of us."

"And in return, I help you with the sluice boxes at your claim up the trail and show you how to care for the dogs?"

"Correct," I said.

"So, I'm free to mine my own claim when I'm not needed to help with the sluice boxes and when we're done with that I can go back to my claim?"

"Right. All you have to do is be here to meet us, with your dogsled team, three days from now."

Richard smiled. A handshake secured the deal before we boarded the steamer for Juneau. "See you in three days."

Chapter 29: A Tarnished Reputation

Nevada, Missouri
January 9, 1898

KNOWING THAT THEY'D BE TAKING MORE RIDES of this sort, Ted had acquired a buggy. He and Eva sat side-by-side, as they took in the wintery scene. The mid-morning sun lingered above the neighboring hills, and the newly fallen snow created a glittering wonderland. A slight chill filled the air as a breeze passed through, but the couple hardly noticed. A blanket was draped across their laps.

Love was in the air.

Leaving them in peace, the twins rode their horses well ahead as they made their way toward town. They would all eventually meet up with their parents at church. William and Ann had left earlier in the family wagon with plans to save seats for the whole clan, which at this time included Ted, who they expected would be joining the family soon.

It seemed that all was right in the world.

At least until the twins came upon five riders grouped together up the street. When they spotted the Schooleys, the one lead rider pulled ahead of the others, as they approached. It was obvious to Sam and John that they were going to have unwanted company.

This is going to be anything but cordial, Sam thought.

Interrupting the serenity of the moment, Stanley Barclay gave the twins a big toothy grin. "Well now. Look at you two," he began, "There's the poor farm boys." This caused the others with Stanley to laugh.

Ted and Eva, were still some distance behind, but they recognized who was leading the bunch. They imagined that the encounter was not pleasant.

"Always looking for trouble aren't you, Barclay?" Sam said.

"I don't know what you're talking about," he said innocently, "I'm just pointing out the obvious; all this time, you've been pretending to be what you're not."

Not taking the bate, the twins sat silently in their saddles.

"Rich," Stanley exclaimed. "You aren't rich."

Now close enough to hear the conversation, Ted pulled the reigns in to slow the horses before halting them behind the twins. They continued to watch, to see what would unfold.

John spurred his horse forward, to close in on Barclay. "You're right, Stanley. We aren't rich and we're not pretending to be."

Barclay hesitated, then looked back at his companions and said, "See, boys. They're admitting to it. There never was any gold," he laughed at his own cleverness.

"Oh, there was gold alright. But we don't claim that it belongs to us. It's our brother's. Just like the news article said. And, by the way, yes, we're farmers and proud of it, too, just like your father," Sam added as he moved his horse up, next his brother.

"Speaking of the news article. It also said he'd be coming home soon, along with the Colemans. Haven't seen them either."

"They're headed back up north to mine some more, or haven't you heard?" Sam said.

"Know what I believe?" Stanley sputtered, "I believe you're all lying, trying make yourselves look good."

Sam crossed his wrists and let them rested on the saddle horn. He looked beyond Barclay for emphasis, "And, do you know what I believe? I believe your friends here know that your ventures are a sham, while our brother's success is real." He then return his gaze back to Barclay.

Seeing that the twins didn't need any help, Ted and Eva sat quietly and listened.

Stanley's face slowly reddened until it looked like he was going to burst. Knowing that he was losing the battle, he didn't want to face his friends until he'd regained his composure. He then did what he did best, he threw out the biggest lie he could imagine.

"You're spreading lies. Just like when you tried to get me to include you in my investment opportunity, when in reality you don't have any money to invest. What were you going to do, have me extend credit and hope you'd be able to pay me after we made a profit? Your whole family's involved," he added.

Now I understand, Sam thought. *He's lying to restore his status with his friends.*

Stanley's cronies were listening closely now.

"You know as well as we do that we never cared about any of your investments. Sounds to me like you're here to try and convince your friends otherwise."

Taking a casual glance at Stanley's followers, John continued, "I think your friends are smart enough to know what the truth really is. The truth, fellas, is Stanley here tried to get close to my sister," nodding toward Eva, "so he could get my brother to invest in his scheme."

"He made that pretty clear to me when I broke it off with him," Eva chimed in, eager to support her brother.

Stanley glared at Eva as she spoke.

"And now he's trying to convince you all that we we're taking advantage of him," John added.

Stanley struggled to contain his composure. He now realized facing all three of the Schooley siblings together was a mistake.

Stanley shifted his attention back to Sam. "I see that you're all in cahoots. You're tryin' to pull the wool over everyone's eyes. Tryin' to become popular with the town folk. You've always been just lowly dirt farmers, and that's all you'll ever be."

Deciding he would not accomplish anything by staying, Stanley lifted his reigns, but decided to take one last parting shot, "Just so you know, I have plenty of investors." He looked back at his little pack and said, "Okay, boys. I think we're done here."

The show was over. Stanley's entourage followed as the Schooley's continued their ride to church.

SEATTLE, WASHINGTON: GOLDRUSH ERA

Seattle's Dexter Horton Bank

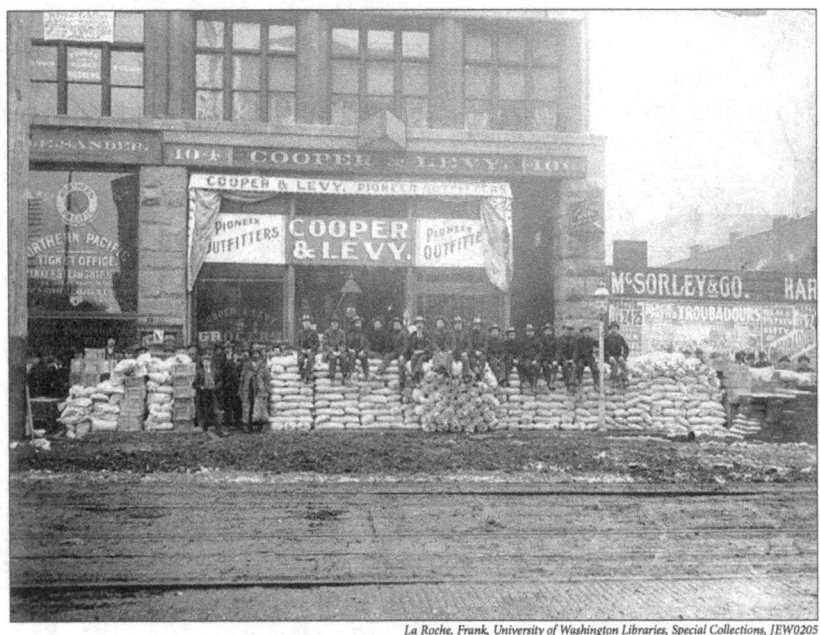

Cooper & Levy Outfitters near Seattle's Pioneer Square.

The steamer Willamette, in 1899, and crowds around the Seattle waterfront. This was not an uncommon scene as they watch the hopeful miners leave for the Klondike gold fields.

SKAGWAY, ALASKA

Skagway Wharves. Moore's wharf is on the right. The Juneau Wharf is next to the Moore's, center of photo.

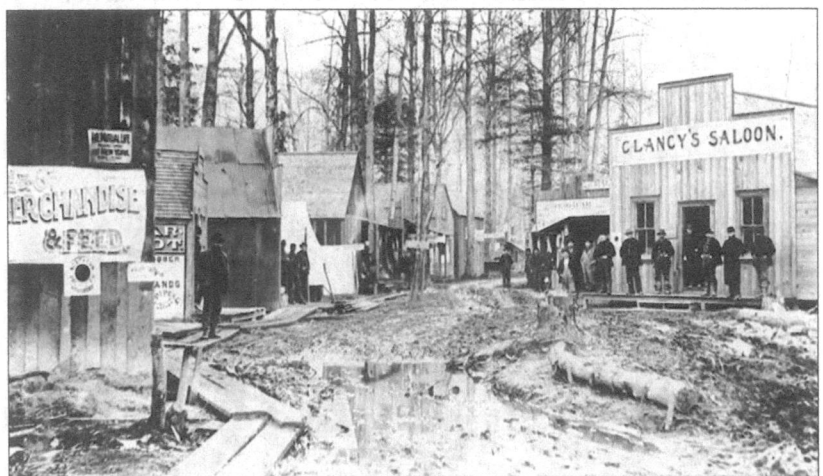

Hegg, Eric A. University of Washington Libraries, Special Collections, HEG086

Entering Skagway

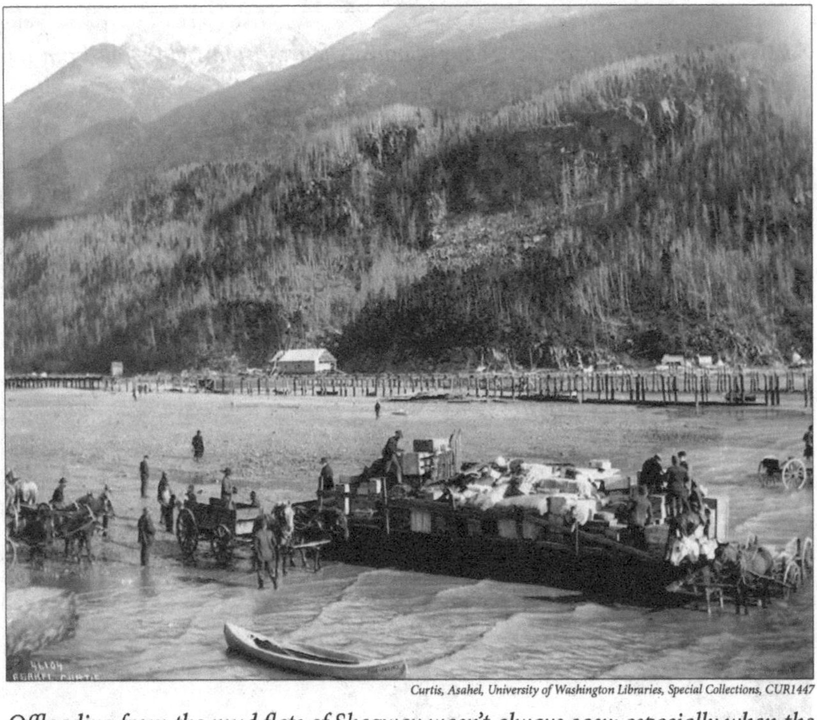

Curtis, Asahel, University of Washington Libraries, Special Collections, CUR1447

Offloading from the mud flats of Skagway wasn't always easy; especially when the tides could come in rapidly.

SKAGWAY, ALASKA, WAS RUN BY CONMEN

Soapy Smith Gang: Jefferson "Soapy" Smith is fourth from right—full brim hat with beard.

Soapy Smith on horseback.

After an episode where some of Soapy's men swindled a miner out of his gold, citizens of Skagway came together to form a vigilante committee. This group was headed by civil engineer Frank Reid. Soapy's downfall would come later during a standoff with Frank Reid and three other guards. Following the shootout, Reid and Smith both died from their wounds.

DYEA, ALASKA

Most of Dyea's structures were completed in 1898.

Dyea's harbor was narrow and had a twenty-foot tide. Klondike stampeders had paid to get to Dyea, but their passage didn't include unloading their supplies and taking them ashore.

SHEEP CAMP

Hegg, Eric A. University of Washington Libraries, Special Collections, HEG055

Sheep Camp, Chilkoot Pass, Alaska, April 1898

SHEEP CAMP SNOW SLIDE

Cantwell, George G., University of Washington Libraries, Special Collections, AWC3838

Palm Sunday avalanche near Sheep Camp

EXHUMATION OF THE BODIES OF THE TRAMWAY MEN BURIED IN THE SNOW-SLIDE ON CHILKOOT PASS. APRIL 3d 1898   202

Aftermath of the April 3, 1898 avalanche between sheep Camp and Chilkoot summit: Sixty-three bodies were dug out from the snow.

SUMMIT

The line on the left—heading for the summit, called "Golden Stairs", was shorter but steeper than the route on the right. Dog sleds would take the route to the right.

Klondikers waiting to be checked by customs and the Northwest Mounted Police at the Canada-United States boundary line.

Many of the Klondikers established a cache site at the summit before moving their supplies across the border, into Canada

LAKE BENNETT

Klondikers camping at Lake Bennett. June 1st, 1898.

Whipsawing lumber in the snow to build boats at Lake Bennett, British Columbia.

The scow with the rear tiller is similar to the one that Schooley and the Coleman's built.

Friday, May 20
"We finished pitching the boat and turned her over right-side up. We built it up-side-down on a frame. It is sixteen feet long on the bottom, and twenty six feet long on top, with a six foot beam. It will weigh about 1500 pounds and we are all pleased with the job."

Saturday, May 21
"I made an oar, and put gunwales on the scow and made a mast."

Sunday, May 22
"We braced the scow, and neighbors helped us to launch her. It leaks very little, and that through knots. The ice is all gone now to a mile below here [Bennett Lake]."
—*William Mace Schooley Diary Book 2, Dated: 1898*

YUKON RAPIDS

Miles Canyon.

Whitehorse Rapids.

Five Finger Rapids.

Dawson City

Dawson City, 1889.

Third Street, Dawson City.

WINTER GOLD – CHICKEN & WADE CREEK, AK

Windlass was used to bring the thawed gravel up from the pits—to be sluiced later, when water is available in the summer. All-night fires were built to thaw the permafrost.

W. M. Schooley's and Coleman brother's cabin near Chicken Creek—used while working Chicken & Wade Creek claims.

The Schooley family
Back row from left to right: John & twin, Sam, William Jr.
Bottom row: William Sr. (father) Eva (daughter) and Ann (mother)

William Mace Schooley
March 15, 1874 – June 13, 1938
Layfayette Co. Seattle, WA

Dog-sled Team

"I think I told you about our investment in real estate here. We have sold all of our property but one lot and house, and made considerable money on the speculation."

"We bought a big outfit and have most of it about nine miles from here [Dyea]. We have six dogs now and are sledding our provisions with the dogs."

"The sleds we use are about six feet long and eighteen inches wide, with steel runners on them. We have harness for the dogs and hitch them up in a line. We take about one half-ton at a load from here to our cache about nine miles up the river, and ride home on the sled every night. It is really great sport."

—Letter to Mrs. W.M. Schooley, January 28, 1898

Dog-sled Team

Chapter 30: Returning from Juneau

Taiya Inlet, Alaska
January 10, 1898

CURLED UP ON A BENCH ON THE SHIP'S TOP DECK, I laid my head on my backpack. I was happy just lying here and gazing at the waterway as the steamer made it up Taiya Inlet, heading toward Skagway. Not until three hours into the ship's five-hour journey was I able to admire the sun rise above the mountains to the east. The air was crisp but I didn't mind. Just resting here was a reward in itself.

From dawn till dark, during the month preceding our trip to Juneau, we had spent each day hauling wood, cutting timbers and building our cabin, only taking a break when we needed to refuel. Except for a few short visits from neighboring miners and old friends, we took little time to relax. We had to keep working. There was limited time to prepare for the cold nights ahead. Shortly after our return to Dyea, we would be getting back to that same routine. I pulled out my pocket watch and saw that we would soon be arriving at Skagway. Holding it, my mind drifted back to home and family.

By the time the ship reached the end of the inlet, I had spent too much time questioning my motivation and drive. For the last three years I'd been able to thrive, knowing that I would succeed. That anticipation had always kept me in a good spirits. I had made friends along the way who were supportive and thought about how proud my parents, brothers and sister would be upon my return.

But now?

I thought more about the days ahead, of endless physical labor, tough conditions, freezing temperatures, climbing rugged terrain, wading in cold water, ice and snow to seek out a few nuggets of gold. I had no doubt I'd be able to endure it. I'd done it before. But, did I truly want to, or even need to?

What's different now, from when I arrived three years earlier? I wondered.

Is it because I've accomplished all that I came out to do?

With the port coming into view, I tried putting my internal struggles to rest as my travel companions joined me. Other passengers also started to mingle on the deck.

Setting his pack on the bench, Frank sat next to me to better adjust his straps and position his load.

"I like the idea of moving our whole inventory on this trip," he said. "Just as soon we get it all done now, rather than drag it on . . . I just hope your new friend shows up with the dog sled team, Bill."

"Can't think of a better way to see how we can move our goods inland," Lafe added.

I watched as more passengers gathered to view the crew securing the ship's lines to the pier. A deckhand announced that we would be able to disembark as soon as the gangway was in place. Sidestepping the crowd gathering at the top of the ramp, I walked to the bow of the ship where I could get a better view of the people on the dock. Leaning on the rail, Lafe and Frank joined me. We all scanned the dock below, hoping to find our new friend.

No sign of Worthington.

Chapter 31: Greeting at the Pier

Skagway Wharf
January 10, 1898

THE CROWD AROUND THE GANGPLANK INCREASED as it was
placed in position. Lafe left, to ensure the porters would be
available to off-load our goods. While we had arranged this earlier,
he wanted to ensure the move would go smoothly.

Frank and I continued to stand by the railing, to keep an eye
out for Worthington. "Bill, do you think he'll be here to meet us?"

"I do."

"You don't think he was just telling a tale? Maybe he want to
raise the price up."

"We're giving him his asking price. He seems responsible enough.
He has a claim. He got sucked into a situation he felt embarrassed
about. He's willing to sell . . . correction, sacrifice something he
clearly treasures, his dogsled team. So, yes. I believe him."

"I sure hope you're right."

Me too, I thought. *We could sure use that sled. Especially right
now.*

The first group of passengers began to disembark.

"Not to mention the extra help building our next sluice box. Especially if we end up selling our lot earlier than expected," Frank added.

"True."

Holding out hope, we continued to watch as more passengers left the ship.

Still, there was no sign of Worthington.

Rather than delay our departure any longer, Frank and I made our way down the gangplank and headed to Mr. Hill's office. Feeling deflated, we knew we couldn't linger any longer. Especially after we saw a lineup starting to build outside his office.

I picked up the pace after I realized that the availability of wagons might be limited. Frank stayed with me as we approached the office on Moore's pier.

Joining the group of men lined up outside the office, I asked the first man I came to what this line was for. He answered, "Seems a lot of folks have some gear that need movin'. This is the place to find folks to get it done."

If I'd only known Richard wasn't going to be here.

"Frank, you stay in line. I'll see how things are going inside."

"Right."

I moved ahead of the others and approached the cabin just as the door opened.

Out walked Worthington.

Shocked and surprised by his presence, I said, "Richard. We've been looking for you. I thought . . ."

"You thought I wouldn't show."

"I didn't know what to think," I stammered.

Seeing Richard, Frank joined us.

"I'm a man of my word," Richard added. "Got here early. I passed the time with Mr. Hill while I was waiting and got two wagons set up for ya. They're big enough to handle all you have in one trip. And if it can't, we can put whatever extra you have on the sled."

"You're a sight for sore eyes," Frank said, looking relieved. "Taking it all in one trip is . . . is a big relief."

Richard talked for a few minutes about what he'd been doing since last talking with us. He also admitted having had some luck panning on his claim. He then walked us to the shoreline and showed us the wagon and dogsled.

When we returned to the ship, Lafe and the porters were just starting to stack our supplies on the pier. The porters hadn't put more than a few boxes down when Frank shared with his brother what was awaiting us on shore.

Lafe immediately redirected the porters to take all our supplies directly to the wagons.

Chapter 32: The New Team

Skagway, Alaska
January 10, 1898

NO LONGER CONCERNED ABOUT HOW LONG it might take to haul our goods to Dyea, we all agreed that we could afford to spend some time relaxing in Skagway. We had plenty to celebrate. Not only had we found a more efficient way to move our goods to the cabin, but we had a new partner, Richard, to celebrate joining us as well. Richard, had made good on his promise, and more. Finding us a couple of wagons that could take all our supplies in one trip was more than we could have hoped for. He even helped move our goods. It was obvious, Richard appreciated our help and wanted us to know we could count on him.

Instead of rushing to get our supplies offloaded in Dyea, we decided to make that trip in a more leisurely manner. Leaving the pier together, Richard and I took the sled while the others rode on the wagons. While they set out for the saloon, Richard and I planned to join them after taking care of a few things related to the dog-sled team. Richard and I planned to stop at the Skagway Merchandise and Feed store to buy rations for the dogs before taking some time to allow Richard to familiarize me with the team. We'd then join the others for lunch.

Worthington took pride in having concocted his own formula for feeding the dogs. We entered the store and he led me straight to a stack of feed bags. He immediately started talking about the ingredients.

"I like to mix chopped up red meat or fish with the dog food," The local native mushers sometimes use beaver or seal blubber. Either way, it's all mixed with water and heated in a big pot with that oatmeal we just bought. It's then served like a kind of gruel.[18] You don't want to give dogs plain water in freezing temperatures. Most huskies won't drink water in the winter anyway."

After determining how many sacks would fit comfortably in the sled, we took what we needed to the front counter. As the clerk weighed my gold, to pay for the feed, I asked Richard what other food he gave them.

"I give them snacks, but we can always get that later," he said, "Usually I give them individual pieces of frozen meat, like whitefish. They're abundant in the inland lakes around here."

We loaded the sacks of feed onto the sled with the rest our gear. Richard directed me to stand on the footboard on the back runner where I could operate the brake while hanging onto the drive bow—the crossbar that I used to brace me. While I'd explained to Richard that I had some experience with a team while at our previous claim, I let him take the lead on how I should manage this team.

Before we got underway, Richard explained a few preliminaries regarding the brakes and verbal commands. "Since mushers don't have reins, everything sled dogs do is by verbal command," he began, "Dog sleds come with brakes. But if a dog team does not want to listen to 'whoa' to stop the team, they'll continue down the trail."

"So. What if the dogs don't hear me, or worse yet, don't obey."

"That's why your lead dogs are so important. You can count on Shep and Watch. They're your two leads. Originally, Shep was

18 **Gruel:** a thin liquid food of oatmeal or other meal boiled in milk or waters.

my main lead dog, but early on I put the two together to ensure I had two good leads—I used Shep to train Watch. And, you have to continue to train them as time goes on. That's important. Working together, they make a great team. They're trained to correctly interpret the musher's commands, but most importantly they're taught to stay at the front. If they turn around the lines will tangle.

"After a lead dog has mastered staying in place, it's time to work on the rest of the commands. It takes a lot of time and patience to train new leads. Eventually, you may want to split the team up or change up the pair. That's how you train the rest of the team."

"Are there a lot of commands?"

"There's three that all the dogs need to know and three others that are important for the lead dogs to know. Ready, Alright, and Whoa. Ready tells the dogs to get ready to run. It also tells them to be quiet, since they can be loud otherwise. When you say alright, that tells them to go and it's okay to make noise."

I laughed at Richard's last comment.

"You may laugh, but that's key to controlling the team when you stop for a quick break on the trail—eat a snack, drink water, or if you need to fix something. This helps the dogs remain alert and quiet so they aren't caught unaware and pulled by their teammates when the musher says alright." After a short hesitation, Richard added, "Also remember, the single most important job for the lead dogs is to hold the line whenever the team is being hooked up or unhooked after stopping. The lead dogs are key in holding back the other dogs from running—which is what they love to do."

"What are the other commands you said the lead dogs need to know?"

"The other three are directional commands that the lead dogs must know: gee, haw, and straight ahead. Gee means go right, haw means go left, and straight ahead means don't turn."

"Alright. What now?"

"Now you know enough to get started, let's circle through town for a short run then we'll put them alongside the building over there," he pointed to Clancy's saloon across the street. I'll stay in the rig. You drive the team.

I did as I was told, and we got underway. Minutes later, we returned to where we'd started. The team of six easily handled the weight of our personal gear, one hundred pounds of feed plus Richard and me.

We circled around the backside of Clancy's, until we were positioned alongside the saloon, with the lead dogs, Shep and Watch, facing the street.

"Don't worry. Your leads will keep the rest in position while we're inside," Richard said.

Once we secured the team, Richard encouraged me to pet each dog as we headed toward the front of the saloon. "It's important that the dogs get to know you," Richard said, as he stood behind the sled.

I stopped at the first pair of dogs, called each by name, ruffled their fur and scratched their neck. Then I walked to the next pair and repeated the process. When I reached the lead dogs, I did the same to Watch. As I squatted down, a loud noise erupted toward the front of the building. It was evident that the front door of the saloon had been opened as the sound of people's voices grew until the door closed again.

I looked up and noticed Shep sniffing the cool air, then begin to growl. I gave the 'stay' command to Watch and walked to Shep. Scratching the back of the dog's neck I said, "What's the matter, boy?"

The dog continued to sniff the air. With me at his side, Shep became silent for a moment. Richard stayed back by the sled, keeping an eye on us.

I heard a few footsteps from the direction of the saloon's front porch. Shep's deep low growl began again.

Chapter 33: An Angry Dog

Skagway, Alaska
January 10, 1898

LOOKING TOWARD THE FRONT CORNER of the saloon, I saw the silhouette of a bearded man. The man took a step in my direction and stopped when he saw that Shep was now baring his teeth and pulling aggressively at his tie lines.

I dropped my arm around the dog's chest worried he'd lead the other dogs in a charge toward the man.

Taking a step back, the bearded man reached under his coat. That's when I detected something familiar about him.

"There's no need for concern," I said. "He's not going anywhere."

The bearded man pulled a pistol from inside his jacket.

"Whoa," I exclaimed. "What do you think you're doing?"

"Step away from the dog," the man said.

I recalled the voice and the silhouette. *Jackson.*

"I'll do no such thing," I replied.

"That dog's dangerous."

"Can't you see that he's tethered to the others and the sled? He's no danger to you or anyone, for that matter."

I watched the man's eyes. They told me all I needed to know. Jackson feared this dog.

They have a history.

"He's my dog, and I won't let you harm him. You have no cause."

Jackson seemed to be considering my words. Wanting to make sure he knew I wasn't alone, I added, "The man behind me is the one who sold them to me."

The man looked behind me. Seeing Richard, he stared at him for a time then lowered his gun.

After a long hesitation, he said, "Sold them, eh? Make enough to pay off your debt, Mr. Worthington?"

"A great deal of it," Richard said.

"You know Mr. Jackson, Richard?" I asked.

"I do."

Jackson looked at Richard, then back at me. He had shown a great deal of bravado when he was with his friends, but he was different now. Even with a pistol in hand he looked unsure of himself. I wondered what had affected him the most, the fact that I wasn't alone, that he was recognized, or something else.

"Do I know you?" Jackson said.

You tried to pick a fight with my friend on Main Street a while back. I was with him."

"You're a friend of that Lafe fella?" Jackson asked.

He remembers his name, I was amazed. "That's right. He's my partner," I clarified.

"The man in the saloon?" Jackson slowly holstered his gun.

"That's him." I couldn't help but wonder if Jackson's odd behavior had anything to do with another run in with Lafe in the saloon. "Or," I considered, "perhaps he's avoiding him all together."

Seemingly anxious to get away from the whole situation, Jackson turned to Worthington and said, "You just make sure you keep that dog away from me."

"What's your problem with this dog?" I asked.

"He'll attack anyone," he stated.

"Maybe it's just you, Mr. Jackson," I replied.

"I've never seen him behave this way with anyone," Richard moved closer to me as he spoke.

Jackson hesitated for a moment then turned to Richard and said, "My prior offer still stands."

"Appreciate it. I really do," Richard showed a tight smile, "but I plan on paying off my debt . . . and keeping my claim, too."

"My offer's only good for so long," Jackson said. "And it's a good offer."

"Maybe to a man who has no other options," Richard said. He looked at me before continuing. "But now, thanks to my friends here, I will no longer be beholdin' to *your* friend, Mr. Jackson."

"Good day, then," Jackson huffed. He started to say something else, but evidently thought better of it.

I stayed silent, letting the conversation fizzle on its own. I could see that Jackson was wrestling with how he was going to deal with Richard, more so than the dog.

I could almost read Jackson's mind, *Worthington is teamed with new friends, now.*

I continued to pet the lead dog. "Well, Shep, I see you can recognize evil when you see it." The dog licked my hand.

Richard came up and joined me.

With Jackson out of sight, Shep was calmer now. I patted the dog one more time, stood, and looked back at the rest of the team. The other dogs sat alert but relaxed.

"I lied to that Mr. Jackson fella," Worthington admitted.

"What do you mean? What did you say to him?"

"That's not the first time Shep has done something like that."

I looked at him quizzically.

"Shep is very protective. He'll bark anytime he's wary of a stranger or feels threatened. That last time I heard him growl is when a stranger came around my camp late one evening. But this is the first time I've seen him growl and want to go after someone," Richard said.

We took some time to get the dogs settle before I said, "We should join the others now. What do you say?"

"Sure thing."

We headed toward the saloon.

Chapter 34: Clancy's Saloon

Skagway, Alaska
January 10, 1898

"How well do you know that Jackson fella?" I asked as we stepped into the saloon.

We paused to let our eyes adjust from the snowy glare of the outdoors. The inside shadows became more recognizable, and I noticed Frank waving at me from the back of the room.

I waved back. Neither of us moved away from the entrance. I waited for Rich to speak before heading over to join the others.

"I don't really know him at all. He was just another guy watching the poker game. He congratulated me when he found out I was celebrating my good luck at gold mining. I didn't think much about it at the time, but later, when I started losing big, he offered to buy my claim, or part of it, to help me pay my debt . . . I guess I thought him a friendly guy."

"You still think of him that way?"

"After Shep's reaction to him and hearing what you said about your friend having a run in with him, I'm more leery now," Worthington said. "I realize that I don't know him at all."

Richard and I started walking slowly toward our group. We arrived at the table where Lafe and Frank and our wagon drivers waited, so I stopped asking questions.

I looked at Lafe and said, "We passed your friend on the way in."

"Which friend would that be?" Lafe asked.

"Jackson," I said.

"Oh, right," Lafe laughed. "That friend." Seeing Richard's look of concern, he added, "We're just being sarcastic."

I explained to the Coleman brothers what Richard and I had just discussed and our experience with Jackson, including our lead dog's reaction.

Knowing that he had just left the saloon, I turned to Lafe and said, "I understand that Jackson was just in here. Did you have another run in with him?"

"Why do you ask?" Lafe said.

"He seemed to be in a sour mood," I said.

"When he was in here, he was talking with those men over there," Frank said, indicating a table across the room where six men were playing cards. Three others sat further back from the table, watching the game.

"Did Jackson say anything to you while he was here?" I asked, wondering if what had happened here might have affected his behavior outside.

"No, not to me," Lafe said. "I saw him, but didn't rightly care. I was mostly interested in getting some grub, something to drink and holding a table."

Frank added, "I noticed Jackson look our way. He stared, rather glared, at Lafe for a bit too, but he didn't say anything or come over here. In fact, now that I think about it, he left in a hurry . . . like he was avoiding being in the same room as Lafe . . . or any of us for that matter. It did seem odd, now that I think about it."

We all looked over to the poker table. Richard had to turn around to see. After he turned, I noticed him flinch.

"What's wrong?" I whispered.

"One of the players and a couple of the men sitting back behind the dealer," Worthington remarked. "They were at that game I told you about."

The man shuffling noticed us looking their way and yelled over to us, "Come and join us if you like." The man smiled. "Just a friendly game of poker." As he spoke, I saw the eyes of the man behind the dealer scan each man in our group, then linger a bit longer on Worthington.

"That's alright. No thanks," Frank said. Richard and I sat quietly.

"Don't care to be snookered," Lafe exclaimed, not looking up at the man.

Following Lafe's comment, the big man behind the dealer, stood and walked toward us. As he approached I noticed a swagger about him.

"Just a friendly game," the man said. "And I assure you, the game is honestly played." He smiled affably.

I saw Worthington stiffen.

Chapter 35: The Pigeon

Skagway, Alaska
January 10, 1898

SEEING RICHARD'S REACTION, I REMEMBERED the story Lafe conveyed from Captain Moore and his son, about how Soapy's gang would use this technique to warm up their next prey, before emptying his pockets. I was dismayed at how gullible the big man must think we were. *Are they all part of Soapy's gang?* I wondered.

Addressing Lafe, The big man then said, "You're welcome to play. Come on, I'll even buy you a drink."

"No thanks. I'm fine with my sarsaparilla," Lafe said.

The man placed a hand on Lafe's shoulder, as if he were an old friend.

"My name's Lenny. Why don't you come on over and join 'em?" the man persisted.

"Do any of us look like one of your pigeons?" Lafe asked.

Looking into his eyes, Lenny quickly sensed putting his hand on the man's shoulder was the wrong thing to do. He quickly pulled his hand back.

It was just like Lafe to invite trouble. I knew he'd always say it like he saw it, regardless of how his comments might be received.

The man seemed unsure about how to react to Lafe. Realizing that pushing further would be no use, he quietly retreated and returned to watch the game.

Lenny sat down near the poker game and started talking to the player sitting to the dealer's left. I realized I'd seen that player before. I looked at Lafe and Frank and asked, "Does that man to the left of the dealer look familiar to either of you?"

Lafe was busy trying to get the waiter's attention. While he and Frank had received their food, Rich and I hadn't had a chance to order yet.

Frank took a cursory glance toward the poker game.

"Why, should he?" Frank asked.

"Wasn't he one of the men following Jackson?"

Frank took another glance at the player next to the dealer. "Yeah, I recognize him now. He was with that Jackson fellow the day Lafe had the dustup[19] with him. In fact, he tried to help Jackson to his feet."

"I thought so," I said.

Lafe got the bartender's attention and waved for him to come over, but I knew he was listening. He never looked like he was paying attention, but he normally didn't miss much.

The bartender sent his assistant over to take our order.

When I looked back at the poker game, I saw the dealer throw out one more card to each of the players. He then looked at Lafe. He had been looking his direction frequently since Lafe's comment to Lenny about the game.

Lafe glanced over and met the dealer's gaze.

The man quickly diverted his eyes and turned his attention back to the players. "Place your bet or fold," the dealer said to the man across the table.

The chips piled on the tables showed it to be a high stakes hand. As I watched, all but two of the players folded and dropped out of the game.

---

19 **Dustup:** a fight or quarrel.

Of the final two, the one with his back to us passed on taking a card. The one Lenny had just talked with placed one card on the table face down and got one in return.

The player who had his back to us yelled, "You're cheating!" and stood up quickly. His chair fell over onto the sawdust-covered floor.

Lenny quickly went to the angry man's side and said, "I know he's not cheating; I've been watching the whole time."

Lafe joined in. "That's not true, unless dealing off the bottom of the deck is acceptable. And it's not the first time," he added. "Seems to me that you're just gathering in players to take advantage of them. Seems we've got a problem here."

That's all the angry player needed to hear. He charged the dealer. Just before reaching him, Lenny grabbed him by his shirt, spun him around, and hit him in the stomach.

The man folded over and dropped to his knees.

"Evidently his job is more than just bringing in the pigeons," Lafe stated while beginning to stand.

"The dealer won that hand fair and square," Lenny said.

Walking with a swagger of his own, Lafe moved to the player who was now struggling to stand.

The man was having difficulty getting his breath. Lenny stood over him, preparing to strike again.

"Hold it right there," Lafe said forcefully enough to stop the man in his tracks.

Lenny turned to face Lafe. "You're walking on dangerous ground here, mister," he exclaimed.

"Only if you choose to make it that way," Coleman said simply. "The dealer made it that way when he cheated him. Like I said, I saw what he did. I suggest you return the man's money."

"Is that right, Lenny?" a voice cried out from the back of the room. We all turned to see the owner, John Clancy, standing next to the bartender who must have run to the back room to get him when the raucous began.

Clancy looked to our little group standing around the injured player and then to the others sitting quietly at the table. They were watching to see what would happen next. The dealer clearly did not want to make eye contact with Lenny, Clancy or anyone else for that matter.

"Hello, Bill," Clancy said.

I nodded back to Clancy and said, "Hello, John. Come out to check on your men?"

"Not my men," Clancy said. "They're . . . my associate's. I let them in here because they bring me business." Clancy turned to Lenny and said, "Fix this, Lenny."

"I'll take care of it," Lenny replied with as much dignity as he could muster. Lenny looked at the most immediate threat. Lafe.

"Make this right," Lafe said again.

Frank stepped up to stand by his brother. Richard and I both stood as well. To our surprise, so too did our wagon drivers. Evidently some of the town's folks were also willing to stand up to these con men. Lenny clearly looked to be in a quandary.

Without saying a word, he walked back to the dealer to talk. They were obviously weighing their options.

Lafe stepped over and assisted the cheated player to his feet.

The dilemma was clear. Lafe was seen as a potentially dangerous element, and they feared losing the respect of the other players. Lenny had supported the dealer who was accused of cheating by both a player and an observer.

If they fought us, they might be able to win, and keep their winnings, but that would also show they were bullies. Fights were not uncommon in the saloons, especially when liquor was involved. But, when the owner was present and a temporary truce had been called to iron out the disagreement, Lenny knew a fight would not be prudent. If word of that got out, potential customers would avoid the saloon and take their business elsewhere. Their reputation was at stake and they wanted to be in good standing with the saloon's owner. Busting up Clancy's establishment wouldn't help, and winning a fight wasn't a sure thing either.

After a short time, Lenny returned to talk with Lafe. "Understand that I'm employed here to prevent trouble on these premises. I'm not saying you're right. And, we don't take kindly to someone claiming we're the cause of another's misfortune, but we are willing to help him out in this situation."

We all waited for him to continue.

"We're letting each player take back his chips from the last hand," Lenny said. "That is more than fair."

Lafe looked at the player who was still holding his stomach. "You okay with that, mister?"

The man nodded, now feeling fortunate to leave with something more than a sore stomach.

The dealer asked the players to remove what they'd bet on the last hand 'before the misunderstanding took place'. The injured man returned to his place and did the same. Once each man agreed on everyone's share, Lafe and Frank escorted the injured man safely to the door, as the other players left the game table.

Lenny stood between the dealer and Richard, our wagon drivers, and myself until Lafe and Frank returned.

As the Colemans rejoined us, Lenny started to returned to sit with the dealer when Clancy, pointing toward the door, said "Lenny, I think it's best if you all give it a rest." He then added, "We'll talk about this incident later."

Understanding his meaning, Lenny, the dealer and three of their other sidekicks left.

We returned to our table just as the waiter set Richard's and my sandwiches and sodas on the table.

Clancy joined us.

Since Frank and I were the only ones who had gotten to know Clancy on the trip north, I introduced him to the others.

The saloon owner looked at Lafe and asked, "You okay with how this all worked out?"

"All except the fact that the dealer didn't acknowledge what he did, and he still seems to be working here."

"He's gone for now, but understand it's a delicate situation," Clancy said. "They work for my associate. He's responsible for them."

"That wouldn't be a fella by the name of Soapy Smith now would it?" Lafe asked.

"Yes," Clancy said. "But it's best to remember that even his own men know better than to call him Soapy . . . at least to his face."

"Looking forward to meeting this man, Soapy, one of these days," Lafe said with a grin.

"Your brother and Bill here, already know him," Clancy said with a smile as he looked at both Frank and me.

I could see that Clancy was amused by our confusing looks.

After a long pause, he simply said, "The man you know as Jeff, who rode up with us from Seattle, on the steamer."

"Jeff?" I gasped. "The sickly thin man with the dark beard, who we hardly saw during the whole trip?"

"That's him," Clancy said. "He spent most of his time in the cabin. But on his behalf, I have to say, that was a pretty rough trip. Many didn't fair well with the ship rocking and rolling like it did."

"When he did join us at meals he hardly said a word," Frank said.

"That's because he wasn't feeling well most of the time. I don't think he felt comfortable leaving the cabin much at all. Even in calmer waters," Clancy added.

That being said, we all went silent for some time to consider the implications.

Chapter 36: Taking Goods Inland from Skagway

Skagway to Dyea, Alaska
January 10, 1898

As we headed back toward Dyea, I found the trip to be effortless. The dogs responded well, with Richard encouraging me along the way, telling me I was a natural.

At the upper part of the city, we crossed over the Skagway River, and continued north leaving the town behind. After a while we turned south, to snake our way around the hill that rose up between the Taiya Inlet and Skagway. The terrain along our route was relatively flat. This made it easier for me to become acquainted with the team. Initially, Richard would remind me of what command to give the dogs when we approached a certain point, like a fork in the road. But after a while, he realized I had full command of the sled and chose to only talk about the beautiful terrain that lay ahead. I became more at ease with the team, and Richard told me about the dogs while we traversed the trails.

"The lead dog, Shed, is the smartest of the lot and independent at times, but you can count on him for good judgment," he said. "He knows how to take care of the others and *you*, too. There will be times when you'll think he's almost human. He might wander off at night periodically, but always seems to find his way back. He's easily the biggest and strongest of the lot. I usually put *Watch* in the second position and *Pincher* in the third." Richard continued to go down the list of names for the rest of the six-dog team and described their qualities.

Traveling north, along the Taiya Inlet, we eventually came upon the Kinney Bridge, which would take us west, across the inlet to Dyea. It was comforting to see that we weren't far from our cabin, but viewing the path that continued on north, had me thinking about we what we might encounter in the near future.

This is where we would be starting the first leg of the long trek toward Chilkoot Pass. That included climbing slopes that would increase with each step, eventually taking us to the Canadian border at an elevation of over 3700 feet. Making the trek doesn't seem too bad until you consider we'd be packing well over two thousand pounds of goods each, and that's not including the extra rations we planned to sell along the way. Having registered two other claims, we carefully planned our trip to include leapfrogging our goods from one claim to another. Using the dog-sled team, in lieu of backpacking our goods, would also give us more time to pan gold as we progressed.

As we got closer to the inlet's crossing point, I could see a small group of men gathered at the near edge of the bridge. I gently put the brakes into play and gave the command to stop when I saw that it would be best to wait until the bridge was clear. I didn't know how the dogs would react to a cluster of men who were partially blocking the crossing point.

The dogs slowly ground to a halt. Still restless, some looked back at me. I figured this was a good time to tend to them while they rested. Richard pulled out some treats and said, "Distributing these will let them know you're the boss."

I worked my way up the line, petting each as it scarfed down a slab of sun-dried fish meat. Approaching the lead dogs, I realized the discussion ahead was getting louder and more heated. From where I was standing, I recognized the toll agent from my earlier passing, but had no idea who the others were standing around him. My attention was quickly drawn to a man with his back to me who was making gestures that included a lot of arm waving. The bridge tender, with folded arms, was looking on in disgust. Without saying a word, the others just stood and watched. It was not evident what the man was upset about, but it was obvious that the toll taker wasn't having any of it.

All the dogs sat alert. Periodically, I would hear a low growl from Shed as he watched the gathering off in the distance. Makes me wonder what's gotten into him lately.

Seeing that the quarrelsome group wasn't getting anywhere, they finally moved on. Slowly, they proceeded north up the Chilkoot trail, away from us and Dyea.

I settled back onto the sled, alerted the dogs and put them back into motion. By the time we pulled up to the bridge, the group was rounding a turn up the trail.

I paid the toll and commented to the toll keeper, "Looked like you were having quite a heated discussion."

"Pretty obvious, huh?"

"I don't recall seeing you that stern with anyone, before."

"You remember a few months ago when some men were not-so-nicely asked to leave Dyea because of their, how should I say . . . shifty business practices?"

"I do."

"Well, that's them, or at least the ones with the same low-down character. They're staying out of Dyea, but wanted to set up shop here, along the trail."

"I take it you said, no."

"In no uncertain terms."

"They tried to bribe me to use the bridge. Can you believe that? They wanted to provide travelers with a little entertainment and offered me a cut of the profits. The man said it might be a good spot, at this crossroads, to provide travelers with a distraction from their tedious journey. The way they try to trick people out of their money . . . I won't have any part of that."

I looked back to where I'd last seen the men disappear up the slope and said, "Looks as though they might be looking for better ground up the way."

The bridge tender just shook his head, "You ought to stay clear of those men."

"Plan to," as I continued watching where they'd disappeared.

Chapter 37: Meeting with the Gang

Skagway, Alaska
January 11, 1898

IT HAD BECOME A REGULAR PRACTICE for Jefferson and his associates to meet in one of his establishments. The most common spot had been Clancy's, since it seemed to be one of the more popular places in town and the most visible, being closest to wharf.

Consistent with Smith's urge to go easy on the violence, he wanted to use this session with his men to emphasize his point. They listened as he talked about lessons learned from activities his people got involved with around town. He often got them involved in the discussions on how things could go better given certain circumstances.

"Yesterday, we had a poker game that didn't end well," Smith began. "Lenny here," he gestured, "could have had a big fight on his hands, and lost a lot of customers if he hadn't handled it the way he did." He then gave Lenny the opportunity to explain what occurred at Clancy's saloon.

Lenny told about how a customer had spotted his dealer slipping a card here and there and called him on it. "He actually demanded that 'I make it right'. Can you can believe that?" emphasizing how nobody had ever had the gall to challenge him before. When Lenny finished telling the story, he ended with, "It's too bad that guy was there in the first place."

"The guy's name is Lafe Coleman," Jackson offered.

Lenny thought about the event and said, "You were lucky, Jackson. You left just before the whole incident began, if I recall."

"It's a good thing I did, too. If I'd still been there when he arrived, I'm sure things would have ended differently," Jackson smirked.

"If I recall," Lenny offered, "You were glaring at that Lafe fella for quite some time. I noticed you left after you couldn't get a rise out of the man."

"Huh. It wouldn't have been worth the effort," Jackson said.

Recalling his words with Jackson earlier, about telling him avoiding that man, Smith chose to make a point without making a big scene in front of his men. "I'm glad to hear you weren't there, Jackson," Smith interjected. "I know about the run-in you had with him a few weeks earlier. I'm sure things would have escalated if you had stayed. Avoiding that man was the right thing to do."

Getting back to his story, Lenny said, "I can't help but wonder about the outcome if I'd stood my ground. We lost everyone at the poker table after that little episode."

You'd probably have caused a brawl on top of losing the customers. Soapy thought.

"What good would it have done you if you'd busted up the place?" Smith said. "It sure wouldn't help my relationship with Clancy, now would it?"

"No I suppose not."

"Not to mention how it would stir up a great deal of public resentment," Jefferson added. "We need to be careful about using intimidation tactics. The less experienced greenhorns are the ones you should be focusing on."

Turning his attention back to Jackson, Jefferson emphasized his main point, again, "In this town, it's important to stay away from the old hands and locals. We don't want to stir them up."

Before continuing, Jackson thought about his conversation with Worthington after leaving the saloon that day. Worthington had become friends with the man who bought his dog-sled team. That included the Colemans.

"But, didn't I hear that you're going to try your luck up the trail again?" Smith asked.

Addressing his audience with a wry smile, Jackson said. "I have some men working on that. We don't expect any problems."

That's what I'm worried about, Smith thought.

"Tell me what you have in mind."

The rest of the men leaned in as he did so.

Chapter 38: Truth Gains Traction

Nevada, Missouri
January 16, 1898

FOLLOWING THE MORNING CHURCH SERVICES, Eva introduced Ted to more of her friends and neighbors, as she had done the previous Sundays. He was slowly getting to know the people around town. Currently, they were chatting with Douglas and Nancy Pepperdine, a newly married young couple who had gone to school with Eva.

"So, you don't think it's a good investment?" Pepperdine asked, while his wife listened at his side.

"All I can say is, investments are not a sure thing," Ted Bohannon said.

"He told us he had other investors," Nancy said.

"You might want to ask him who has invested. And, if he gives you a reference, you may want to talk with them personally," Ted said.

"So, you don't think he's telling the truth?" asked Douglas.

"I'll let you be the judge of that. He may have more investors by now, but he sure didn't have any earlier."

"You've certainly given us something to think about," Nancy said.

"Thank you, Ted. It was good meeting you." They shook hands and left. Ted and Eva began walking over to join Sam and John, across the foyer.

On the way, they were stopped by another young couple, Tom and Janice Harding. Eva, again, made the introductions. After they had a short conversation about how they knew each other and where they lived, Eva's twin brothers walked over to join them. Being long-time friends, Sam asked what the latest news was. Tom said, "Not much, other than . . . rumor has it that your brother striking it rich was just a hoax. Is that true?"

"That seems to be the question of the week. No. It's not a hoax," Sam continued, "He did well in Alaska and sent us a letter from Seattle telling us he was heading home. Then, they decided to try their luck in the Yukon, according to the letter he wrote to us later."

"Now I understand," Tom said, "I have to admit, I wasn't sure what to think, at first. I was surprised someone would start a rumor like that. That's why I decided to ask you directly."

"It's sad to think that as soon as someone passes along information, others assume it's true, but in reality, it's based on rumors, not facts," John offered.

Ted said, "Gossipers just pass on what they hear and even add a few tidbits of their own sometimes."

"I wonder who started that story?" Janice asked.

"Who did you hear it from?" Ted asked.

"I heard it from Stanley Barclay," Tom offered.

The couple were summoned by other family members and excused themselves.

Once Tom and Janice left, Sam said, "Now we know where the rumor came from."

Eva, after listening quietly, looked pensive and said, "What do you think we should we do about the rumors?"

"Nothing," Ted said. "Actually, we are already doing it."

"What do you mean, 'already doing it,' Ted?" Eva asked.

"People ask us. We tell them the truth. They'll be the judges," Ted said, "Eventually, they'll see things as they are."

"You mean the truth," Eva stated.

"Yup."

"Like dad always says," John added, "'actions are louder than words'. When Bill does return home, they'll all see for themselves. And in the meantime, if they believe what they're hearing now, that's their problem not ours."

"People will believe what they chose to believe, especially if their friends believe it. But eventually, the truth comes out."

"I can't imagine why Stanley's been doing this," John said, not aiming his comment at anyone in particular.

"He's trying to get back at us," Eva said.

"Ever since the picnic I'm sure he's felt the sting of people losing interest in that investment of his," John added.

"So he's rebuilding his base," Sam said, "He chose to challenge us in front of his friends, which didn't end well for him. He probably feels that if he says his lies out loud, enough, his buddies will believe them to be true."

With all the tales he tells, good luck with that, Ted thought.

Chapter 39: Establishing Cache Sites

Canyon City, Alaska
January 16, 1898

"RIGHT HERE, LAFE?"

"Yup. Right here."

Dutch looked at the rest of his friends, a dozen standing together admiring the open space, tucked away behind some trees.

"What do you think, boys?"

This question was met by a chorus of "greats."

"Anxious to get started," Dutch said, directing his comment to Lafe, Frank and me. "Appreciate you offering your lot for our next cache[20] site. Miller, Jake and Guy have their goods by mine, just north of the toll bridge. We set up camp there a few days ago. The others aren't far from us."

"We plan to get started tomorrow," I said.

"If that's your plan, stop by whenever you like. Maybe get a bite to eat and a little rest before you move on."

"Stopping for a short spell sounds like a good idea," Lafe said. "But it'll probably be after we get most of our goods moved."

"Okay. Whenever you can make it."

---

20 **Cache:** a collection of items of the same type stored in a hidden or inaccessible place.

Turning to Worthington, Dutch added, "You are always welcome too, Richard. Even if you're not moving any of your goods."

"Appreciate it Dutch," Richard said, "But I know we'll be visiting a great deal when you bring your supplies up to my claim, which isn't far from Sheep Camp ."

"Well, boys." Dutch addressed everyone present. "Looks like we're set for a spot where we can stash our goods, at least until we get to the summit."

Worthington was a good worker. His teaming with us to erect the sluice boxes and set up camp at Canyon City had helped a great deal. That in itself made our arrangement with him worthwhile. Sitting around a fire at our Canyon City camp site, I could see that he had connected with Dutch and the Sunrise crew, as well. He seemed to fit right in with our bunch. It was comforting to know any one of these men would be willing to lend an extra hand when needed.

We learned quickly that working together, with friends, was the best practice if we wanted to be successful. Lafe, Frank and I felt fortunate to have hooked up with Dutch and some of our other neighbors while working our claims in Sunrise. Dutch was a well-organized, hard-working, well-read, older gentleman. We often came together, as neighbors did, to mingle and socialize with each other. It evolved into helping each other by sharing ideas and problem solving, which made us all better gold miners.

On Dutch's thirtieth birthday we celebrated what he referred to as his becoming an old man.

From that time on, we often refer to him as that, *the old man*— the rest of the team were in our twenties. Being the most senior member of the group, we all respected his educated ways and mining experience. Dutch was a man of few words. Anytime someone outside our group asked him if Dutch was his birth name or nickname, he'd just say, "It's what everyone calls me," and say no more.

"Lafe. Any idea what conditions are like up at the pass?" Dutch asked.

"I'll let Frank and Bill tell you about that. They went up a couple of days ago. Just got back."

Dutch and his friends all looked expectantly at the two of us.

"Not much to tell," Frank began, "Too windy and cold for us." He then began to explain how, after selling our Dyea claim, instead of moving all our supplies numerous times, we'd planned on storing a portion of what we wouldn't need during the trip in Canada. Leaving two of the six dogs with Lafe, who stayed to fix up the site, we packed up our three-hundred-pound camping outfit and set off to look for some town lots near Lindeman Lake. "It had seemed like a good idea," he continued. "However, not everything went as planned."

Frank then told of how unpredictable the weather had become and how they made it to the summit. But there the temperatures had dropped to single digits with high winds freezing any exposed flesh straightaway. No sooner did we talk about continuing on into Canada when we met a man who had his feet badly frozen. His experience with the easterly winds over the pass convinced us it would be more prudent to stay the night at the summit and make our way back to Canyon City in the morning. We also decided it was best to leave our camping outfit at the summit. At least that's three-hundred pounds of equipment we won't have to move multiple times in the weeks to come. Also, with our camping outfit, we were able to established a site for our cache at the summit, that later might be difficult to acquire once the rush of other miners arrive. The next morning, we returned here, at our campsite by Canyon City.

While January was the time we planned to start moving our goods, we now wondered if we'd waited too long. The weather we'd encountered was eye opening, as was the influx of arriving miners. The steady stream of men arriving had increased from hundreds each day to thousands. The worsening weather conditions and swarm of miners racing up to the summit would inevitably be quite a challenge.

Little did we know what additional problems we'd run into along the way.

Chapter 40: First Leg Up the Trail

Canyon City, Alaska
January 17, 1898

RISING EARLY, LAFE, FRANK AND I finished our breakfast by 5:30 a.m. Having packed everything we needed the previous evening for this day's test run, we were almost ready to go. At least Frank and Lafe were. Since I'd prepared everyone's breakfast, I first had to clean up the cooking pots, pans and stove, get the dogs hooked up and secure the cabin before I could head out.

This third Monday of the new year, would be our first run from Dyea to Canyon City. During this trip, we'd be able to see how well we could handle moving our supplies and how much we could accomplish during the limited daylight hours. Having made a number of trips by sled already, to the summit as well as to and from Skagway, I was already aware of the team's capability. So far, I knew that the team could handle about 1100 lbs. plus Worthington's and my weight without difficulty. Now I'd be able to gage how the team could handle a slightly steeper slope.

While we'd left some supplies on the pass, to prepare for setting up our campsite in Canada, we still had another outfit for camping along the trail on this side of the pass. On the first stretch to Canyon City, and each new location thereafter, we would be packing our duplicate camping equipment as well as those items needed for everyday use. Our first runs would have to include at least our basic kit. It consisted of a tent, stove, cooking utensils, tools we'd need on a daily basis, as well as enough food to last us for a few days in the event of an emergency. Snow conditions could abruptly change, sometimes overnight.

We knew we'd have quite a challenge ahead of us having already withstood the Alaska winters for the last three years. But we'd not experienced having to move so much up through a mountain pass in such rugged conditions. One thing we did learn while mining in Sunrise, Alaska, was the cold, windy weather should never hold us back from getting things done. Although our first leg of the journey would have its own difficulties, I knew it would be a breeze compared to what we'd have to endure at the higher altitudes and steeper slopes.

With Lafe and Frank now ready to leave, my thoughts ran through any possible item we may have overlooked. "I can't remember if we packed the stovepipe last night. Either of you know where it might be?" I asked.

"I packed it alongside the stove on your sled," Frank replied.

"How about the cutting tools?""

"Same place as the stove pipe," Frank said.

"Do we have enough emergency rations?"

"Enough for us and the dogs," Lafe responded.

After hearing no more questions from me, Lafe and Frank picked up the backpacks that they'd packed the previous evening and headed for the cabin door.

"See ya up the trail," Lafe said.

Frank and Lafe both waved as they left. Even with the chores I had to complete before leaving they knew I'd be catching up to them soon enough. With six dogs pulling the sled, I'd probably catch them before they got too far up the trail.

This routine went on through the rest of the month.

When we first started out, Lafe and Frank were envious of my being able to ride the whole way. But as time went by, they not only appreciated how great a load I'd be taking up with each trip, but they looked forward to riding down with me on the return trip.

On each return trip, the Colemans sat in the sled, bouncing with joy while I put all my energy into controlling the team. The brake came in handy. Without it I could not control the sled on the steep downhill slopes and sharp turns. I also had to be careful not to allow the sled to overtake the dogs when they needed to maneuver at a slower pace, especially on the steep grades and turns. Avoiding travelers coming up the trail became tricky at times as well.

Once we got to the flatlands, I'd let the dogs loose, at least if the pathway was clear of travelers. I believe they enjoyed our return trips as much as we did. We'd then have lunch at the cabin and rest for a spell before loading up more supplies.

We quickly learned that two trips in a day was plenty, for this time of year. Typically, we'd finish our runs around 3:00 p.m., when darkness was setting in. This still left us enough time to pack for the next day, have dinner and get a good night's sleep before rising early the next morning and starting the routine all over again.

Our final trip to Canyon City was the last day of the month. That's when we were scheduled to meet our friends at the campsite of Dutch and Guy.

Leaving Dyea

"The customs here are very different from back there. Here, there is no trouble over nickels and pennies. All the little things you buy are twenty-five cents. If a man cannot come within that amount of making correct change, it goes anyway."

"If a crowd of us Alaskans would suddenly appear in Nevada, Missouri, dressed in our usual garb, we would create no little sensation. Our coats, called Mackinaws, are square cut, they have great collars, a belt to buckle around the waist, and are made of heavy wool—like a blanket. They are all loud colors. My present suit is yellow, the last one was like Joseph's, of many colors, red and brown striped. That is the Indians' favorite color. Our caps are made of fur, usually of marmot, squirrel, rabbit or sealskin. Our mittens are the same."

—*Letter to brother John Schooley, December 30, 1897*

Historic Gold Rush Trails from Skagway and Dyea

Lake Bennett

Bennett

Bennett Station

CANADA

Lindeman Lake

Lindeman City

Bare Loon Lake

To Carcross, Alaska Highway, Yukon Territory

Deep Lake

Log Cabin

Deep Lake

Long Lake

CHILKOOT TRAIL NATIONAL HISTORIC SITE OF CANADA

Happy Camp

Historic route of WHITE PASS TRAIL

Crater Lake

BRITISH COLUMBIA ALASKA

Fraser Canada Customs

Chilkoot Pass

The Golden Stairs

Bernard Lake

The Scales

UNITED STATES

Summit Lake

CHILKOOT TRAIL

Sheep Camp

Pleasant Camp

White Pass

Dead Horse Gulch

KLONDIKE GOLD RUSH NATIONAL HISTORICAL PARK

Canyon City

KLONDIKE GOLD RUSH NATIONAL HISTORICAL PARK

CANADA

Finnegan's Point

South Klondike Highway

White Pass City

White Pass & Yukon Route Railroad

Laughton Glacier Trail

United States Customs

Skagway River

Taiya River

AB Mountain

See Dyea map at upper right

Chilkoot Trailhead

Historic Dyea Townsite

Denver Glacier Trail

UNITED STATES

Dyea Road

Reed Falls

Icy Lake

TONGASS NATIONAL FOREST

Skagway

Lower Dewey Lake

Upper Dewey Lake

Devil's Punch Bowl

TAIYA INLET

North

0   1   5 Kilometers
0   1   5 Miles

△ Backcountry campsite

Chapter 41: Leaving Dyea

A Few Miles North of Dyea, AK
January 30, 1898

A s PLANNED, WE VACATED OUR CABIN in Dyea and headed for Canyon City. Along the way, we'd planned to stop at the campsite of Dutch and Guy, just north of the toll bridge. Some of the others we'd worked with in Sunrise, would also be joining us.

The Colemans left first, as usual, but only after helping me clean and pack up our cooking gear. All I had to do now was rouse the dogs and get them harnessed to the sled.

In the darkness of this early morning, I made one last check around the cabin, to see if there was anything I overlooked. Once I vacated our quarters, the cabin would belong to the new owners. I took my time, understanding this would be our last load. We put a lot of effort into building the cabin. I wanted to acknowledge what we'd accomplished here.

Before stepping on to the sled's rear footboard I checked the dogs' riggings and ensured the supplies were secured. It took very little time for the six dogs to get the sled moving. Leaving the neatly laid out streets of Dyea behind, I looked back at the town's scattering of cabins while entering River Street. Heading north, I mushed the team parallel to the Taiya River. The sound of the river and light from the moon helped guide me.

Since this day would be my last trip packing our goods out of Dyea, my senses were keen to take in my surrounding. I wanted this trip to leave an imprint on me. In a short time, I found the well-used, snow-packed ruts that led me through the flatlands toward the Chilkoot trail. The dogs were excited to get moving again, and I had become even more confident in my lead dog. Shed had taken the route up the valley enough times to know where to direct the pack. I caught a whiff of the sweet aroma of burning cedar. Miners across the valley were beginning to rise, make their meals and face the chores of the day. The light of day was beginning to peek over the hilltops. I admired the silhouette of the snow-covered mountains as the light slowly revealed them.

As I got further inland, I saw tents sprinkled across the flats, many with smoke coming from their stovepipes or burning camp-fires. But mostly I noticed the barren spaces. During my time in Dyea, I'd seen a great deal of the scrub brush and trees disappear. Any timber that couldn't be used for building materials was used for lean-tos, tent poles, wind barriers or burned for cooking or keeping the miners warm. I wondered how long it would take for the forest to start reclaiming the land after the travelers passed through. Looking across the valley, I noted the remarkable changes from months earlier. When I first arrived, Dyea had only been par-tially been surveyed for lots. Then, it was forested and had very few inhabitants. Now it was quite different.

I took in the peacefulness of the morning. The serenity of this rare windless moment invigorated me. I enjoyed watching the sun rise, glistening off the snow-capped hills as it peeked over the mountain tops. I savored the tranquility of the moment as I left the multitude of cabins and campsites behind.

I was glad to beat the crowds that would soon begin to make the climb. If I were to rise when the bulk of the other travelers did, the trek would not be as exhilarating. It would be crowded with those making their way on foot, carrying whatever they could on their backs while trekking up the slopes. Everyone heading this way was destined for the pass, and all had to leapfrog their goods if they were going to bring the two thousand pounds of food stuffs required to enter into Canada. Although I would make better time, riding on a sled, I learned early on that getting behind the back-packers on a narrow path would significantly slow my progress. As a result, I found myself enjoying the early morning quiet. I believe the team I'd grown to trust enjoyed this time as well.

Here in the flats, the dogs made their way without difficulty. In fact, I was holding them back a bit, they were happiest when running full out. Still, it didn't take long to come upon the bridge, at the Taiya River.

Approaching, I could see a group of men starting to cross. Pulling up closer, I saw that the Colemans as well as three other Sunrise friends made up that group.

They all waved as I arrived.

I joined them, braked, to slow the dogs, and settled them into a walking pace.

"Good timing," one of our Sunrise friends yelled, "Dutch's campsite is just up the rise."

"Go ahead," I responded, "I'll follow." I kept my attention on the Colemans, just ahead of me.

As we got closer to Dutch's camp, a somewhat muffled yelp pierced the air, followed by another person's agonizing yell.

Someone was in distress.

Chapter 42: Stolen Goods

North of the Taiya Bridge
January 30, 1898

"**M**ISSING? WHAT DO YOU MEAN, MISSING?" the barrel chested stout man bellowed. Dutch was responding to the cries of three of his fellow miners.

"Our box of tools, axes, shovels and saws, are gone, Dutch," Guy said.

"So are some of our foodstuffs, the jerky, flower, sugar, and who knows what else," Miller added.

"They were right here," Jake said forlornly, gesturing to a crate with a detached lid laying at its side. "I put 'em here myself."

These three men were close with Dutch, having met him during the long trip north aboard a steamer out of Seattle, six years earlier.

Stepping out of the trail's compacted snow, Dutch made his way around the stack that was covered by snow drifts, to where his three cohorts had made the discovery.

"Hmmm," Dutch mused, as he walked around to where Jake was standing. "Let's brush off the snow from the neighboring crates and see if any of them have been tampered with."

Finishing their inspection Dutch said, "Seems whoever did this was either looking for particular items or chose to take whatever they could get away with while hiding behind the stack. They only emptied the three crates in the rear, furthest from the trail."

Hearing a noise not far off, Dutch and the others stopped to listen. Not knowing if it was the thieves leaving the area or the flow of prospectors passing by, they waited. A moment later, a procession of backpackers trudging up the trail, came into view.

Dutch recognized the first two and figured he would know those following behind. They were part of the same group he'd been working with over the last three years, in Sunrise.

This procession of hikers followed Dutch back along a side trail and into the woods where they could unburden themselves from their packs.

By the time Lafe, Frank and I pulled up alongside the storage site and gotten the dogs settled in, Dutch had returned.

"We've got a campfire going just outside my cabin," he said. "Come on back whenever you're done here."

Lafe and Frank went first. After getting the dogs settled, I started to follow then stopped when I saw a box with its lid removed in the back of the pile. Having heard Dutch's friends grumbling about a theft when we first arrived, I looked in the empty box and picked up the lid. I wondered if this was what they were talking about. Since I was late joining the others, I started to toss the lid back when something caught my eye. I took a closer look at one particular nail sticking out of the lid. It had something hanging from it. I pull it off, put it in my pocket and left to join the others.

Lafe and Frank had already joined the rest of the crew. They were participating in a loud discussion about the theft. Everyone was settled around the fire when I arrived, so I filled my cup with coffee, took a strip of jerky from a pan by the fire and sat on a log nearby. Staying away from the hubbub, I listened to everyone's concerns as tempers flared.

Dutch let the venting go on, hoping that eventually it would burn out. During this time, he stayed seated and listened.

When the men around him got to the point of repeatedly making the same complaints, Dutch stood. He looked expectantly, waiting for them all to quiet down and listen to what he had to say.

"I'm no less angry than you are," he began. "All we can do now is resupply what's been lost, pass the word and ensure it doesn't happen again." He waited for the grumbling to simmer before continuing. "At least we've made a good choice to work together over the next couple of months. Consolidating our cache as we approach the summit will help us to better attend to our supplies, too."

The men nodded quietly, knowing he was right.

"Who knows. Maybe we'll even find those who did this," Dutch said with a wry smile. "You all understand we should be attending to our stockpile of goods from here on?"

Hearing a loud murmur of assent, Dutch stepped away and joined me.

"What did they end up taking, Dutch?" I asked. Dutch and I had become good friends over the last three years. We had a lot in common, we were both inquisitive, had a strong desire to understand things better and a thirst for reading, which we often shared. Once he filled me in on what was taken, I asked him if he had any suspicions about who or when the theft might have occurred. He told me what he knew.

When he finished, I said, "I saw the empty box up there." I then pulled my discovery from my pocket and filled him in on where I'd found it. I told him what we'd learned up at the pass, "Thefts have occurred at the summit as well." After that, we sat quietly considering the implications of the matter.

After a time, Dutch responded, "You know it's not going to stop till they're caught."

"We've got plenty of folks going up and down the trail the next few weeks. We'll just have to keep alert."

I returned the find to my pocket and thought about Dutch's comments.

Be alert and keep going.

Chapter 43: Retribution

Nevada, Missouri
January 30, 1898

BARCLAY QUIETLY SNUCK HIS HORSE ALONG the back pasture and tied the reigns to a fence behind the barn. The bright stars made it manageable for him to find his way, but the clear sky brought the temperatures so low, it chilled him to the bone. Now, he needed to get inside the barn where he could more covertly view his target. The cause of his floundering enterprise.

He had always thrived on his reputation as the bad boy in town. He friends were all of the same lot. But lately, he found that some of his group had become more distant. They had trust issues. He learned this after overhearing two of his buddies talking. His friends were few, not that that bothered him. But losing investors and not gaining any new ones was costing him. Now he was driven to get even. Maybe what he had in mind wouldn't change anything, but he'd get some personal gratification as a result of his actions.

They must be punished.

Entering through the barn's back door, he found it too dark to see inside. Feeling his way along the wall, he located a gate to a stall, followed along the short wall and headed for the front of the barn.

Reaching the second stall, he heard voices from the direction he was walking and froze in place. Hearing the rattle of the barn's double doors being unlatched, he scrambled across the center corridor and fell over a bale of hay. He lay still, not knowing what to do. When the door swung open, light from a lantern allowed him to see a tall stack of hay bales not far away. Stanley carefully and quietly crawled behind them. He lay still for what seemed like an hour, afraid to move as the twins prepared the horses for a ride into town. Two horses were saddled and another was hooked to the family wagon. Once done, the boys lead them to the front of the house.

That's when Stanley took the time to find a more comfortable position up in the loft, to keep an eye on the house. His plan was to wait until the family left for church before driving their livestock out into the freezing outdoors. It didn't take long for them to leave. A carriage arrived out front, and Eva ran out and climbed in. The rest of the family exited shortly after that. The husband and wife boarded the wagon and the two youngest mounted the horses that were tied to a railing nearby. He watched as they all went off to church, as he knew they would. Like clockwork.

Seeing that one of the twins had placed the lantern on the back porch, before entering, Stanley decided to make good use of it. Although it was starting to get light out, it was still difficult to see inside the barn. The mid-twenty temperatures felt colder now that the winds were picking up.

He quickly snatched up the kerosene lantern, lit it, and returned to the barn. Although his horse was partially covered with a saddle and blanket, he retrieved it and walked it back into the barn. The increasing winds would have taken its toll on his horse, otherwise.

The family will pay.

He then took the time to prop open the barn's double doors. Returning to the stalls, he opened each gate and began to shoo the horses outside. This wasn't easy since the they weren't excited about leaving the comforts of the barn. When Stanley started hustling the cows out, the livestock had no choice but to go out into the cold.

Anxious to complete the task before church services were over, Stanley hurriedly returned to the house to place the lantern back where he originally found it. Before setting it down, he check his watch.

Good. Church services are just now finishing.

He started to slide the lantern back onto the shelf when he heard a loud bang. He froze, thinking someone from the household had returned early.

When he realized the wind had caused a shutter to bang on the side of the house, he continued. Unaware that he'd set the lantern on the edge of the shelf, he pulled his hand away. The next noise he heard was the shattering of the lantern as it bounced off a metal milk cannister and landed on the floor.

A whooshing sound followed.

The flames spread rapidly across the spilled kerosene as it flowed over the wooden planks. Trying to stomp the fire out only caused one of his trouser legs to catch fire. He jumped back, off the porch, quickly pulled off his coat and beat at his trousers. Smothering the fire, he turned his attention back to the house and tried using his coat on the flames.

With kerosene streaming under the door, he quickly found that the coat was not enough. The flames continued to spread. The inside of the house was now ablaze.

Seeing no alternative, Stanley fled to the barn to get his horse. With a fleeting thought about covering his tracks, he made cursory look around the barn before fleeing.

Chapter 44: House Fire

Nevada, Missouri
January 30, 1898

MINGLING WITH FRIENDS IN THE WARMTH of the church, following services, was always a pleasant pastime, especially
during the cold winter months. But now Sam and John needed to
set out into the cold and make their way home. Their parents had
already left, their sister too, with Ted. The twins waved to the pas-
tor, who was helping to tidy the pews, and headed to the front of
the church.

As they stepped out onto the front porch, they heard someone
yell, "Look. It's the fire boys."

Their attention was immediately drawn to the distinctive clop-
ping noise made by two draft horses pulling a rattling wagon. Two
men sat in the buckboard up front, and a third perched on a small
platform at the rear. All present watched in wonderment as the
wagon rolled down the street.

At their leisure, Sam and John mounted their horses and headed
in the same direction. Riding side-by-side, they stared after the
fire wagon as it pulled away, further down the street. It eventually

turned off at a major intersection. Once out of sight, Sam and John turned their attention back to their discussion about the family activities of the day.

The Sunday morning routine didn't change much. This was quiet family time, when they'd read by the fireside and play games following a hearty lunch. Their only chores this day were having to ensure the fireplace was adequately stacked for the day's fire and the indoor wood pile had been replenished. Other than that, this was a day of rest. They looked forward to this time.

The winds had died off since the early morning. The twins took little notice of a smoky aroma that filled their nostrils. It was an odor not uncommon during cold weather as people in homes throughout the town warmed themselves by fireplaces.

Turning south onto Main Street, they once again caught sight of the fire wagon, but this time it was even further off in the distance. They went quiet, their full attention on the wagon, watching in admiration.

When they neared the turn and headed east toward their home, both John and Sam saw the smoke rising into the sky. The realization came to them simultaneously.

"It's our place," they said in unison. With hearts beating faster, they spurred their horses to a gallop.

Arriving at their house, they could see that the fire fighters had already off-loaded their hoses and were completing the process of hooking them together. A number of volunteer fire fighters had also arrived and were helping.

Among the fire fighters, they saw their father trying to enter the house. A sole police officer was keeping him back. Sam jumped off his horse, draped the reins over a nearby fence, and ran to join his father. John pulled up next to Sam's horse, dismounted, and led both animals to a neighbor's fence to better secured them before joining them.

By the time Sam got there, one firefighter was bringing the nozzle around to the back porch while others were securing the hoses spread across the yard. The volunteer manning the hose pulled hard at the nozzle, but the weight of the hoses lying on the ground were too much for him to handle. William Sr. and the twins immediately ran over to help. They pulled at the lines lying on the ground, allowing the man at the nozzle to maneuver more freely.

Once the volunteers attached the hoses to the tank, they started the hand pump. The back door was kicked in and water began streaming in. A couple of volunteers, not needed on the pump, relieved the twins and their father. At this point, William and the twins could only stare in disbelief as the smoke billowed out the back door.

In a short time, the thickened smoke began to lighten and thin out as it intermixed with steam.

That's when William Sr. and the twins went in. They were accompanied by the fire chief.

Inside all they could do was stare at the charred remains of the soaked and scorched cabinets near the kitchen stove and cabinetry along the side wall. While William Sr. was assessing what could be saved and how much repair work might be necessary, John and Sam followed the fire chief's lead to see if any hot embers could reignite. The Chief also wanted to figure out how it started.

Looking at the cluttered mess in front of them, Sam said, "It probably started from the stove. At least that seems the only possibility."

"Or at least the only thing that makes sense being that that's the only place we might have left a fire burning," John added.

"It certainly seems to be in the center of everything that's burnt," the chief replied.

"You don't sound convinced," John said.

"I'm not. Something here doesn't quite look right. Look here," the fire chief said. He then stood back, letting the twin's curiosity take the lead. "Look out there. Compare the inside to the outside," he challenged.

John stepped out onto the porch while Sam inspected the inside. "What do you see?"

John knelt down to look more closely at the door. "The door's scorched the most, but that's to be expected. It's the closest to the stove."

"Keep looking," the chief urged. "If the fire came from the stove, how would it spread? What else looks the most charred?"

Sam took his time and looked more closely around the stove. After a moment, he started thinking aloud. "The metal area under and around the stove doesn't seem to have any damage. No surprise there. But when I look at the cabinet and compare it to the door . . . I see that the door was been fully engulfed—it's the most charred. The cabinet, too, has been burned but not nearly as much."

John, thinking about his brother's comment said, "You'd think that the cabinet would burn a lot faster than a thicker door. More like kindling. Wouldn't you think?"

"My thoughts exactly," Sam responded.

"So, that means . . ." the chief began.

"The fire started outside the house," the twins said in unison.

"But how?" John asked looking at the decking of the porch.

"We need to keep looking," the chief responded.

One of the volunteers came around to the back porch. "Chief, we've done about all we can do in here. We've started loading our equipment back in the wagon."

"Alright, thanks Andy," he said as he took a step toward the back porch. John moved over to let the chief get by.

As John was moving, he looked at the porch and spotted something glimmering under the edge of the deck's overhang. "Hey Chief. I found the cause."

"What'd you find, son?" the chief asked.

"There's a broken lantern there. It must have dropped and broken then rolled off and under the porch."

The chief bent down to take a closer look.

"We need to tell Dad," Sam said.

Not to mention the police, the chief thought.

Chapter 45: The Cleanup

Nevada, Missouri
January 30, 1898

SEEING THAT THEIR FATHER WAS NO LONGER in the house, Sam and John left the back porch and went searching. They headed for the front of the house and found him a deep in conversation with a fireman along the side of the house.

They patiently stayed back, not wanting to interrupt his conversation.

Looking across the street, Sam and John saw a small crowd of neighbors gathered. Their mother, Eva and Ted, stood in the front of the group, watching with their neighbors, keeping a safe distance from the firemen working in their yard. Eva seemed the most upset as she leaned into her mother's arms, weeping. Ted stood next to her, comforting her as well.

Sam began to walk across the street when John grabbed his arm. "Look. Over there, by the Healy family. Is that who I think it is?"

Sam did a quick scan of the crowd and stopped when he saw who his brother had been referring to.

The moment Sam spotted him, Stanley walked away, climbed on his horse and rode off.

William finished his conversation with the fireman and caught up with the twins as they crossed the road. The three of them gathered together with Ann, Eva and Ted.

Ann said, "At least we're all safe."

Looking at his family, William Sr. said, "From what I understand, we have a lot to be thankful for. Thanks to the Healy's, it could have been worse. They had their son contact the firemen as soon as they spotted the fire."

"Mr. Healy provided the buckets and I joined him in throwing water on the back porch until the fire wagon arrived," Ted said.

"I think that may have stopped the fire from crawling up the side of the house," William added. Wanting to put his family at ease, he gave a rundown on what the fire chief had told him, ending with, "All I've heard so far is that it most likely started in the kitchen area."

Sam and John didn't interrupt. Seeing the fire chief talking with a police officer Sam whispered to his brother, "Let's tell him later." John agreed.

Their father continued. "And, although there's going to be a strong smell of smoke throughout the house for some time, the damage was contained mainly to the kitchen area and back porch. We have insurance for the house, so that will help, but it might be a while before things can be repaired."

Turning to Sam and John, he told them they'd need to help close off the kitchen area from the rest of the house and figure out what else needed to be done during that process.

Ted added that he wanted help as well.

"Thank you, Ted," William Sr. said.

"The Healy's have offered to let us stay with them if need be," Ann added. They're preparing a meal for all of us," she added.

Others had gathered around the family to give support while the fire was being fought. Blankets were provided by nearby neighbors to help fight the cold while they stood outside. Others offered their homes as well.

It was decided that they'd accept the Healy's invitation, at least for a short time. Once the smoke cleared, they'd get a better feel for what was needed to make the house habitable.

Once that was decided, Ann and Eva entered the Healy household to get warm and help to prepare the Sunday meal. William Sr., Ted and the twins stayed outside until the firemen completed their cleanup and left for the station.

That's when Sam and John shared their findings and the fire chief's suspicions. During their conversation, the twins also shared their confrontation on a previous Sunday while riding to church with Ted and Eva.

As they talked, the group entered the kitchen. There, William Sr. was able to see what the twins and fire chief noticed earlier. Hearing what they had to say and seeing the evidence, William Sr. came to the same conclusion.

The fire could have started by accident, but it wasn't from anyone in this family.

"I think I'll have to look into this more," William Sr. said.

Thieves on the Trail

"We made our cache on a high point of rock so the wind would sweep the snow away. Some of the fellows have their outfits deep under the snow and cannot find them."

—*William Mace Schooley Diary, February 7, 1898*

"We moved 750 pounds to the scales today. Sledding is good and the trail was lined with men. Part of the day it was clear, and I could get a good view of the scales. Getting provisions over the Chilkoot Pass is a hard proposition. In December last, about 1000 pounds of provisions were stolen from a cache six miles from Dyea. Today, the thieves were caught with the goods near the summit and brought to Sheep Camp."

—*William Mace Schooley Diary, Thursday, February 10, 1898*

Thieves on the Trail

Chapter 46: Sheep Camp

Sheep Camp, Alaska
February 1, 1898

A FTER SPENDING A NIGHT AT CANYON CITY, we began moving our goods to what we would consider a more permanent site—at least until we made the crossing into Canada—it was called Sheep Camp. As usual, we left in the darkness. Dutch's comment lingered in my thoughts, "stay alert." As a result, I inspected our cache to ensure no tampering had occurred during the night, before leaving Canyon City for higher ground. This, and staying alert, would become a common practice.

By the time we completed our six-mile trip from Canyon City, climbing to an elevation of a thousand feet, it was clear we would not be admiring the landscape any time soon. The higher altitude brought on increased winds that limited our visibility. My full attention went to just watching the trail ahead. These conditions would haunt us in the days and weeks to come.

On our first trip up, we only brought our kit up—camping gear— to Sheep Camp to get our camp set up. As a result of the conditions we faced on our arrival at Worthington's lot, we only met up with Richard long enough to have him show us a good location for our cache. Once we identified where we'd be storing our goods, we shoveled out a place nearby for our tent. By the time we finished, the winds had intensified, making it difficult to put up any kind of structure.

Setting up the tent was like working with sails that were flapping on a ship. The three of us secured it the best we could in the four-foot deep snow. After that, Frank and I worked on making our quarters more comfortable while Lafe set up the stove and got out the cooking supplies. Lafe would be the first to rise in the morning since he'd be preparing breakfast.

Exhausted as we all were, it didn't take us long to bundle up and settle in for a good night's sleep.

The next morning, I awoke at the usual time and became vaguely aware that Lafe was moving about the tent, preparing breakfast. I lay listening to the wind blow, muffled somewhat by the snow, and drifted back to sleep.

It wasn't until I heard a clanking noise that I began to stir. Peeking out of my cozy wrap of clothing and blankets, I saw Lafe clambering around, stove pipe in hand, fiddling with the stove.

Seeing that he wasn't anywhere near getting our breakfast made, I asked, "Is there a problem?" He explained that he'd just returned from searching for the stove pipe. The wind had blown it away, and it had gotten buried in the snow. He was trying to refit the pipe to the stove, but was having no luck.

I immediately got up and shook Frank.

Working together, we eventually got the joints cut, so it fit more snuggly. But, after getting the fire started, Frank and I had to hold the stove in place to allow Lafe to cook breakfast. When the fluttering tent caught the pipe it would jerk the stove so that cooking became difficult. Even after breakfast, we still needed to help steady the stove while Lafe cooked some cornmeal mush and tallow[21] for the dogs. This day was the windiest weather we'd ever experienced.

---

21 **Tallow:** a hard, fatty substance made from rendered animal fat, used in making candles and soap

By two o'clock, the wind had abated enough for us to seek out a site more protected from the high winds. While Lafe kept the fire burning and prepared our late afternoon meal, Frank and I located a spot deeper into the timbers. It took the better part of the afternoon to shovel away a space for our new camp site. The new location, tucked back in the woods, was about 400 yards from the original site.

By day's end, we had accomplished a great deal. Frank had put in a puncheon[22] floor in the front half while Lafe and I spread about a foot of hemlock boughs in the back to soften and insulate our sleeping area. Later in the evening, the three of us dug a hole in a snowdrift near the tent, which we covered with a tarpaulin and boughs, for the dogs.

This was probably the most comfortable camp we'd had during our Alaska stay. Even the dogs' quarters were nearly as good as ours. Unfortunately, conditions outside were getting worse, to the point where we had to let the dogs sleep in the tent with us.

In spite of the weather, which had been hovering around eight degrees above zero, we continued to move a number of loads to our new Sheep Camp site.

Getting creative in how we could harness the dogs to the hand-pulled sleds, we broke up the dog team by pairing them up, two per sled. This not only allowed us to more equally share the workload, but help train other dogs to take on lead-dog responsibilities. Despite the steeper grade, the smaller teams worked fine. They even seemed to revel in the challenge of running loads up the hills without being a part of a six-dog team. Even with the frigid temperatures they seemed happier when they were running.

To fight the cold, we stayed busy, but from reports we were getting from those we'd passed on the trail, our current mackinaws would not protect us from the stormy conditions at the summit. While it was only four miles away, it was another twenty-five hundred feet higher in elevation with little protection from the winds, since it was above the tree line.

---

22 **Puncheon:** a rough board or other length of wood, usually with one flattened side, used for flooring.

Returning to our campsite, we came upon a couple of others who'd just returned from the summit. From them, we heard that three men had their faces freeze near the scale at the summit. Another took a slide down the scales with a pack on his back and was badly injured. While, in the past, we'd discovered that some stories were not true, one thing was clear, it was unsafe at the summit—where there was a dangerous mix of high winds and even lower temperatures.

Instead of taking advantage of a somewhat clear day, we had to delay our plan to complete our last move up to Sheep Camp.

Lafe was feeling ill.

Chapter 47: The Arson Suspect

Nevada, Missouri
February 2, 1898

WILLIAM SR. HAD BEEN BUSY SINCE THE FIRE. For the next two days, he and his two sons closed off the damaged portion of the house, tore out the scorched cabinetry, and cut out or shaved off as much of the burned wood as possible. While he knew the odor would linger for some time, their actions made it less pungent. He added reframing of the door to the boys' farm chores while he went in to town to talk with the fire chief and insurance agent about the incident.

It wasn't until the third day following the fire that William Sr. decided to approach the police chief. Although the insurance agent determined there was no indication that the fire was anything other than an accident, he wanted a thorough investigation, in particular regarding Stanley Barclay.

When William Sr. arrived at the police station, he found that Chief James Bridgeman had already been made aware of the facts from the fire chief. Two days following the fire, he had received information that indicated Barclay could very well have been involved. Chief Bridgeman had not only been looking into it but had officer David Bateman working the case. What initiated the investigation was a report from a companion of Stanley's who had a few drinks with him the day after the fire.

While the Schooleys were busy with their farm duties, Stanley Barclay was participating in one of his common practices. During his off hours, from helping his father on the farm, he could be seen in one particular local saloon on the edge of main street. This is where he'd gather with his companions, have a beer, talk about the latest gossip, and boast of their escapades. The most popular topic was the fire at the Schooley farm.

Well aware of the grudge Barclay had with the Schooley family, Stanley's cronies brought up the topic at the first opportunity. Unaware of the multiple beers Stanley had put down before their arrival, his friends teased him about how he must be happy about their misfortune. Inebriated and feeling uncomfortable about his unfortunate gotten-out-of-hand prank, he initially stayed quiet. Unaware of Stanley's condition, they pressed on, teasing him about having probably been the one who started the fire. Following that statement, an argument ensued between his cronies. The cause of the fire was up for debate.

One companion, named Bart, stated he'd heard it was arson. Another friend said, he'd heard it was an accident; that someone in the family dropped a lantern on the porch. And still another said that the fire had started when nobody was at home, and that the family had arrived from church after the fire had started. Tired of hearing all this discussion, and wanting to put the conversation to rest, he blurted that he'd witnessed the fire and found it to be an accident.

Curious and concerned about his behavior, as well as his comment, Bart decided to sit with him for a bit after the others had moved away. When Stanley started sulking and walked over to the bartender to order another beer, Bart led him to an empty table. Once there, Stanley went from moping to rambling and then mumbling about what he'd done.

The next day, Bart stopped by the police station and shared his previous day's experience with Barclay. He explained to the officer that a number of things had been off about Stanley, causing many of his friends to stay away from him. For weeks now, he'd been drinking more heavily. He hadn't seen him this depressed before. That's why he'd decided to stay with him in the saloon and heard his story about chasing the livestock out of the barn and accidently dropping a lantern.

"Chief, let me get this straight," Schooley said looking across the room at officer Bateman who was seated at his desk. "Are you saying that Stanley Barclay admitted to officer Bateman that he started the fire at my house?"

"Not directly to Bateman, but yes. Barclay mentioned it to one of his cronies while in an inebriated state in the saloon. That man then passed on that information to officer Bateman."

Bateman, hearing their discussion, walked over and stood off to the side of Chief Bridgeman's desk.

"So what do we do now?" Schooley asked.

"We wait, Mr. Schooley," the chief said before nodding his head toward his officer. "Officer Bateman is allowing Barclay to come in voluntarily on his own this afternoon. He's promised to arrive after helping his father at the farm. He didn't want to bring undo attention on himself. Being brought in by the police is not something he wants people to know about."

"The guy who brought this to my attention," Bateman interjected, "said he wasn't interested in making things any worse than they had been for him already. Barclay's friends already have trust issues with him. At least, that's what he told me."

The chief nodded, then looked out the window. "There he is now."

Schooley and Bateman both looked. Barclay was angling his way across the street, heading for the police station.

How do you plan to handle this, David?" the chief said to the officer.

"I've given it some thought. When he comes in, he'll see Mr. Schooley here and his reaction will tell me how to proceed."

The chief said, "Okay. Just give me a sign if you want me to assist."

Not surprisingly, Stanley was taken aback by Schooley's presence and hesitated at the door, before entering. Officer Bateman immediately motioned Barclay to follow him into a back room, which he did.

Thirty minutes later, the two reentered the main office where Chief Bridgeman and Mr. Schooley were still sitting, passing the time. As Bateman stepped forward to address them, Barclay stood warily behind the officer.

Looking at Mr. Schooley, officer Bateman said, "Mr. Schooley, are you aware of on-going hostilities between Stanley Barclay and your boys and daughter?"

"I am. It's been going on for a while now."

"Do you know what it's all about?"

"I'd gotten an inkling, from my children. Evidently there's issues with Barclay regarding some money-making scheme. My boys called him on it and, in retribution, it's believed that he's been the one behind rumors about our family."

"Evidently," Bateman began, "It's escalated to him wanting to get back at you even more." Looking at Chief Bridgeman, and then back to Mr. Schooley, he said, "Chief, Mr. Schooley, Stanley Barclay has admitted to accidently starting the fire. And he has something he'd like to say to you, Mr. Schooley." Bateman stepped to the side, to allow Barclay to come forward.

Schooley, looking calm but stern, listened as Barclay apologized for the damage and hardship he had caused. He also explained why he had been at their farm. "Yes. It was dumb of me . . . in so many ways," he admitted. "I . . . I didn't want to hurt anyone. I just wanted to strike out . . . to hurt those who I felt were the cause of my troubles." He paused to gain the strength he needed to say what was so painful to admit. "Since doing what I did . . . I realized that

I'm the one who's to blame for my problems, not anyone else. I'll do anything I can to make up for what I've done."

After Barclay went silent, Officer Bateman picked up where he had left off. Bateman explained how Barclay admitted to him that he had arrived at the Schooley farm early in the morning and waited until the family left for church. "He knew the family's routine," Bateman explained. "He even watched your boys come out to the barn to take care of the morning chores. When they left, that's when he borrowed the lantern. He said he figured that letting the animals out of the barn would cause your family some problems when you had to round them back up later."

"Did he say anything about wanting to cause the animals to freeze as a result of his actions?" Schooley said, sarcasm obvious in his voice.

"No he didn't," Bateman said, looking over to Barclay.

"I didn't think . . ." Barclay began, then stopped, realizing nothing he said would help.

"As it turned out, the animals are smarter than you." Schooley added a tight-lipped smile.

Puzzled with his comment, Barclay showed a blank expression.

"I checked the barn," Schooley declared. "Yes, all the stalls and barn door were open, like you said." Not until he saw Barclay's confused expression did he continue. "All the animals were in the barn. It seems they didn't care for the cold much. They returned to the comfort of the barn, on their own."

Stanley lowered his head and slowly turned it from side to side, realizing how stupid he'd been. He didn't even remember to close the barn after shooing the animals out. "Dropping the lantern was an accident," was all he could muster.

Saddened by Barclay's behavior, Schooley could only stare at him in disbelief. Realizing how idiotic his actions had been, Stanley refused to make eye contact.

"Well, shall we take this to the judge?" Officer Bateman asked.

Barclay looked alarmed. "My dad will kill me."

"I think we should," the chief said.

Schooley, seeing the devastated look in his eyes, waited for a spell before commenting. "What other option do we have?"

"That's up to you, Mr. Schooley. But let me make a call first," The chief said, reaching for the phone.

Chief Bridgeman spoke with the judge's secretary, Mary Bullock. After hearing what the chief had to say, he was asked to wait on the phone while she conveyed the situation to the judge.

It didn't take long for the judge to confirm a hearing date the following Monday.

Chapter 48: Change of Plans

Dyea, AK
February 6, 1898

UNDER NORMAL CIRCUMSTANCES, we would have been able to bring the last of our goods to Sheep Camp this day. Especially with the improved weather conditions. But when Lafe started feeling ill, we changed our plans. That evening, we'd decided he needed a day of rest while Frank and I would go to Dyea to get clothing better suited for the higher elevations. Unfortunately, by morning Lafe had a higher than normal fever. So, Frank elected to stay with his brother and encouraged me to go on my own. We all felt that it was imperative to get parkas before dealing with the harsher conditions at the summit and not leave Lafe unattended.

Taking two dogs, I sledded down the icy trail. With the ice conditions and the wind at my back the trip went quickly. The winds coming out of the north benefitted me, but I could see that those traveling up the trail were having a tough time of it.

Although it wasn't as windy at the lower elevations, I decided not to return to Sheep Camp until morning, hoping that the winds would die down by then. Before going into Dyea, I'd drop in to

see Dutch and Guy, to see if they had room for me for the night.
I knew they were still staying at their claim, just north of the toll
bridge. They'd started moving their goods to Worthington's claim
about a week after we'd made camp there.

As I neared their camp, my attention was drawn to a group of
men gathered alongside the trail. It wasn't the fact that they were
walking north that caught my curiosity. It was that each was pulling an empty sled.

Why the empty sleds? I wondered.

As I got closer I recognized some familiar faces. Some I'd seen
at the wharf, looking to con passengers leaving the ship. A couple
of others I remember seeing arguing with the man tending the toll
bridge, a few weeks earlier.

They stood clear of the trail and waited for me to pass.

I slowed the team as I passed and looked at each man more
closely. "Something about these guys didn't look right," I thought.
Most travelers going up the trail would be miners packing their
goods, never empty handed. *Why go up toward the Canada border without moving your goods?* I thought. Their presence in the
wilderness wasn't just unusual, it was fishy, at best. The men I recognized would rather put their energy into swindling others than
engaging in the hard work of mining.

Then I set eyes on the last man in line.

Jackson.

They're all Soapy's grifters and friends of Jackson.

They paid me no heed as I passed.

"Dutch's cache." I wonder if . . . Could they have . . ." Realizing
there was nothing I could do about them, now, I looked away,
released the brake and commanded the team to pick up the pace.
I felt secure knowing that I was not only protected from the winds
but my face was covered, which kept me from being recognized.

I directed the dogs toward Guy and Dutch's lot and tried to put
thoughts of these scoundrels out of my head. I was just minutes
away from my next stop.

Dutch must have heard the dogs barking, or he was just attentive to strangers lurking about the campsite since the theft, for he
was quick to greet me before I even got the dogs settled. Once he
heard my plans, he invited me to stay the night.

"You're lucky," Dutch said.

"Lucky?"

"Right. Another day or two and this place would not be ours."

"You've got a buyer?" I exclaimed.

"Yup."

"Where's Guy?"

"He and Jake are taking a load up to Richard's, as we speak.
Figured you'd have passed them on the way down."

"If I did, I didn't notice them. Everyone I passed had their faces
covered to guard against the cold winds."

"He'll be setting up camp and staying up there tonight. You're
welcome to use his bed, if you like."

"Appreciate it. What are your plans for today?"

"I'm going to take a jaunt into Skagway to sign some papers at
the surveyor's office, to transfer my claim. After that, I'll be coming
back here."

"How about I give you a sled ride into Skagway?"

"That would be great," Dutch smiled.

"But I need to stop at the dry-goods store in Dyea first."

"That's fine. That'll save me a lot of time." Dutch admitted. "I'll
go find Miller and tell him. He'll be staying here to watch over our
stuff while I'm gone."

Dutch talked with Miller, grabbed a few things to stuff in his
backpack, and came back, ready to go.

Heading into Dyea, we made our first stop at the dry goods
store. Once there, I paid for three duck parkas and arranged to
pick them up in the morning. The $12 price was pretty stiff, but
the coats were a necessary expense. I also bought two yarn caps,
some tallow and some cooking utensils. The prices seemed to soar
each time I entered a store, driven up by the influx of people. I

would have been able to buy all these goods many times over if I were back home in Missouri. It seems the rush is on in earnest. The word I got from people traveling up the trail was that about 1500 people landed in Dyea just this day alone.

Thinking about that, my anticipation of traveling into Skagway waned for just a moment as I considered the throng of travelers I'd be passing on the trail.

Just another motivation to move our goods up the trail sooner, rather than later.

Chapter 49: Soapy

Skagway, AK
February 6, 1898

O N ARRIVAL, WE FOUND REID TO BE BUSY with one customer with a few others waiting ahead of us. "Business must be good with all the newcomers coming in," Dutch commented.

"I imagine so," I said. "Not only is Reid busy with the new claims that he surveys, but they also come to him to handle their real estate transactions."

Seeing that it would take some time before Dutch could take care of his business, I told him I was going to check on the dogs and walk about town. He encouraged me to take my time, and said if he finished up early he'd just wait here until I returned.

I gave the dogs a snack and checked their riggings then walked toward the waterfront. Seeing Clancy's Saloon up ahead, I decided to see if he was around.

Entering, I noticed John Clancy immediately. He was standing at the far end of the bar, watching a line of men who were having a spirited conversation. Seeing me enter, he beckoned me over.

"Hello, John, good to see you. Entertaining clients, I see."

"Actually, Jeff's entertaining *us*. He's telling us about his new venture." Clancy gestured to the man standing next to him and said, "You remember Bill don't you, Jeff?"

Hearing his name mentioned, Jeff turned. With immediate recognition, Jeff reached his hand out and said, "I do. And the not-so-pleasant trip we took up here from Seattle."

"Don't remind me," I said.

"I don't plan on heading back down again until I'm guaranteed blue skies and clear sailing," Jeff responded.

"I'm in favor of that. So, what's this venture John mentioned?"

"If you recall, I've spoken about having some business ventures here in Skagway. I've partnered up with a few others, besides John here, but I've always wanted a place of my own."

"You're opening your own saloon, I gather?"

"Yup. It'll be called *Jeff Smith's Parlor*," Jeff said with pride. "I've acquired a lot and will be building soon."

"That's great," I said.

"What have you been doing with yourself?"

"Bill has a claim in Dyea," Clancy interjected.

"Had a claim," I corrected. "Just sold it. Frank, Lafe and I have been moving up toward the summit. Should be able to get there within the next week or so, weather permitting, of course."

"Congratulations, Bill," Jeff said. "I wish you well."

"Thank you."

I thought back to when I first got to know Jefferson. While the trip was long, so too were the storms. Jefferson Smith spent most of the time in his cabin due to seasickness. He didn't start joining Frank and I at meal times until after the fire we had experienced aboard ship and the waters had calmed. During the few discussions we did share, I found him to be charming and charismatic, always civil. Both he and his business partner, John Clancy, were amicable and unassuming in discussions about their profession and business ventures in Skagway. While Clancy warned of the makeup of the township and those tending saloons, it wasn't until my arrival in town that I learned about the nature of the man named Soupy Smith, who ran Skagway. Little did I know at the time, that 'Soupy' was Jefferson Smith, the same Jeff Smith that I'd met aboard ship. It took some time for me to adjust my view of the pleasant man I'd met during our travels and imagine him as a conman who ran the township of Skagway. I was now viewing Jefferson as an enigma.[23]

Typical of his frankness, Jeff said, "Is your friend, Lafe, the one who had a run in with one of my men a little while back?"

"You mean, Jackson."

"That's him."

"That's right. He's Frank's brother. You remember him from aboard ship, don't you?"

"I do. Sorry to hear about that incident," Jeff said. He waved at the bartender who quickly came over. "A sarsaparilla, for my friend, here." Turning to me, he added, "That is your drink of choice if I recall."

"Good memory," I said.

"Comin' right up," The bartender responded.

"I want you to know, I talked to Jackson about his . . . behavior," Smith said. "I know too well that he and some of his men can be a bit too aggressive at times."

The bartender set my drink in front of me.

"Downright hostile, if you ask me." I took a swallow. "You should have seen him when he ran into Lafe, and I mean literally."

"Yes, I heard the details from Jackson and some others who were also there. That's unfortunate. It doesn't reflect well on me or what this town should represent."

"Yes, I've become aware of your concerns about running this town."

"I wouldn't exactly say I run it, but I do want to uphold this upstanding community's reputation and make it prosperous."

Remembering Reid's comment about how Smith urges his men to go easy on the violence, I wondered what he might know about their exploits outside the town.

---

23 **Enigma:** a person or thing that is mysterious, puzzling, or difficult to understand.

"On my way down the slopes, I passed Jackson and a few of his ... associates heading up the trail this morning. I have a bad feeling about what they're doing up there."

"Why do you say that?"

"They were all pulling empty sleds."

"Why would you be concerned about that?"

"The only people I've seen going up the trail with sleds are miners, and they wouldn't be wasting their time taking a sled up the slopes unless it was packed full of their goods. Jackson's group looked out of place out there. And, I know what shenanigans they've been expelled for in Dyea."

"Oh, you know about that, do you?"

"Yes, Lafe told me about how they were basically expelled from Dyea for their tricky ways of getting money from the townspeople. Besides, there's been enough thefts from some of the miner's caches to make me wonder about that as well."

Seeing some discomfort, I stayed silent. Jeff looked curious and concerned. After a solemn moment, he looked at me with a somber expression, slowly shook his head and said, "If they break the law, they're on their own up there," Jeff said.

During this whole discussion, I felt that I was talking to the man I originally thought I knew aboard ship.

After a time, I peered at my pocket watch and realized Dutch could be finished with his meeting. So I informed Smith and Clancy that I had to leave, to meet up with a friend, and that I'd be going back up the slopes.

They wished me well.

I thanked them, downed the last of my drink, and excused myself.

Chapter 50: Courthouse

Nevada, Missouri
February 7, 1898

STANLEY BARCLAY FELT NUMB AS HE RODE on the family wagon with his father at his side. It wasn't until he approached the courthouse in the town center that he felt a chill run down his spine. Seeing the grand white columns of Nevada's two-story brick courthouse, he'd come to the realization that he might be dealing with something greater than just the wrath of his father.

Entering the buildings vestibule with his father, Stanley kept his head down, not wanting to make eye contact with anyone. His demeanor didn't change until the judge called him up to the bench. As he approached, he sheepishly looked back at the spectators who had been sitting behind him and his father. Some were family. Others included the Schooley family, the fire chief and Officer Bateman.

"You are Stanley Barclay?"

"Yes, your honor."

"I understand all are present who need to be here, is that right?" the judge asked, looking at his bailiff.

"Yes, your honor," said the bailiff.

"Very well." Looking at the defendant, the judge said, "I've read the police report, and I understand you've confessed to the charges before you. Is that correct?"

"Yes, your honor."

"Is there anything you'd like to say?"

"Yes, your honor. I've already apologized to Mr. Schooley, but I would like to apologize to everyone in the Schooley family for my irresponsible actions."

After Stanley had his say, the judge said, "There is no excuse for doing what you did, but I want to hear from the Schooley family. For starters, Mr. Schooley would you tell me about the damage from the fire and what it's going to take to make your house habitable?"

William Schooley stood and explained what damages had occurred, the cleanup, the status of the insurance claim and where they were currently living. He finished with how long it might take to make all the necessary repairs.

Following his comments, the judge addressed Mr. Barclay, asking, "Mr. Barclay, understanding that your son is no longer a juvenile, can you tell me more about what we can expect from him in the future?"

"Yes, your honor. He's knows that he must comply with my rules while living in our household, if that's what you're asking."

"That's part of what I'm looking for, Mr. Barclay."

Mr. Barclay then described the various roles each family member had taken and the increased responsibilities Stanley would be assuming around the farm. He also admitted having a heart-to-heart talk with his son about what changes needed to be made.

When Mr. Barclay finished, the judge turned his attention back to Stanley. "You agree to the terms your father just laid out, young man?"

"Yes, sir." Stanley head dropped slightly.

"From what I understand, I don't need to hear from any of

the witnesses. But I would like to speak with Mr. Schooley and Stanley's father. Would the two of you approach the bench?"

"Young man," the judge referred to Stanley, "you can be seated for the moment."

Mr. Schooley and Mr. Barclay came forward as Stanley went back to his seat.

The judge spoke quietly with both gentlemen, then said, "I will now go back in my chambers and consider my ruling."

Upon returning, the judge asked Stanley to standup. He then spoke loud enough for all in the courtroom to hear. "Considering the seriousness of the offense, your guilty plea, and the information I've received today, I will wave jail time for a probationary period of one year. During that time you will serve community service. He then handed Stanley a document that stipulated the fine he'd have to pay and requirements of performing his supervised community service. He finished with, "Remember, your probation period may be extended if you do not follow these requirements. Additional jail time is also a possibility if any of these terms are not met. Part of your time will include doing chores on the Schooley farm.

"If there is no further comments . . ." slowly the judge scanned the group, then said, "Court is adjourned."

Chapter 51: Weather Permitting

Near Sheep Camp
February 8, 1898

W HILE I WAS HAPPY I COULD STAY THE NIGHT at Dutch's and wait out the high winds, I had to endure a sleepless night in a cold cabin, in a bed that was too short for me. It was so cold I didn't take off any of my clothes, not even my fur cap. My feet were so cold I had the dogs sleep on them. It was nice to know they could be useful in other ways.

Bidding farewell to Dutch the next morning I headed back up to our campsite. The winds were much calmer compared to the previous day. The dogs towed me and my small load seventeen miles to an elevation of a thousand feet to Sheep Camp at a remarkable pace. It only took two and a half hours.

Upon my arrival, both Frank and Lafe came out to greet me. I was pleased to find that Lafe was back on his feet again.

"Feeling better I see."

"Yeah, but I still feel a bit weak and tired," Lafe said.

"I think you were just to dehydrated," Frank began, "and exhausted from those long days packing our goods."

"We probably need to consider pacing ourselves better," I responded.

"And drink water and rest between trips," Frank added

We all agreed.

"Considering how many around here have died from meningitis, typhoid fever, scurvy and other illnesses, I feel fortunate," Lafe said.

"Frank, if you think your brother is good enough to watch over our camp, you and I can get our last load up here from Canyon City."

Frank looked over at Lafe.

"I'm fine," he said, "Go ahead."

"Leave right after lunch?" I asked.

"Sure," Frank replied. "Lunch sounds like a good idea."

"No surprise there," Lafe added.

By the time we returned, it was getting dark. Instead of unloading everything at Sheep Camp, we left the packs and sled as they were for when we would move them to the summit.

We planned to leave first thing in the morning, but awoke to high winds and fresh snow. All we could do was 'bide our time'[24] while hunkered down. This was not only good for Lafe, but for me as well, having not slept well the last couple of nights. This downtime also allowed me to enjoy my pastime, reading. We had a number of works of fiction that a friend of Lafe's sent to him, to help us pass the time during our travels. This day, I started reading *Twenty Years After*, by Dumas. Thankfully, our accommodations were reasonably comfortable, compared to staying in Dutch and Guy's cabin.

One day later, the temperatures reached twenty-two degrees Fahrenheit. Although warmer than the eight degrees we had been experiencing, Lafe and Frank were still appreciative of the new parkas. Now that Lafe had recovered and all of us were appropriately attired, we were able to move a few loads to the Canadian border. Our first stop would be the scales before taking our loads to our cache site at the summit.

---

24 **Biding My Time** (Idiom): to do something else while you're waiting for something that you're looking forward to.

While waiting at the scales, I saw an almost unbroken line of men moving their goods to the summit using the shorter but steeper line on the left. I felt fortunate not to be packing our supplies like those in that line. Instead, we took the route to the right that was more manageable for the dogs. Seeing the hikers on the left slowly trudge up the slopes, I could only imagine how much more exhausting it was for them, not to mention how stiff and sore they'd be feeling at the end of each day. With the sled, we were able to move three times the weight with greater ease than the others who walked, and after each trip up, I could make good time riding back down to camp. I felt fortunate to have my sled. Along our route, I saw horses, oxen as well as dogs being used. I was amazed when I saw a lady helping her husband moving their goods.

Lafe, Frank and I learned quickly to make adjustments after watching other's mistakes. Seeing them struggle to find their goods after they'd gotten buried deep in the snow, we learned to stash ours on a high point of rock. Doing that ensured that the wind swept the snow away.

We also learned that we couldn't control all mishaps. One old man had both of his legs broken after being run over by a sled that got away from a miner at the top of the pass. We'd also heard that another had some goods stolen at the summit. I couldn't help but think of Dutch, and how he and the others felt when he discovered some of his supplies were missing.

Returning to Sheep Camp, Frank and Lafe had begun to prepare our mid-day meal, using the small cache of dry wood we'd stored in the tent. Worthington would be joining us for this meal. This was one way of showing our appreciation for his allowing us to camp out and store our goods on his claim.

Typically, most travelers either established a camp at Sheep Camp or Stone House—halfway between our camp and the scales. We picked Sheep Camp knowing we were below the timberline where the trees would provide firewood as well as some protection from the wind.

Whenever I did go out scouting the local area—often to gather wood, I would typically let the dogs run loose. They were used to this routine. They normally didn't stray off too far from me while I traipsed through the forest. They knew that once I'd finished these chores, I'd give them a treat. It might seem bad to hitch them up without any breakfast in the morning, but experienced dog teamsters say that was the proper way. Their big meal was at the end of the day. They rested better that way.

While gathering wood this day, I was determined to explore the outermost portions of Worthington's claim on the eastside of the Chilkoot Trail. After securing my snowshoes, I crossed over the beaten pathway and headed for a forested area that had yet to be picked over by travelers. There, it would be easier to snap off some of the lower branches. Digging for underbrush buried in snow was not an option.

Just as I reached for a limb, the dogs dash ahead of me.

Chapter 52: Hidden Stash Site

Near Sheep Camp
February 8, 1898

THEY SEEMED TO PICKED UP A SCENT almost in unison and scurried off as a pack. Figuring it was probably some small animal I ignored their barking. At least until it changed into a loud snarling uproar. Following the path the dogs had taken, I hurried awkwardly in my snowshoes to see what the fuss was about.

Coming across a small clearing, I could see the dogs clambering down the bank. Not far ahead of the pack, I saw what looked to be Shed. Near him, I saw a large silhouette then heard a loud yelp. Worried that they could have cornered a bear, I called for them to return. When I stepped out to get a clearer view, I went down on my face.

Struggling to get up out of the snow bank, I found that my snowshoe had caught on something. By the time I'd regained my footing and scrambled back up, the dogs were heading my way. The last one to return was Shep who was matted with blood from a cut across his front left leg. He wasn't bleeding badly, but his fur was matted down. All I could think about was the claws of a bear. I removed the scarf that I used to protect my face from the wind and secured it around Shep's leg and chest. Once I secured the scarf, I checked on the other dogs as they sniffed around the area. None of the others seemed to have any injuries.

Seeing the dogs pawing at the ground, I became curious about what drew them back to this site. One of the dogs was using his teeth to pull something out of the snow. It was the kind of wood used for containers that stored food stuffs and other supplies. The dogs were most likely searching for food that had once been in the container. I looked back at where I'd fallen and saw a similar slat sticking up. It became clear to me, now.

That's what my snowshoe caught on.

I also wondered why anyone would store their goods here, on Richard's claim.

Why here, and why so far off the trail? I could see why travelers would want to hide their cache, but not this far off the main trail.

Exploring further, I walked along the route the dogs had traveled, eventually coming upon the spot where they turned back. Beyond this point, I followed what looked to be a pathway that had been used recently. The packed snow appeared compressed by snowshoes and sled runners. A number of travelers had been here.

Following the route, I came upon a broken ski pole with blood on the end of it. I considered Shed's injury while following the path further down the hill.

It wasn't a bear.

The path eventually merged with the Chilkoot Trail, curving downhill, to the south. No movement could be seen at least a hundred yards to where the trail dropped from sight. Clearly whoever was here was long gone.

I returned to the abandoned cache site and filled my arms with as much wood as I could carry. Once collected, I headed back toward camp, dropped off the boards, grabbed one of the hand-pulled sleds and returned to gather more wood.

By the time I'd returned, Worthington had joined Frank and Lafe and were preparing to eat. I joined them, grabbed some grub and immediately shared my findings. We discussed the mystery cache on his property. That included wondering if any of this was related to stolen goods from other cache sites. Once again I thought about Jackson and some of his friends pulling empty sleds up the slope.

"You don't suppose those goods are the ones that we heard were stolen from the summit, do you?" Lafe asked.

"Considering the location, I wouldn't be surprised," I responded. "That's not a bad place to hide something, assuming you'd plan to sneak it down the hill at the next opportunity and sell it somewhere along the trail where travelers gather, like Canyon City, or even Dyea or Skagway."

"Who would do such a thing?" Frank said.

"Richard. You don't suppose that's one of the reasons those con men wanted to get your land, do you?" I asked, thinking about how Jackson had made an offer on Richard's claim.

Richard went silent, thinking about how Jackson had pressured him to sell after losing his money in the poker game.

Are all these incidents tied together?

The only conclusion we all came to was we needed to stay alert, and hopefully things would be better across the border.

Chapter 53: The Scales

Below the Summit, Chilkoot Trail
February 9, 1898

ANXIOUS TO GET OUR OUTFIT OF SUPPLIES up to the pass, we were determined to at least make our first trip to the scales—a one thousand-foot climb short of the summit. The distance from our Sheep Camp campground to the summit was just four miles in distance—as the crow flies—but is another 2500 feet in elevation. It would be nice to have this chore behind us. We would save the half-mile climb to the Canadian customs house for another time. That's where the storms often rage.

As unpredictable as the weather had been below the summit, we knew we'd need to take advantage of every opportunity to get things moving. This would be that day. While it was cloudy, it had warmed up to 22 degrees, with little snow. In the morning, Lafe and I each backpacked 150 pounds to the scales.

In our absence, it was Frank's turn to look after our campsite. He also needed to look for our lead dog, Shed. The dogs had been prone to go off on their own at times, but this time Shed had been gone since the previous evening. They were conditioned to return to our campsite for food and comfortable sleeping quarters.

But on returning to camp, we found that Frank still hadn't found Shep. We could only hope that he'd return on his own, knowing he'd done this before. At least Frank had lunch ready for us when we arrived. After our meal, Lafe and I took another three hundred pounds of goods to the scales.

With less snow falling and more travelers compacting the route up to the scales, we considered using the dog sled for future trips. Pack animals and sleds could be used to this point, but not beyond. The scales location was nothing more than a small, flat basin along the Chilkoot Trail, located at the base of the "Golden Stairs"—the nickname came from the steps that had recently been cut into the hillside, making it easier to climb the 1000 feet up the last half mile to the summit.

Lafe and I agreed that making it to the base of the "Golden Stairs" would be good enough for now. It was difficult enough getting to this point. We were beginning to worry more about Shed's absence.

Chapter 54: The Thieves

Sheep Camp, Chilkoot Trail
February 10, 1898

W E WERE IN LUCK. SHEP RETURNED IN TIME for the evening meal, which allowed Lafe and I to put the full team
together and move our goods with greater ease. We left first thing
in the morning. Rather than making two steep climbs, trudging
up the slopes with 150 pounds on our backs, we looked forward
to taking three trips by sled, allowing us to triple our expectations
for the day.

Our first jaunt went reasonably well, considering that we left
early enough to beat the crowds. The second trip had more travelers on the trail, but it was still pleasant, considering what it would
be more difficult walking with packs on our back. Our return to
Sheep Camp went smoothly. We even had an interesting diversion
as we got closer to camp.

Passing through Sheep Camp we came upon a group of men
heading up the hill from the south. Normally, it would be quiet
on the trail, partially because sounds were muffled by the snow
and most of the time travelers were too tired to converse. But this

group was abnormally lively and looked to be taking up the full width of the trail.

As the leading procession got closer, we pulled off to the side of the trail to let them pass. Those in front seemed to be herding three men who had their wrists restrained with ropes. A crowd was following close behind. As they neared, I could feel the excitement in the air. A few in the crowd were loudly passing the word to everyone they passed that these men were thieves caught with the goods they'd stolen. They also announced that they were going to Sheep Camp to set up a trial.

As they marched by, Lafe and I admitted to being curious about the thieves, but quickly dismissed following since we had to take care of business while the weather held.

We headed back to our campsite, packed up our supplies and headed up the slopes for our final trip of the day. It was near dusk when we returned. Feeling good about delivering seven-hundred and fifty pounds in one day, we were optimistic about what would could accomplish in the next few days, if the weather held.

We could get all our supplies to the scales by mid-month.

As we headed toward the scales, sledding on the main trail through the center of Sheep Camp, we noticed a group of people milling around outside a saloon. A number of them were trying to peer inside. This structure, like many other buildings, was still under construction. It consisted of two timbered walls secured to a plank floor. The first wall to go up was completed and blocked the winds coming out of the east. A tarpaulin provided a roof and siding for the rest of the saloon. It was obvious, this hastily built spot was constructed to cater to the miners for only a short time.

Lafe and I agreed that this place was more than likely where the trial would be held. We decided to stop only long enough find out what we could. Settling the dogs alongside the trail, we approached the saloon and mixed in with the crowd.

The people there were chatting to one another. The first two men we approached were excited to share what they'd learned.

"The people inside are preparing for a trial that's going to be here," one man said.

The man standing next to him added, "Three men were caught with about one thousand pounds of provisions that they stole last December from a cache six miles this side of Dyea."

My immediate thought went to the theft at Dutch's. Although the location wasn't far from his place, this theft was a month earlier. I heard that thefts were becoming a common occurrence. Robbery and murder were also on the rise.

"What are they doing now?" I asked.

"They finished electing the committee members a little while ago," the first man said.

His friend added, "They're just discussing how they are going conduct the hearing."

"When does the trial start?" Lafe asked.

"Sometime tomorrow morning," the first man offered.

Satisfied we'd found out what we wanted to know, we thanked them for the information and left to complete our final trip for the day.

Returning to our campsite, we got the team settled and fed, and prepared our packs for the early morning run. Frank had a meal ready for us. During dinner, we had a lot to share with him about the coming trial and the possibility of our getting all our goods to the scales by the middle of the month.

Since the trial would begin in the morning, we looked forward to checking on their progress, between runs.

Chapter 55: Trial Begins

Sheep Camp, Chilkoot Trail
February 11, 1898

LAFE AND I FINISHED TAKING OUR FIRST LOAD to the scales early in the morning. On the return trip, we stopped at the saloon where the trial was being held.

Sticking our heads inside, we saw a guard sitting near the front door eating a sandwich. Seeing that the trial was in recess for lunch, we were able to see the layout of the saloon, now converted into a courtroom. Another guard sat near a side entrance, located next to the bar. A pair of chairs were positioned next to a single table in the center of the room. Another chair was behind the table. A few neatly lined-up row of chairs faced the front of the room. Since they weren't in session, we returned to camp, loaded our sleds and took a second trip to the scales.

By the time we returned, we knew the trial would be under-way and wondered how it was progressing. As we made our way back toward camp, we heard what we thought were gunshots in the distance, down toward Sheep Camp. Then a little while later, another single shot. Not thinking much of it, we continued on. In the past, we'd often hear someone either celebrating, target practicing, or shooting at an animal. So hearing a shot now and again wasn't uncommon.

However, as we got closer to the edge of the new boomtown, we saw a commotion just outside the saloon. A number of people had congregated around the building. Included in the group was our friend, Dutch.

"What's the commotion all about?" I asked him.

Dutch said, "One of the accused shot himself."

"When?" I asked.

"Not long ago."

"I wonder if it was that gunshot we heard?"

"More than likely."

"What happened?" Lafe asked.

Dutch then began to tell us the full story of what had occurred during the morning session.

"When I arrived," Dutch began, "I found a place to stand in the back corner of the saloon. Once everyone was settled, a guard brought in the first of the three accused men for questioning. He was seated in the chair beside the front table. The guard sat next to him. A man seated behind the table stated that he was the person voted by the committee to preside over the trial. He then proceeded to ask the committee members to raise their hands and be recognized. Those people were seated in chairs in the middle of the room. They raised their hands and a man then clarified that they were voted on by the community to be the committee that decides the verdict for this hearing."

Then the trial got underway.

"The first accused man was sworn in on a Bible, and was asked a series of questions. A second man was brought in to replace him and was asked the same questions. Then the third suspect followed. Since there was conflicting testimony between the first and the other two defendants, the first defendant was brought back in. When the first defendant's lies came to light, the suspect realized he'd been discovered and decided to run. He grabbed the guard's pistol and fired wildly before running out the side door. It happened so fast, no one moved. Those present were too stunned to take any action."

The guard then gathered a group of men to help him chase the defendant. A short time later they returned. By the time they'd reached the trail heading out of town, they found the man lying in the snow. He had shot himself."

Once Richard finished sharing his recollection of the events, we approached the saloon and found a body displayed outside.

Chapter 56: Vigilante Justice

Sheep Camp, AK
February 11, 1898

BANG. BANG. BANG.

I was still gawking at the body near the front entrance when I heard the gavel hit, then, "THIS COURT IS CALLED TO ORDER."

I looked inside, surprised to hear the presiding officer calling for order in the courtroom. I stepped in as he announced, "It is at the committee's insistence that we reconvene this hearing, despite our . . . disruption, to ensure we serve justice to the other two men."

Evidently the whole episode was considered nothing but a 'disruption'.

Everyone in the room was aware of the significance of getting justice—even if it was vigilante style. Emotions ran high, and I could see why. Most in this room were in the midst of moving their required 2,000 pounds of goods into Canada. And it was wasn't easy doing it. Having fought through the high winds and low temperatures to climb the 3,500 feet of elevation that marked the border between our two countries and get to the Klondike, they had little sympathy for someone who was willing to steal.

Before any of those who had congregated outside could enter, Lafe, Frank and I stepped in. As much as I wanted to watch the hearing, I was leery of vigilante justice. I also wondered if any of the thieves being tried were associated with Jackson's crew.

"There's going to be limited seating," Lafe said, as we entered the saloon. The chairs were already occupied and others were beginning to jostle for a good place to view the spectacle. We moved forward, along the left wall. Others were pressing for us to move further. We stopped half way down the wall and allowed others to pass. Frank gave both Lafe and me a nudge and nodded for us to look across the room, toward the back.

I saw four men shuffling along the back corner of the room. Two of them I recognized from the crooked poker game we'd all witnessed. Another I'd seen with Jackson when I passed them pulling their sleds. As the next suspect was being brought into the room, I kept focused on one last figure who had slunk behind his cronies.

Jackson.

The trial was underway. The defendant was reminded that he had sworn to tell the truth. Rather than make eye contact with Jackson, I tried to turn my attention back to the second defendant. He looked scared. But with each question he answered, it became obvious he was trying to be cooperative. When providing details about his involvement, he claimed not to know where the goods came from. He was being paid to help move the supplies. He'd assumed it belonged to those who paid for his help.

He was then dismissed and returned to a back room, accompanied by a guard who returned with the third suspect.

The third suspect, more than likely affected by his friend's tragic demise, looked contrite. When asked about his relationship with the second suspect, he confirmed that that man was innocent. He had only been paid to help them relocate the stolen goods. After further discussion, it soon became apparent that this was his sole connection to the two thieves.

The third accused man appeared to want to cooperate, but as the questioning continued, there was something about him that was disquieting. His constant fidgeting made me curious. His answers were particularly evasive when asked who he was working for. He denied working with anyone other than the first defendant who was now deceased. The man looked more nervous with each response. He didn't seem to be lying, but he sure wasn't telling the entire truth. The more I watched him, the more I wondered. He seemed to be holding back. His eyes darted back and forth, to the guard, the chairman, the committee and beyond.

I followed his quick periodic glances, to the back of the room, and saw that he was looking at Jackson.

Jackson was glowering at the defendant. When he saw me, he lowered his head, and spoke quietly to the man standing on his right.

I looked back at the defendant. His panicky actions increased. He looked at his hands, and tugged on his coat sleeves and periodically straightened the bottom of his coat. After the umpteenth time of pulling at his sleeves, I noticed a ragged tear.

I wonder . . .

I recalled what I'd discovered some time ago. Something I'd put away and forgotten about. I reached in my pocket to see if it was still there.

It was.

I pulled it out and looked at it closely. The material seemed to match the man's coat, but that dark brown and black tweed was common here.

But not the size of the torn fabric.

After completing his last line of questioning, the chairman called for deliberations, and explained to the audience what would be occurring shortly. "The committee will now meet in the back room and carefully weigh all the evidence before reaching a verdict." After a pause, he added, "If there's anyone here who would like to offer further information in this case, feel free to provide it at this time. While we're not a formal court, we do want to make sure everyone has a chance to be heard." He then directed the committee to file into the backroom, behind the bar.

Once the members made their way into the room, the chairman rose, declared the courtroom to be in recess and stepped away from his chair to stand next to the committee room's open door.

That's when I pushed myself away from the wall and approached the chairman, leaving my confused partners behind.

Seeing me approach, the chairman looked at me expectantly. I handed him the piece of cloth and told him how I'd acquired it at a different cache that had been raided. "If I'm right, this may show that he's been involved with at least one other theft."

The chairman asked me to wait near the door, in case the committee had questions. He stepped over to the guard who was sitting next to the accused, just feet away. After a few words to him, both the guard and the accused got up and followed the chairman into the back room. The chairman still had the fabric in his hand when he joined the committee and closed the door.

Seeing that I wasn't returning, Lafe and Frank joined me and started asking questions. By the time I'd caught them up on what I'd found at Dutch's cache site, and answered a few other questions, the defendant and his guard returned to the courtroom.

As he passed, the guard stated, "I don't think they'll be needing you." He and the defendant returned to their seats. The defendant looked distraught.

I was not sure if the guard meant I should no longer wait or go, so I stayed.

Not long after that, the committee and chairman returned from the back room. The chairman stopped to talk with me as the members took their seats in the courtroom. "Thank you for sharing this," The chairman held up the torn piece of fabric, "Do you mind if I keep it?"

"You're welcome to it," I said. "Just hope you find it useful."

"Oh, it was useful alright. I presented the torn fabric to the committee as additional evidence and took the time to see if it matched the missing part of his coat. It did. He immediately fessed up. We didn't need you in there after all."

Before ending my conversation with the chairman, I told him about the suspect's nervous behavior and how he had been watching a particular man in the back of the room. "The man goes by Professor Jackson," I said, "He works for a man in Skagway who heads up a gang of confidence men."

"You must be talking about Soapy Smith," the chairman said.

"Yes. You know about him?"

"Only by reputation."

"Then you know he has a number of others who work for him?"

"Yes. I'm aware of that."

"Jackson's been standing back there," I pointed to the back corner of the saloon, "with three of his associates. I can only assume they're up here to see if they can protect their friend."

When we looked back at Jackson, he was watching us. I knew he recognized me. Realizing we were talking about him he broke eye contact, lowered his head, and nudged the men next to him.

"Just one more thing to address, I see." The chairman thanked me and excused himself before returning to his chair.

Lafe, Frank and I moved back to our old spots, along the wall, as the chairman called the courtroom to order.

Looking at the committee, the chairman said, "Would the foreman please rise?" A man sitting in the front left seat, stood. "Has the jury made a judgement?"

"We have, Mr. Chairman." The foreman first announced which of the two men was innocent and declared that he should be set free. He then explained that the other man was guilty and should be tied to the stake, to be whipped by anyone who wished to do so. With emphasis, the foreman then said, "He should then be branded a thief and run out of the area."

Once the verdict was announced, the chairman announced to the gathering, "The guilty sentence will be carried out tomorrow." He then paused for a moment before adding, "I wish to have you know that . . . I have learned that the guilty men did not work alone. Others who may be in this room, with us now, also worked with them."

The chairman waited as people looked around the saloon and grumbled to one another.

"We will be looking into that," he emphasized. "In the meantime, if the guilty man's partners-in-crime find it appropriate to leave the area and never be seen again, that would be a wise choice."

I looked at the back corner of the saloon to see Jackson's reaction. He initially put his head down to avoid eye contact. Then thinking better of it, he looked around, like many others were doing.

While the chairman was bringing closure to the trial, four men in the back quietly slunk out.

After the trial was adjourned, Lafe, Frank and I followed the crowd out. Spotting Jackson and three of his men not far off, we kept them in our sights. Trying to look nonchalant, they picked up their pace as they made their way south.

Seeing that there was nothing further to be done, we watched as they went down the trail and faded from our view.

"Don't know that they learned a lesson," I said, "but I do know Jefferson Smith can't protect his associates up here. And, I can guarantee that someday it will all catch up to them."

That was the last we saw of Jackson and his men.

Chapter 57: Punishment

Sheep Camp, AK
February 12, 1898

WE WERE BUSY TAKING OUR SUPPLIES UP to the scales when the convicted thief's verdict was being carried out. What the locals had witnessed was the talk of the town. News here traveled fast. We had barely gotten back to the edge of town when we first heard about the lashing.

The thief was stripped to the waist, tied to a post and given seventeen lashes—the whip consisted of a new rope tied to a handle. After it was over, he was marched down the trail toward Dyea, led by guards who held a sign that read "A THIEF, SEND HIM ON."

The Colemans and I agreed that although we didn't care for vigilante justice, we felt a weight had been lifted from our shoulders. Concerns about Soapy and his gang hadn't yet been alleviated, but it was comforting to know that we were distancing ourselves from the corruption that greeted the miners in Skagway, and that the gang was being dealt with. The downfall of Soapy's gang was now inevitable. Through communication with Frank Reid, we knew that the committee he was part of would deal with that town's problems. Not only was there a group of men who were willing to stand-up to Jefferson Smith and his army of thieves and tricksters, but Jackson's men, who were acting outside of Skagway, were being dealt with as well.

I realized I could no longer fret over what I couldn't control. It was time for us to move on. Witnessing as much as we had, I was glad to see that at least there was some justice in the world. I'd seen enough lawlessness. Vigilante[25] justice wasn't much better than corrupt law. The people mean well, but are governed pretty much by emotions. I was still bothered greatly by those who retrieved the body of the suspect who had committed suicide and brought back to the saloon to be displayed.

With the disturbance now behind us, the citizens of Sheep Camp were able to return to their daily routines. For us, that meant we would continue to get as much of our supplies up to the scales as possible. The next eight days we made a dozen trips each, to bring four thousand pounds of supplies up to the scales. We'd hoped to move the other two-thousand pounds up there in the next few days.

I was looking forward to moving out of this place, and viewed each step north as one step closer to reaching our goal. We would put our full attention into the new challenges that lay ahead in Canada, exploring the Yukon and seeking gold.

While I knew it wouldn't be easy, I didn't know the next leg of the journey would bring more horrific events.

---

25 **Vigilante:** a member of a self-appointed group of citizens who undertake law enforcement in their community without legal authority, typically because the legal agencies are thought to be inadequate.

The Border Crossing

"Today we moved to the timber and have the most comfortable camp we have had during our Alaska rounds. Ours is a ten by twelve tent. The bed is spread in the back on about one foot of hemlock boughs. Frank put a puncheon floor in the front half. This eve we dug a hole in the snowdrift near the tent for the doghouse and covered it with a tarpaulin and boughs. The dogs have about as comfortable quarters as ourselves now. Last night we let them sleep in the tent with us it was so cold."

—Letter to mother, Mrs. W.M. Schooley, March 8, 1898

"The English flag floats on the summit now, meaning they will collect duty there. So many people are on the trail now that it looks like the main street of a crowded city. We remarked this while looking down from the summit. It was clear this morning and we could see a long way toward Dawson. A good day for sliding down the mountain."

—William Mace Schooley Diary, Monday, February 28, 1898

Chapter 58: Crossing the Border

The Summit, AK
March 18, 1898

UNFORTUNATELY, THE NEXT DAY, temperatures dropped to nine degrees below zero, and blizzard conditions made it impossible to travel beyond the tree line. All we could do was rest and read. Over the next few weeks, we tried to make a trip or two but got frustrated as the conditions got worse as we neared the summit.

We were able to stay busy by helping others move their goods at the lower elevations, where the weather was more manageable. At least that routine kept the dogs as well as ourselves active. We also found that getting paid to move supplies, instead of sitting around, made a lot of sense.

To prepare ourselves for the next jump, we loaded only the camping outfit we would need to set up camp at Lake Lindeman, nine and a half miles into Canada and headed for the border, despite the winds. To accommodate the dogs, Frank and I had used the longer "Peterson route" to get from the scales to the summit, in lieu of the steeper "Golden stairs." We both had left

Sheep Camp this morning, each with a sled, blankets and three dogs. Although it was a bit gloomy when we left, it was calm. But, by the time we'd arrived on the summit it was snowing with gale-force winds. Thankfully, the wind was at our back. Otherwise, we'd have been completely blinded by the flurries and would have had to turn back. We'd already faced frostbite and snow blindness a number of times over the last few weeks and learned that facing icy winds was dangerous. We'd also seen others become incapacitated from their experience. We loaded the camp outfit, stashed at the summit two months earlier, and proceeded to seek out the inspector's shack. We knew we were near but not sure if we were on the right track.

"OVER HERE!"

I could hear a man's voice bellowing, but I had difficulty seeing whoever it was. Visibility was about twenty feet at best.

"OVER TO YOUR RIGHT, BILL!" Frank yelled from behind me and gestured with his arm.

Following his gesture, I could barely make out a Union Jack[26] flag flapping in the wind, its blue colors waving in the blowing white snow. Behind that was a mound of snow that blocked the view of a structure—only a rooftop could be seen. Not far from the flag, I could see someone waving us over.

We descended down a pathway that led us to the buried structure. Down below the snow mound, we joined the Canadian officer. Once there, we found the pounding winds to be less prominent and could more easily hear the inspector.

"Welcome. I'm Inspector Belcher," he said.

As Frank pulled his team up next to mine, the man added, "Just the two of you?"

"There would normally be three of us, but his brother," I nodded toward Frank, "Is tending to our campsite at Sheep Camp."

"Where are you headed?"

"Dawson City," Frank exclaimed.

---

26 **Union Jack:** The Union Jack, or Union Flag, is the national flag of the United Kingdom. The flag also has official status in Canada.

The inspector smiled.

"But we're going to set up our next campsite at Lake Lindeman," I added.

"Alright. You know what you're required to have, right?"

"Yes. Two thousand pounds of provisions for each of us. Today, we're just bringing three hundred pounds of camping gear. Once we set up camp, we'll start bringing the rest over."

"Seems like a sound plan," The inspector took an invoice of what was on the sleds and after careful consideration, said, "That'll be ten dollars, for the outfit."

Incredulous, Frank and I looked at each other. Frank shrugged. Knowing we had no control over the situation, I paid the fee. I figured we'd talk about this later.

The inspector then started looking at the dogs.

Inspecting, or appreciating, I wondered.

Seeming to read my mind, Frank said, "We don't have to pay for our dogs do we?"

"No," the inspector laughed, "Just admiring your team. No duty on the dogs. Welcome to Canada."

Wasting no time, we sledded the dogs down the trail toward Lindeman. The trip down went fast, but the snow was so heavy that we couldn't see the mountains on either side. At one point, due to the snow drifts, we got lost and had to backtrack about a mile before we eventually found our way again. Later, after crossing some open spaces, we realized that we'd traveled over two frozen lakes—Long Lake and Deep Lake. The snow-covered flat lands and lakes all looked the same. Thankfully, Alford, a friend in Sheep Camp, provided directions that included key landmarks for us to follow. Eventually, they led us to his tent on the banks of Lake Lindeman, where Alford encouraged us to stay.

Once settled in, Frank said, "Can you believe the price he charged us for our outfit?"

"Ten dollars for three hundred pounds of goods, is exorbitant," I agreed. "At that rate, by the time we bring the rest of our goods, we'd be paying well over what it cost us to buy our three lots in Dyea."

That put us in quite a dilemma.

"Bill, our plan was to not just set up camp here but to store our good, too. Paying those prices isn't reasonable."

"I agree with you, and that bothers me, too. I can see them not wanting us to go into the wilderness unprepared, but it feels like we're paying for our goods twice. We'll just have to hold off going into Canada for now. It'll still be a while before the ice breaks free on the rivers and lakes anyway."

In the meantime, we've got plenty to do here, getting our campsite put together."

The next morning it was clear and warm, and we got a good view of the country. A wall of mountains were all around us. I could even see clearly in the direction we'd come from. Hooking up the dogs, we went across the lake to find firewood and logs, to better secure the base of the tent. After we'd shoveled away four feet of snow near the lake and set up our tent, we collected more boughs for us and the dogs to sleep on, and dug a house in the snow for the dogs. As we finished up, the weather got worse. It took a few more days before our lakeside campsite was fully ready to live in.

It wasn't until six days later that the weather allowed us to return to Sheep Camp. Once there, we picked up an encouraging rumor, the duty needed to cross the border into Canada might be lifted come April.

Just need to bide our time now, I thought.

Back at Sheep Camp, when Alford found out about our situation, he made a proposition, "I've got five tons of goods I could use some help in moving to Lindeman. Can you give me a hand?"

"I think that can be arranged," I said.

"Name your price."

I gave the going rate, and warned of our need to get reimbursed for paying the duty, which he accepted, and we were in business with a handshake. Shortly after that, other neighbors began asking for the same service. Not only were the dogs paying for themselves, we were staying engaged in something useful while biding our time.

For a while, everything was going well.

Then disaster struck.

In Mourning

"A disaster to be remembered occurred today. A number of people were camped at the foot of the scales in tents running lunch counters and working on the summit. Two or three small snow slides came down the mountain and buried up some of the tents and people in them. They were dug out alive. But things looked so dangerous that about forty took hold of a rope so as not go get lost and started for sheep Camp. They had come about one half mile when a big snow slide came down from the mountain side and buried all but two.

This was about twelve o'clock. Then the weather got better. The news spread to sheep camp and hundreds turned out to dig for them.

We started to the place and were passing Stone House when three dead bodies were dug out of their tent. A slide had come down during the night and buried them in their beds. Eleven dead bodies were taken from under the big slide, and five or six others who were brought to life. The dead, 14 in all, were brought to the morgue for identification. One woman is among the lot. A meeting was called tonight and an executive committee was appointed to take charge of the dead and to oversee the excavation, which will continue. Music has ceased in the dance halls and freighting will stop tomorrow. Sheep Camp is mourning."

—*W.M. Schooley Diary, Book 2, April 3, 1898*

Chapter 59: In Mourning

Sheep Camp, Alaska
April 3, 1898

UNTIL THIS DAY, WE'D SPENT OUR TIME, weather permitting, moving goods for other travelers, either from Sheep Camp to the summit or from the summit to Lindeman Lake. We'd acquired a number of friends along the way who not only admired the capabilities of our dog sled team, but with whom we had a number of things in common—common goals as well as common backgrounds.

With many, we quickly became friends similar to what we had with Dutch and the boys in Sunrise. We found them to be trustworthy, and helpful, sharing tents when needed during our travels. Having shelter available when stuck along the trail due to bad weather was always a blessing. I found that connecting with these folks renewed my faith in my fellow man, contrary to the type of people we'd encountered in Skagway. Not until this day would I understand how much these folks were willing to pull together.

Throughout the night, until noon the next day, we waited out the weather in our tent. This was the heaviest snowfall of the winter—over two feet deep. We hadn't been up long when we heard a lot of yelling outside. At first, a number of voices echo across the landscape. Then one voice stood out from the others.

"LAFE, FRANK, BILL. WE NEED EVERYBODY WE CAN GET." It sounded like Alford.

Lafe stuck his head out first. "What's going on."

"Avalanche. Bring whatever shovels you've got. We got some folks buried under the snow."

"Where?"

"Up the slopes, near the scales."

As quickly as we could, we dressed, grabbed our gear and headed up. As we passed Stone House, just below the scales, we came upon another, smaller slide that had just occurred. We caught a glimpse just after we heard rumblings but didn't know where the people were who were affected by the avalanche. A man nearer to the slide yelled to us. Motioning to where the avalanche had hit a tent, the man pointed to a couple of areas where we should start digging. About a dozen of us immediately lined up abreast of each other, faced the center of where the tent was considered to be and began digging.

After about a half hour of shoveling I looked up out of our trench and saw that a number of men gathered around us. They were ready to help as soon as anyone asked and carefully stayed back from where people could be buried. It was backbreaking work, but nobody complained and nobody wanted to quit digging as they worked alongside the family and friends of the lost. Another hour went by when someone yelled.

"I'VE FOUND A TENT POLE." Hearing this, our line of diggers converged closer together, and started working closer to where the tent might be. Some of the men watching from above were able to join our outer ring of diggers. Once we found the tent flaps, all the effort went into lifting the tarp and locating those inside. After almost another forty-five minutes of burrowing had passed before we'd uncovered three bodies. Seeing that there was nothing else we could do here, we moved up the trail to see if we could help in other areas. As we traversed through the scales and up to the Golden Stairs, we found that a series of disasters had struck.

Initially, a number of people at the foot of the scales as well as some who were working on the summit, were buried after being hit by some small snow slides. Those enveloped by the smaller slides were dug out alive, but things looked so dangerous that about forty took hold of a rope so as not to get lost and started down the slopes toward Sheep Camp. They made it about a half-mile down the slope when a slide buried most everyone on that rope. That's when the cries for help traveled throughout Sheep Camp.

As word spread later, music ceased in the dance halls and the movement of goods below the summit came to a standstill.

All of Sheep Camp was in mourning.

By the end of the day, eleven bodies were recovered from the large slide, and five or six others survived after being dug out. Of those who died, one was a woman.

It wasn't until late in the evening when it was announced that rescue efforts were no longer feasible. At that point, a meeting was called, and a committee was appointed to take charge of the dead and oversee the excavation that would continue in the morning.

Chapter 60: Putting It All Behind

A Week Following the Avalanche
Lindeman Lake, Canada

FOLLOWING THAT TRAGIC DAY, other than the mammoth undertaking of those still excavating, the southern hillside was vacant of freighting activities. Frank took his turn watching over our campsite for the next few days, while Lafe and I went to check on the conditions elsewhere.

With all of the snow that had fallen, we first needed to check on our supplies at the summit. We got an early start and saw that the excavation crews were just starting to arrive as we passed by the scales.

"Evidently, there's still a number of people unaccounted for, Lafe."

"Not to mention all the supplies that may never be found until the spring thaw," Lafe added.

Without much that could be said about those still missing, we continued on, to the summit and eventually found our cache.

"This pile here should be our stuff," Lafe gestured to the snow-capped mound.

Looking at the snow drift that had covered much of our stash, I said, "It could have been worse. If we'd done what many others had done, we'd be spending at least a couple of days searching under the snow. Hard to believe that what we're seeing is still on the high point of a rock. We'll need to do some digging but that's a great deal less than what many others have to do."

"Since we can't do much about bringing more supplies up here from Sheep Camp, at least we can take whatever we can from here to Lindeman Lake. We should at least take advantage of the favorable weather we have now."

Taking our first load to the border, we found that the duty hadn't been lifted, but at least the fee was lower, almost half the price for this day's load. The inspector seems more accommodating, too. More than likely due to the tragedy that affected all of us.

We made decent time getting our load to Lindeman. As we passed through the scales, on our way to Sheep Camp, we talked with a couple of the men who were part of the recovery effort.

"Can you tell us how things are going up here?" I asked, after coming upon a team of men taking a break from digging.

"Over the last few days, we've uncovered twenty-one more bodies," one of the men said.

Another man with the group offered, "Those victims were all tramway company workers who were returning from work when the slide covered them."

My mind flashed back to my previous days' experience.

I shuddered at the thought that it could have been any one of us. I also thought about the victims and their families, those who had yet to be found, and what they'd already sacrificed just getting this far. Even the buried outfits might never be recovered or at least claimed. The loss was too profound to think about.

As tired as I was, after our trek over the pass to Lindeman Lake and back to Sheep Camp, I did have a few hours of fitful sleep. The next morning, Lafe and I made a trip to Dyea to check on the sale of our other lot. Planning on staying two nights in Dyea's

Lindeman Hotel, the first day there we walked around a town that was now dead. Most who had occupied it had moved north, up the Chilkoot Trail. We quickly grasped why our lot hadn't sold. The best we could do now was leave it in the hands of the real-estate dealer. After two nights in Dyea, we found no need to stay longer.

Leaving for Sheep Camp, we refocused our energy on getting the rest of our goods to Lake Lindeman. Anxious to put the tragedy behind us, Lafe, Frank and I hastened our move to the summit.

Keeping ourselves tightly wrapped in our parkas and taking advantage of the wind at our back, we found conditions manageable. However, at times, when the conditions were not safe outside, we found it more comforting to play whist and cribbage with our Lindeman friends rather than fighting the elements of the outdoors.

A week later, however, our desire to get our goods off the summit drove us to move them regardless of weather conditions.

Chapter 61: Danger on the Slopes

April 12, 1898
Chilkoot Pass, Alaska

LAFE, FRANK AND I AROSE AT 2:45 a.m. The snow was falling, but the winds were calm. Thinking we were getting an early enough start to beat the crowds, we were surprised to see about two hundred hikers ahead of us on the trail. Evidently, others thought it a good idea to rise early, too. Considering the time it took us to follow the crowd and climb to the summit, we quickly changed plans. Instead of taking our goods to Lindeman, on a long, busy trail, we would go to Crater Lake instead. It was a shorter distance and, although we'd have to move our supplies twice before arriving at Lindeman, at least we could get everything off the crowded, stormy summit more quickly.

As our determination to get the job done increased, so too, did the winds. By the time we finished loading for our last trip of the day, the weather had become concerning.

"The winds are strong, but I think we can do this," Lafe said.

Frank and I both agreed, knowing this last trip would complete what we set out to do this day. But, by the time we secured our loads and started down the hill, the high winds had turned into a blizzard.

"We're committed now," I said.

"Thankfully, we don't have far to go," Frank added.

Regrettably, we didn't get much further before the snow became overwhelming. I was blinded to the point that I could not to see the ruts made by my sled. Leading the others with my seven-hundred-pound load, I tried to push on.

Struggling, I made it another half-mile or so when the sled bottomed out.

It was all I could do to turn the sled in such a way as to blocked the wind so I could view how my partners were faring. When they pulled up near me, I could see they too were also struggling.

I hollered, "DON'T THINK WE CAN RIDE THIS ONE OUT." I checked my watch and added, "IT'S ALREADY FIVE O'CLOCK."

"I THINK IT'S BEST IF WE TURN THE SLEDS ON THEIR SIDES," Lafe said.

"WHY DO THAT?" Frank asked.

"WE DON'T WANT TO MAKE IT TOO EASY FOR THE SLEDS TO RIDE DOWN THE HILL WITH AN AVALANCHE," his brother responded.

Working together, we pushed the sleds over and unhook the dogs.

Taking notice of some key outlying features, we took our bearings before trudging down toward Lindeman.

Halfway down the hill, I heard a rumbling and saw a rush of snow coming our way.

"SLIDE!" I needlessly yelled, as we all instinctively ran while the snow crossed between us. The dogs stayed with us.

Coming upon three other men, I yelled again just as another small slide caused the three of us to stumble and fall. We quickly recovered and continued on.

Reaching the foot of the hill, we turned another three men back after quickly explaining the situation, and our group of nine continued toward Lindeman. Using the numerous caches along the Lindeman shore as landmarks, we were led to a tent that belonged to one of the men we'd just turned back. As soaked as we were, we were invited inside. The lunch-house was cold and damp with a snow floor. A cookstove stood in one corner and blankets were spread on boughs. There were only three sticks of wood available to provide heat and the tent felt as if it was ready to blow away. But, at least we weren't fighting the storm. A few of the men rolled up in blankets. Still freezing, the rest of us gathered around the stove. I was unable to feed the dogs, but without a protest they gathered together under a counter.

Trying to sleep that night wasn't easy. By five in the morning, the wood was all gone, at least until the cook took the blocks that the stove was resting on and chopped them up. Those pieces provided enough fire until noon. Despite our wet clothes, Lafe, Frank and I slept until the fire went out.

By that time, the storm had calmed enough for us to venture out. As miserable as conditions were, we were all thankful for our stay in the tent and paid the dollar fee for spending the night. Putting down some bread and coffee before heading out, we didn't get back to our campsite until late in the day.

That evening, we got the stove lit, ate a decent meal, got clean dry clothes on and wrapped ourselves up before getting a good night's sleep.

The next day we spent our time patching and drying our clothes. Feeling uneasy about the loads being left on the hillside, we discussed whether or not we should wait for the snow to stop before going after them. We'd already witnessed too many outfits lost from the slides on the southside of the summit. During our discussion, I took a peek outside then said, "It's showing no sign of letting up. But, I think it's best that we get them as soon as we can."

"Otherwise we may never find them again," Lafe added.

"It's another early start, then?" Frank said. Both Lafe and I agreed.

Rising the next morning at 1:45, we set out immediately, even though the snow hadn't let up. At least we were able to find our way. It was a good thing we had all looked closely at the surrounding area before abandoning the sleds. Once we agreed on the right location, we were able to determine that the three uniform humps we were looking at were what we were after. We then started digging. Even after digging them out it wasn't easy getting them upright and hooked up to the dogs. We didn't get back to our Lindeman camp until two o'clock in the afternoon.

It wasn't until a week later that we were able to bring the rest of our goods from Crater Lake to Lindeman. The breaks in the weather allowed infrequent trips to the summit and Crater Lake. Between trips we either rested, read, played whist or cribbage to pass the time.

When the final trip was completed, we celebrated by taking a bath and washing our clothes. It felt good knowing we would no longer need to fight the steep terrain.

Our next challenge was to make our last move to Lake Bennett, before the thaw.

Chapter 62: The Wedding

Nevada, Missouri
Saturday, April 16, 1898

"YOU SEEM TO BE ENJOYING YOUR punishment."

Stanley smiled at that, "I've got to tell you, Sam. I didn't expect this."

"What? A spring wedding?"

"No. Me being a part of this . . . helping to decorate, and even being invited," Stanley answered.

"You've worked hard around here . . . and even seem to enjoy the hard work." Sam thought for a moment. "It's been two months now, since your court order. You've been to our home every day that you were required, always on time and often earlier than expected. You haven't complained once while cleaning out the stalls, helping to repair the damages to the house or putting out hay for the livestock. The repair work on the house looks great. Even better than before."

"I learned a great deal about carpentry," Stanley admitted.

"That's good to hear. I even heard your dad say, you've been working harder around your farm, as well."

"I have to admit, I've never felt more appreciated . . . I even feel a change in how my father treats me . . . a higher regard."

"I understand your father's always been strict."

"Yeah. That's just him."

"Other than the circumstances that got you . . . in trouble, I think we've all been able to appreciate what kind of a man you actually are."

John approached his brother, looked at Stanley, and said, "You might want to take your seats now. It'll be starting shortly."

"Will do," Stanley said.

"I'd best be getting back to helping get folks seated," John said, before walking to the back of the church. The twins were in their Sunday best, as was their father, who would shortly be walking his daughter down the aisle. Their mother was already seated in the front row.

On this day, Eva Schooley would marry Ted Bohannon. The Nevada city church, was decorated with flowers, and it seemed like half the town was there. Many brought potluck dishes for the wedding reception following the ceremony.

Waiting for the organ to declare the start of the processions, Eva stood with her father, in the back of the church.

"So my little girl is getting married," he smiled forlornly.

A tear trickled down Eva's face as she reached out and hooked her arm into his. "I only wish Bill could be here with us," she said.

"I'm sure he's thinking about you, too," he said.

"All I can hope is that he's safe and enjoying his adventure."

"We all hope that," her father said.

Chapter 63: Two Camps

April 20, 1898
Lake Bennett, Canada

WHEN WE STARTED MOVING OUR GOODS to Lake Bennett, we quickly discovered that the conditions in the valley were far more pleasant than what we'd experienced on the summit and Lindeman Lake.

The mountains protected us from the winds, and the temperatures were warmer. These travel conditions allowed Lafe, Frank and I to discard our parkas and take advantage of the longer daylight hours.

I was tired even before this day began, so it was nice to find that being on flat land made it easy to move even our heaviest loads. The frozen lakes allowed us to make the fourteen-mile trip without difficulty. But making more than one trip each day was wearing on all of us.

Exhausted, we brought our last load of the day to Lake Bennett late in the evening. It was all we could do to set up our two stoves on a gravel bar and spread our beds under a fir tree before feeding the dogs and turning in for the night. The dogs needed the rest more than we did.

We waited till the morning breakfast to discuss the day's activities.

I sat on a log with not enough energy to do anything but stare off toward the hillside.

"I know we should be getting started on our boat right away, but I'm still feeling pretty worn out," I said.

"Yeah. Me too," Frank responded. "I know there's a lumber mill nearby. I heard some other men talking about it. Maybe we should just have one of them cut the boards for us."

Lafe said, "I've also been listening to other travelers. From what I've heard it's very costly to get lumber from the commercial sawmills.[27] Since we've got the skills, we should just mill our own. Especially since we've got plenty of time before the lake is free of ice."

"Even as tired as I am right now, I agree," I said. "More than likely it will be at least a month before the ice breaks up. What do you think, Frank?"

"I suppose it's better to be involved in building the boat than just sitting around, watching the ice melt," Frank responded. "Now we just need to find the right trees."

Scanning the hillside, I noticed where most of the tents were located and what wooded area seemed most suitable. "Right over there," I pointed. "That seems like the closest area to us that still has trees worth working with."

"Not real convenient," Frank responded.

"Maybe not, but I don't see anything closer where we can find the timbers we need," I replied. "We'll more than likely have to set up camp over there."

"What? Have two campsites?" Frank said.

"Why not?" We keep our supplies here by the lake and bring the lumber here when we need to put everything together."

"We only have our camp there long enough to get what we need. It's better than traveling over there every day and coming back here

---

27 **Sawmills:** While there were commercial sawmills operating near both Lindeman and Bennett, the cost of milled lumber was beyond the means of most. The majority were forced to resort to milling their own lumber by hand. Chilkoot Trail National Historic Site—Boat Building.

in the evening. We'll get a lot more done if we just stay over there," Lafe offered. "We can set up a saw pit at both locations. Once we cut the logs to a reasonable size we can sled the lumber back here."

"I like it," Frank said.

"Alright," Lafe said. "Let's set up camp here first, then we can go over and see what the hillside has to offer."

We found a spot where we could cut and store the logs we'd be harvesting before moving them to the assembly area. Lafe and I prepared the campsite while Frank retrieved our tent from the Lake Bennett site.

It wasn't until the next morning that I finished making a saw pit by the timbers and at our lakeside camp before feeling too weary to continue. Too many long days of strenuous work had taken a toll on me. I spent the rest of the day in bed. While I was recovering, Frank and Lafe made runs to Lindeman, to bring more of our supplies.

Feeling worse the next couple of days, I completed less-demanding chores while the brothers brought more loads from Lindeman. I filed the whip and crosscut saws, made bread, cooked some potatoes, pears, and set some yeast. When I finally felt better, I was pleased to hear from Frank and Lafe that the last few days had provided ideal conditions for sledding. But, as the temperature warmed up, the lake became too slushy to travel on safely.

That was just as well since, as promised, I sold two of our dogs to Brinson, a man whose supplies we helped move. He would be picking up and paying for the rest of the team before our departure on the scow.

As I started feeling better, the three of us spent the next few days cutting a series of logs that we stockpiled on the hillside until we had a chance to transfer them to the lakeside camp.

With the woods already clear of snow, we knew it wouldn't be long before the open areas would be losing the snow as well. That's when we started sledding our logs to our waterfront camp. It didn't take long to get the lumber and camping outfits from both camp-sites consolidated at the lakeside location.

Shortly after that, Brinson retrieved the other dogs.

We were ready to shape the logs into beams and whipsaw the timbers into planks[28] using the sawpit[29] I'd created at the Bennett site. Working in unison the three of us slowly started laying out the pieces.

---

28 **Whipsaw planks:** For the inexperienced, the physical demands of the job, combined with the inherent difficulty of keeping the saw straight enough to produce a usable plank – plank, after plank, after plank—proved more of a frustration than the hardships of the trail. Klondike Gold Rush journals are liberally laced with accounts of partnerships forged on the trail, dissolving in the sawpits of Lindeman and Bennett. Nonetheless by the spring of 1898 a makeshift armada had assembled on the shores of Lindeman and Bennett Lakes, impatiently waiting for the ice to go out. Chilkoot Trail National Historic Site—Boat Building.

29 **Sawpit:** This involved laying a log on a scaffold and then sawing the log lengthwise using a whipsaw. It was a two man operation. One man would stand atop the scaffolding straddling the log, while the other would work underneath. The man on top would pull the saw on each upward stroke and guide the saw on the downward cutting stroke. It was both a physically demanding and exacting job. The man on the bottom meanwhile would provide the power for the downward cutting stroke, an equally exhausting job. Chilkoot Trail National Historic Site—Boat Building.

The Launch

"This forenoon it was snowing and disagreeable so we did not work. It moderated some this evening so we finished pitching the boat and turned her over right-side up. We built it up-side-down on a frame. It is sixteen feet long on the bottom, and twenty six feet long on top, with a six foot beam. It will weigh about 1500 pounds and we are all pleased with the job."

—*William Mace Schooley Diary, Friday, May 20, 1898*

"We braced the scow, and neighbors helped us to launch her. It leaks very little, and that through knots. The wind is blowing pretty hard and she is on a lee shore but I guess we will be all right. We did not work this afternoon. The ice is all gone now to a mile below here."

—*William Mace Schooley Diary, Sunday, May 22, 1898*

Chapter 64: The Launch

May 22, 1898
Lake Bennett, Canada

IT WASN'T MORE THAN A WEEK EARLIER that we awoke to cries of excitement. Word had traveled from the north end of the lake. The ice there was starting to give way in places that allowed boats to be launched. The ice that had become too dangerous to sled or even walk on was starting to give way. There were still chunks of ice that were large and dangerous if they hit a boat, but the possibilities of launching soon were real.

The excitement was palpable.

As I finished my lunch and waited for our neighbors to join us, the reality of actually making it to Dawson City was on my mind.

It wouldn't be long now.

"HEAVE . . . HO . . . HEAVE . . . HO . . . HEAVE . . . HO!," In unison, the men droned rhythmically. The fifteen-hundred-pound scow slowly made its way to the water. The dozen or so neighbors who helped launch it all clamored along the shoreline as the boat finally floated free.

"NOW, THAT'S WORTH CELEBRATING," one of them yelled.

Everyone cheered.

"Looks sturdy enough," another commented.

Hopefully strong enough to get us to Dawson City," Frank said, while tethering one of the lines to a nearby stump.

"Timing's good, with the ice breaking up and all," this, from another neighbor.

"Feel good about that, too," Lafe said, then added, "Took some time to get to this point."

"I know exactly what you mean, Lafe," Alford said.

Securing my line to a tree and having just heard Alford's voice, I turned around to see him standing not far from me. Behind him, were three other friends who Frank, Lafe and I had gotten to know since setting up at Sheep Camp. Over the last few months, we'd either helped to move some of their supplies, allowed them to borrow some of our dogs or just worked together as friends do.

"Alford, Thanks for the help," I said. Turning my attention to those standing behind him, I added, "You too, Eakin, Brinson, Ellis."

"A lot easier when we work together," Alford said.

"So true," I said. "We learned a lot working beside you while you built your boat."

"Time to get back to work now. See you later."

I waved to the men as they turned to leave.

As they left, I recalled our talk earlier, concerns about the spring thaw and all that we set out to accomplish. We got all our supplies to Lake Bennett while we could still travel over the frozen lakes. And, we aimed to get the boat built by the time the rivers and lakes were free from ice. We didn't want anything to impede our progress in staking a claim near Dawson City.

"We're looking into getting a boat soon, too. How long did it take you to build yours?" I looked to see a new arrival, who assisted in the launch. "I mean, from the time you arrived to today," he added.

"Let's see," I began. "We sledded from Lindeman to this spot on April 21st. It took us two days to get both this campsite and the one closer to the hillside timbers set up."

"Did you start cutting logs right away?"

"Close to it. I had the deck planks cut by the end of April. That was after I made a whipsaw^{30} pit at our hillside campsite as well as here. I cut the logs near the timbers before sledding them down here. Then, we cut the planks for the deck here. I finished making the deck planks about the same time they finished moving our supplies from Lindeman. The three of us worked together on the rest."

Seeing the conditions of the ground, he asked, "Did you have any difficulty sledding, here?"

"We called it pretty close," I said, "The snow was already gone from the woods when we sledded the logs here. Another day or two later, it would have been a problem, especially considering the weight of the logs on the little snow we had left."

"So, my timing's not that good in regard to what I'll need to do to get the timbers on the shore then?"

"Could be some folks around here could give you a hand with that," I said. "It's not cheap, but you can always find a local sawmill."

"I'll keep that in mind. How about the ice on the lake?"

"As you can see there's still some out there, but none of its safe for sledding. Even the first two weeks into May, when the ice was two-feet thick, sledding on the lake wasn't safe. By that time we no longer needed to sled across the water, thankfully. That's when we'd heard three men had broken through the ice and drown about three miles up the lake from here."

"We heard that, too. I haven't seen your dogs around lately," he added.

"We sold them, and the sleds, to some friends," I replied.

"So, from the time you arrived here, the three of you got everything done in about a month?"

"That's about right. We got the framework completed and attached the bottom and ends in a week. After we flipped the scow

30 **Whipsaw:** a saw with a narrow blade and a at both ends, used typically by two people.

right-side-up, It took another week to caulk and pitch it, make an oar and put gunwales on it. I still have a few things I need to complete before it's ready to sail, though."

"Wow. That's a lot when you consider its size."

"Well, it's got to hold the three of us and six tons of supplies. So yes, we'll need all that," I then added, "The bottom's ten feet shorter, but provides a stable base."

"That's a lot to get done in a month. Will you be staying around awhile? Are you available to help us build our boat?" He quickly added, "We'll pay you of course."

"Sorry, right now, we're planning on leaving within a week's time, as soon as I make a mast, a canvas sail and another couple of oars."

"Well, thanks for the information," the man said as he walked away.

Building other boats . . . I'll have to keep that in mind for later. Gotta long ways to go. Just hope this one holds together, I thought.

Chapter 65: Joining the Flotilla

End of May, 1898
Between Bennett and Tagish, Yukon Territory

OUR MORNING BEGAN WITH A HARDY BREAKFAST before tearing down our camp and loading the scow. It wasn't until 10 a.m. that we finally pushed off from the shore of Bennett Lake. The winds were fair and the sky clear, making the day pleasant, but it didn't make moving the scow out into deeper waters any easier.

No different than any bulky barge, carrying a few tons of supplies and three men, it took a great deal of effort to move. More accurately, it was slow to respond to what we wanted it to do. Initially, it took a lot of effort to put the scow in motion with the three of us using our oars. Lafe started as the tiller, using his oar at the aft end to steer, while Frank and I rowed from the sides. The three of us worked together to manipulate the boat as we drifted along with the current. When the wind was favorable, we used the sail to assist.

Leaving the shores of Bennett Lake was exciting and significant. It marked the next phase of our journey. We were now getting deeper into the Yukon Territory, and the rest of our trip would be by water. That in itself would be quite an adjustment.

As we worked our way along the waterway—a series of connected lakes and rivers—a number of other boats joined us along the way. All of us following the currents to the north. It took us six hours to travel almost sixteen miles. Soon, we started to seek out a favorable place to tie up along the shore but quickly found that finding a good anchor point would not be easy.

After spending our first night on the beach, we hiked further down the waterway and chanced upon several of our Sunrise friends. From them, we discovered that the vessels were all clustered here because ice had gathered and clogged the mouth of the Tagish River. Apparently fifteen boats had been smashed on the ice in the river. It was speculated that we might not be able to pass through for another week.

We decided to return to our boat and seek out a site where we could be more comfortable in our tent.

As we rounded the corner an amazing and discouraging site came into view. There were hundreds of boats of all types and just as many camps spread along the shore. Pushing on, we found the next three potential sites, Nares Lake, Wendy Arm and Tagish Lake were just as crowded. The few areas that were available were either covered with ice, too close to rapids, or in an open area that was exposed to the high winds.

It took a while, but we finally found a spot where we could tie up and pitch the tent at Windy Arm along with several hundred other boats that settled on its smooth waters. Here, at least, we were able to sleep through the night instead of having to constantly push big chunks of ice away from the scow. We'd learned earlier that some sites were open to wind gusts that caused swells that would break up the ice and caused havoc on the boats, not to mention our sleep.

Frank and Lafe set up the tent while I baked some bread. We then visited with neighbors who told us of an area nearby that was covered with wild onions. Borrowing our neighbor's boat, Lafe and

I found the onion patch, gathered a pail full and brought them back to camp. This night we found the onion stew quite a treat compared to our typical mundane rations.

The first day of June, we sailed across Windy Arm toward Tagish, but found that most everyone else was doing the same. It was quite a sight seeing so many boats, around a couple thousand, with mastheads displaying flags that represent many different nations. They were all headed, as we were, to a place where the boats were inspected and numbered. We arrived, to find a line of men a half-mile long.

Taking turns standing in line, Frank finally acquired a number—276—that allowed us to get out of line but still be in the same position in the morning.

It was the end of the next day that we paid our dollar for the inspection of our goods and boat before being granted a boat number[31]—12513. We immediately sailed down the river across Marsh Lake and reached the lower end about ten on the evening of June third. There, we were quick to find that regardless of the winds, the mosquitoes were plentiful.

While we put the dangers of ice behind us, we knew there were other challenges ahead of us.

---

31 **Boat number:** North West Mounted Police assigned a number to each boat, carefully recording the names of the passengers—in order to facilitate notification of next of kin. *Smithsonian National Postal Museum.* "As Precious as Gold."

The Rapids

"We are at the famous White Horse Rapids. In order to be on the safe side we camped about 1-1/2 miles above the canyon. After dinner we took a walk to the canyon and rapids. A wonderful sight it is! Most of the boats are shooting the rapids and with different results. Yesterday two men struck the rock at the head of the canyon and the boat was broken to pieces. Both of the men were lost. An hour ago three men were thrown into the waters but they were saved. It is very common to see a boat torn to pieces. This is the most exciting thing I ever witnessed. Pilots charge twenty or more dollars apiece to run a boat through and many are making $100 per day."

—*William Mace Schooley Diary, June 4, 1898*

Chapter 66: Smooth Sailing
and Rough Waters

June 4, 1898
White Horse Rapids, Yukon Territory

HAVING HEARD ABOUT THE PREVIOUS DAY'S tragic incident, we packed up our basic camp outfit and hiked the upper banks of the canyon to view the rapids below. Not more than a half mile into our walk Lafe pointed to the upper-most part of the canyon, "From what we heard, that's got to be where the two men drown yesterday after their boat busted up. See that whirlpool there? That's most likely what caused them to lose control."

"They probably didn't know it was even there until they were in it," Frank said.

"There's no way they could have survived after they fell into the drink," Lafe then pointed at the narrowest portion of the canyon. "Even if you're a good swimmer, the water moves too fast going through that narrow channel for anyone to survive. And there's plenty of rocks to navigate around, too."

"Now I see why the White Horse Rapids[32] are considered the most treacherous of the ones we'll be facing during this trip," I said.

Continuing on along the bank, we watched three men who were navigating a cluster of rocks. No sooner had they made it safely past the first one when their boat drifted broadside and collided with the next couple of rocks. It was all the men could do hang on to the wreckage as they floated away. Running to the edge of the canyon walls, we watched as the men drifted down the rapids. In the nick of time a scow just ahead of them, spotted the mishap, and positioned their boat to pull them aboard.

"THEY MADE IT," Frank yelled.

"Only because they stayed with the scow's wreckage," Lafe said. "Without the wreckage to keep them afloat, they wouldn't have stood a chance."

"We should be able to make it," Lafe said. "With the three of us and our sturdy scow, we can do this,"

I said, "I can see why some travelers are willing to pay to have an experienced guide take them through the canyon, but I'm not willing to pay $20 or $25, when we're just as capable of doing it ourselves."

"I understand some of the pilots make as much as $100 a day. Perhaps that's something we could do, if we found a need to stick around here for a while," Frank offered with a laugh.

His brother added, "Seems that at every turn throughout our travels there's always someone offering a service for a price. Just like those at the mill who offered to build our boat." Once again, all three of us agreed that we could do this on our own.

Hiking well beyond the rapids, we found a good place to set up camp. From this site we could still keep an eye on the boats coming through the canyon. While setting up and during our evening

---

32 **Yukon Rapids:** With the thaw in May 1898, about 7,000 boats of all types began the 500-mile Yukon River journey from the lakes to Dawson. This journey took about three weeks, but it was not an easy ride. Wild rapids tested stampeders. The worst were Miles Canyon, White Horse, Five Fingers and the Rink. Stampeders lost boats and outfits, and some drowned, but most arrived safely in Dawson by the summer of 1898. *University of Washington Libraries.* Riding the River Exhibit: Klondike Gold Rush - The Perilous Journey North.

meal, we watched a series of boats exit the canyon. From what we'd seen and heard, while many were successful in running them, some were not. A few were torn apart by the rocks, and a few were fatal. We were all anxious and excited to take on the challenge.

Once camp was set, we gathered moss for under our beds. While spreading it, Alford, Eakin and Ellis arrived. They'd offered to help us run the rapids. Not knowing how much progress we could make, the six of us went to the scow and ran her to the head of the canyon. By the time we got to that point, we decided not to run the rapids since it was so late in the day. Instead, we planned to get up early the next morning, to beat the rush of other boats that were expected to be there as well.

Getting up at four in the morning, Alford and his two friends ran their scow through the rapids first. While they were gone, another group proposed putting some of their stuff into our scow and then help us with the run. Accepting their offer, two of them took the oar in the bow, another took the oar in the stern, and Frank, Lafe and I rowed. The six of us got through in good shape, taking on very little water. The ride was exhilarating. Something I wouldn't have missed for anything. We all felt the same.

Once we were done, Frank helped Henry's group run their smaller boat through. During this whole process we saw more wrecks between the rapids and our campsite, three miles below start of the rapids.

It was a few days later, that we experienced a calamity of our own. Where the river made a short turn, we came upon some unexpected rapids. While traversing across the rapids, we spotted a large barge grounded on a sandbar. It became immediately obvious how they got there for the current swept us broadside and pushed us toward the sandbar and the barge.

Pulling hard on our oars, Lafe and I redirected our scow but not in time to miss the barge that was prominently positioned ahead of us. Glancing off the large structure while making the turn, we successfully regained control and continued to ride the rough waves downstream. Pulling away from the barge I saw that it was twice our size and wasn't harmed at all, other than a stovepipe that had fallen off the barge onto our scow.

It wasn't until we floated on smoother waters that we were able to see results of our collision. Assessing our damage, we found a broken oar and hold pin. All considered, I think we got off easy, although we didn't know what to do with the stovepipe since we'd more than likely never see that vessel again. As we got to the end of the rapids, we discovered others had also experienced problems.

Passing a big scow, we saw four men trying to gather their goods that had flown off the boat after it hit a boulder. We could only watch as we passed by for it was all we could do to handle our own fifteen-hundred pound scow. Continuing on, we passed a number of other wrecks as well.

At the end of the run, we saw what had happened to the supplies lost in the turmoil. A group of Indians were gathering the spoils.

It was a bit more exciting than we'd expected, which contrasted with the smooth sailing that preceded this event. Between these unexpected rapids and those of White Horse, we'd made good time sailing down the river and halfway across Lake LeBarge, a distance of about thirty-five miles. The sail was up and the wind in our favor the whole way. Following a night of sleeping on the scow we covered the remaining fifteen miles of Lake LeBarge plus another twenty-five miles to Hootalinqua.

We learned that after a period of clear sailing, we still couldn't put our guard down. We had to be prepared for anything.

Following the unexpected rapids, we stopped for a couple of days to repair the damage to our boat. That's when we decided to take advantage of the stop. We erected a sawpit and cut lumber. Taking the time to do this allowed us to build a poling boat while in route to Dawson City. We figured we'd need it later to explore the smaller tributaries ahead. Once done, we lashed the boards to the side of the scow, readjusted our load and set up our tent. The purpose of the tent was to protect us from the pesky mosquitoes. They were such a big problem that we even kept our heads covered with cheese cloth when working outside.

Once all this was completed, we took the time to report in, as required, with the Northwest Mounted Police at Little Salmon River, before heading for Rink Rapids. The headwinds hindered our progress, but the next day we more than made up with winds blowing in our favor. We traveled about sixty miles, just a few miles short of Five Fingers, near Fort Selkirk, where we stayed the night. At least now we'd be able to get a good night's rest before running the next set of rapids.

Once we got close enough to hear the rapids, we stopped to make the same observations before making the run, similarly to what we did at the White Horse. Shortly after we arrived, we saw a man standing on a big rock in the middle of the river. His boat had broken apart on the rock he was standing on. The Mounted Police were in the process of getting a rope to him. As we watched, we could see that the water was as rough as White Horse Rapids, but the rocks were less dangerous.

Thanks to viewing the rapids beforehand, we were able to run them without incident.

Now that we were free of rough waters, and within reach of Dawson City, we could start searching for some good ground to stake a claim.

Dawson City or Bust

"We did nothing much but take in the town [Dawson]. I did a little cooking in the morning. Steamers May West and Alexandria are here. None have arrived from St. Michaels yet and old timers say they may not. The river is unusually low.

I went to the theater with Frank this evening."

—*William Mace Schooley Diary, Friday, June 17, 1898*

". . . we all made another trip up Forty Mile[33] and built a cabin on Chicken [creek]. Frank stayed there, and Lafe and I came down in the boat a month ago. But we have not been idle. Hearing of a strike on Wade Creek, we hastened there just in time to get some good ground. I, and everybody else, think that Wade is all right. we will try and find out for sure this winter."

—*Wm. M. Schooley, Letter to Mother, from Fort Cudahy, dated: October 25, 1898*

---

33 **Forty Mile:** (Seattle P.I., Monday, Aug. 22, 1898)—There was great excitement in Dawson over a reported strike of great richness on the north fork of Forty-Mile Creek. Over 500 people left Dawson for the new diggings on Aug. 2 and 3rd.

Chapter 67: Prospectors Converge

Latter part of June, 1898
Dawson City, Yukon Territory

UNFORTUNATELY, TOO MANY OTHERS ARE SEEKING the same thing we are.

After coming sixty miles, from Five Fingers Rapids to Fort Selkirk, we camped at the mouth of a little stream called Pearly Creek. On arrival, we found that all the good ground was no longer available throughout the creek area. So, we continued on to Stewart River, about sixty miles, where we saw hundreds of boats and many people building caches and smaller boats with the intention of going up this stream.

Once again, we continued on, to another small stream below Sixty Mile Post. There, we pulled to the bank and completed some needed repair work on our scow before continuing on to Dawson City. During that time, we were able to connect with others who'd explored the area. They too, had little luck finding good ground.

We were quickly discovering the best areas, along the rivers and streams, had already been claimed by the sourdoughs.[34] The newcomers had to settle for the margins of the creeks that were

34 **Sourdough:** an experienced prospector in the western US or Canada; an old-timer.

already staked. Some were fortunate to secure bench claims—land above the creeks, on the hillsides—which the sourdoughs deemed worthless.

Arriving at Dawson City, we found many prospectors. They too, were disgusted with what they'd found—the crowds, the lack of good ground,[35] the good claims were already staked. The Canadian government limited the size of the claims, charged import duties on miners' equipment, and levied a 10% royalty on the miners' earnings. While at Dawson, we met a number of old friends. Some had success in staking a claim, while others didn't. All seemed to be cursing the country, some were preparing to leave.

The next few days we did nothing more than explore and enjoy the town and speak with the locals who had been around for a while and knew the terrain. During this time Frank and I even went to the theater. While continuing to glean information about the territory, we also built a workbench, to plane boards for our boat. The going rate for buying a boat was about $300. It's nice to know we could always sell ours if we found no further use for it.

While working on the boat, the three of us decided how we might go about exploring the region. We finally concluded that splitting up would be the best approach. Frank was content to stay in Dawson, to watch over our scow and listen to other prospectors' comments as they pass through Dawson. Lafe and I, each with a companion, would explore the north and south Yukon waterways for a period of five weeks before rejoining Frank in Dawson City. We would then decide if either of us thought it was worth returning to a particular site.

Of the friends who we'd typically gather with in Dawson, Lafe paired up with a seasoned prospector friend of ours who had two horses. They planned to travel by land, south to the Stewart River region, while I headed north down river, with another friend, toward Alaska, using our pole boat.

35 **Lacked good ground:** "American miners realized that most of the good claims were already staked The Canadian government, moreover, limited the size of the claims, charged import duties on miners' equipment, and levied a 10% royalty on the miners' earnings." Gold in Alaska: A century of Mining History in Alaska's National Parks.

If something in the Yukon Territory looked exceedingly promising, we'd more than likely take a careful look at it, but considering
the ten percent that would go to the Canadian government, we felt
it more profitable if we spent most of our time in Alaska where
all the profits would be ours. Hence my desire to head toward the
border.

Lafe and I wished each other good fortune, literally, and went
our separate ways.

Chapter 68: Five Week Separation

July, 1898
Yukon River, Yukon Territory

SITTING ON A BOX OF SUPPLIES, I used my pole as a tiller as we drifted north down the Yukon River. My partner, Pettit, was sitting at the bow, ready to use his pole to redirect our boat if needed. With the rapids behind us, the river was much smoother for traveling.

"This is the most peaceful and scenic trip I've been able to enjoy for some time," I remarked.

"A lot better than trying to go up river," Pettit laughed. "Look there," he pointed. "There's the steamer Monarch heading for Dawson."

"Looks like it just left the town of Forty Mile," I said. "Seems the steamers are the only boats that can handle going up river. Otherwise many couldn't make the trip."

"I feel badly for those on board who have high expectations for when they reach Dawson City. The situation there hasn't gotten any better since we first arrived. If anything, it's gotten worse," Pettit said.

Seeing the first structure on the west side of the Yukon River I said, "I think that's the Northwest Mounted Police outpost where we need to check in. Doesn't look too busy right now. Might as well get that out of the way before we explore the town."

We tied our boat just outside the Mounties' building and went inside. With nobody ahead of us, and considering how we had a much smaller boat than I was used to, it didn't take long for the inspector to check our goods and complete the custom's inspection. During our discussion with the inspector, he asked a number of questions about our travels and where we were headed.

After telling him of our experience south of Dawson, how discouraged we'd become after traveling so far, he ask about our future plans. We informed him that we were hoping to prospect in Alaska. After learning that our plans included leaving Canada, he told us that although we would be out of country, we could still register our Alaska claims here, at the police station. That was helpful to know.

Once done, we left to walk around the town and talk with the locals.

We chatted with whoever we met. It was surprising to see what the place had to offer. The North American Transportation and Trading Company was well stocked with mining needs. There were a number of saloons, a library, billiard room, a couple of restaurants, a theater and an opera house. They even had a watchmaker and a number of distilleries.

In talking with many of the locals, we found that most of what we saw had been here for only a few years. Many businesses arrived after the first gold was found in the area, sometime after 1886. The boom towns seemed to come and go up here, one man had told us. Everywhere we went, we asked the same question, "Are there any places you'd recommend for prospecting for gold?" We then carefully considered what seemed most promising. Going up Forty Mile Creek, appeared the best option, although we'd also heard some of the business owners here had relocated to Dawson once word of gold that direction became public.

"We should head up Forty Mile River and find a spot to stay the night. That will give us an opportunity to get a feel for how much headway we can make going up river before we get some sleep," I said.

"Good idea," Pettit responded.

Less than a mile upriver, we spotted a couple of Mounties tying up their boat to another scow.

"Wonder what's going on there?" Pettit said.

"I saw that boat ahead of us just after they made the turn off the Yukon River. I'll bet they bypassed the customs outpost without reporting in."

Passing by more closely, we saw the Mounties carefully going through all the supplies the travelers had onboard.

"Interesting. The Mounties were hiding their boat under that canvas over there," I pointed at their hideaway. "Seems someone is keeping a sharp eye out for those trying to get a free pass on paying duty."

A few miles later, we found a good place to tie up and set up the tent for the night.

All I could think about was, *We've got five weeks to find good ground. We'd best move up river as quickly as we can.*

After a few days of moving west, Pettit and I arrived at a spot where Forty Mile split to a northern and southern tributary. Following the recommendations most mentioned in the town of Forty Mile, we took the south fork, and eventually reached a smaller creek that took us west once again. We were told that the creek was named Chicken, since the gold found there in 1886, was said to be the size of chicken feed.

Once there, we set out to find ground that was worth setting a claim on. Our interest was finding bench claims,[36] that met placer claim[37] specifications, similar to what we'd worked along the river banks in Dyea. We set up camp nearest the ground that seemed the

36 **Bench claim:** A placer claim located on a bench above the present level of a stream.
37 **Placer claim:** A mining claim located upon gravel or ground whose mineral contents are extracted using of water, by sluicing, hydraulicking, etc. a unit claim is 1,320 ft^2 (122.6 m^2) and contains 10 acres (4.1 ha).

most promising and explored the opposite sides of the creek where the ground was undisturbed.

For five weeks, we prospected as much as we could before reuniting with our friends back in Dawson City.

Upon our return, I found that Lafe had arrived the day before without finding anything promising. All he could say was, "Everywhere I went, all the good ground had already been taken." Frank, who'd been grilling any prospector who was willing to share their thoughts about prospecting, said he'd gotten similar responses.

Once I shared our success up north, we all agreed that Chicken Creek seemed the best bet. We all were especially pleased that we'd have a claim to work on in Alaska.

Chapter 69: Code of the North

Summer, 1898
Dawson to Forty Mile River, Alaska

WE SHARED OUR PLAN WITH OUR SUNRISE GROUP and some of our newer friends we'd met along the way. Since there was so much interest in joining us, we set up a meeting to discuss it further. It was natural to come together for a common purpose. Whether it was giving advice about prospecting, needing supplies, building a boat, sharing shelters and tools, or working on and sharing a claim together. We then passed the word about having a meeting so we could talk about what we needed to do prior to striking out to the north.

During our gathering, it was clear that everyone present was anxious to get away from Dawson's growing crowds, and were glad to hear we'd be well away from most of the throng of prospectors we'd already found along the southern and local tributaries. Most of what we discussed was about the best way to make the trip down the Yukon and up the smaller tributaries. While we no longer needed to pack the massive amount of supplies that we needed to get into Canada, we still had to consider how much we could manage on the boats and what supplies we could expect from local towns. While the steamer was a nice way to travel it didn't stray much from the Yukon River. We'd also be spending a good deal of time poling up Forty Mile River and possibly up a number of other smaller waterways.

Before leaving Dawson, we wanted to ensure we had the boats and supplies needed. Selling our scow was uppermost in my mind. Fortunately, it sold quickly. Knowing that the North American Transportation Trading Company at Forty Mile was well stocked allayed any concerns about our need to have all the supplies we needed after leaving Dawson. It was only a few days later that everyone was ready and able to get underway.

Arriving at Forty Mile, we checked in at the Mounty outpost, then headed upstream. As Pettit and I had already experienced, the heavy loads made it difficult to pole our boats in the shallow waters of Forty Mile River. After a long day of poling, we made it to Alaska.

Once it was clear we'd left the Yukon Territory and were well within the limits of Alaska, part of our group broke off to explore the earlier tributaries of Alaska's portion of Forty Mile River. We then had a group of eleven. Our original Sunrise group.[38]

One unstated understanding with all miners is that group ties can change at any time. If anyone in the group wants to go a different direction, that's always an option, but while we're together, we all pitch in and share whatever we can to get the job done— whether it be cooking, building a cabin, hunting for food or panning for gold.

Continuing on, we made our way up the south fork of the Forty Mile, eventually arriving at Chicken Creek. We all found a site to settle on and got busy splitting time between establishing and improving campsites, and working the claim. In our case, we

---

38 **Sunrise Group:** These names were listed as having traveled back to their claims together: L.D. Pettit, Jake Christensen, Arnold Dehous (Dutch), William Davis, W.A. Press, Orval Davison, Miller Thostesen, George Heely, Louis J. Korter, William Bunge. W.M. Schooley's Diary, Books 4, dtd: June 10 & 11, 1900. They arrived back at Wade Creek on June 13, 1900. W.M. Schooley's Diary, Book 5.

quickly got involved in building a cabin. We knew we'd be here for a good length of time. Working our claim became our top priority.

Going by the "Code of the North,"[39] everyone did his part to prepare a comfortable camp or get wood for the big campfire, after which we sat about, partaking of a hot dish prepared by the various members of the party. When we didn't work together, we still shared the tools that could be found at a common cache site nearby. Everyone was welcome to borrow from it as long as the item was returned in good shape. During this time, each of us ventured out and prospected various portions of our claim.

Once the cabin was completed, we switched all our efforts toward working the most promising test-pan areas. Throughout the rest of the summer, we continued working our claims.

At least, until we heard of a big strike on Wade Creek.

Lafe and I hastened there and immediately began prospecting while Frank stayed at Chicken. A few of the other Sunrise friends joined us after we staked out two claims along Wade Creek. Fortunately we were able to record our claim through a U.S. Commissioner who was stationed at Jack Wade Creek. That was helpful, especially considering that we'd otherwise have to travel as far as Forty Mile or Eagle to record them.

Soon others arrived. Many from Dawson, having gotten word shortly after we did. As more arrived, we also heard that a number of miners were diverted to the north fork of Forty Mile having heard of another strike there.

At Wade, we had great confidence in the ground, and it had proven itself to be better than our expectations.

So we worked through the winter, there.

---

39 **Code of the North:** MODERN MAN TO HUNTING BAND: A READAPTION. The Social Organization and Dynamics of the "Old Tiers" of the Yukon. 1882-1898. By Margaret Don Power, Simon Fraser University, 1974. Department of Sociology & Antrhopology.

EPILOGUE

"I am drifting with the current without any notion of whether smooth water or dangerous riffles are ahead. If next year closes me out of Alaska there is yet time for the second course; if not —well, it is a pity that things are so arranged in this life that one cannot always take up the work that he likes; then there would be few idlers and no pessimists, I think. The fight for a livelihood, for something to put down one's gut to crowd out hunger not only makes one selfish and mean, but even blinds him to the beauties of nature; in fact pinches to death all the finer nobler feelings."

—*W.M. Schooley's Diary, Book 5, September 19, 1900*

Chapter 70: Blessed Spring Thaw

The Gold Season of 1899
Chicken and Wade Creeks, Alaska

ONCE THE SNOW FELL AND TEMPERATURES DROPPED, we had to adapt. We'd pick ground that we hoped would be rich in gold and start digging a shaft. Due to the permafrost, we set fires in the ground we wanted to work and let them burn all night. By morning we'd be lucky to thaw a depth of about fourteen inches. This was done in a number of locations. Any gravel that we dug that potentially contained gold would be put aside, to be sluiced later. Since this process needed water, it wouldn't be possible to sluice until the spring thaw. The shafts we dug didn't need extra support because of the permafrost.

After a while, Wade became too cold. By the end of October the temperatures drove us back to Chicken Creek, where we still continued the winter-way of gold mining, but at least there we had the cabin.

Although life wasn't easy in these conditions we felt fortunate to be away from crowded towns, like Dawson. Through our local news boy, who would provide a wide selection of newspapers, we stayed apprised about what was going on elsewhere. Dawson's paper told of the town's problems with a typhoid outbreak, crowded conditions and poor sanitation. Many had died of influenza, tuberculosis and pneumonia as well.

That wasn't the only reason we appreciated spring arriving.

Once the rivers thawed, we began sluicing the gravel that was stockpiled from our winter work. After the stockpile was cleaned, we turned to summer prospecting, setting boxes for sluicing near our mining sites. This work continued through the warm months.

Our greatest success was on claim #13. It was doing so well we received a cash offer of thirty thousand dollars for it. Our confidence in the ground was high, and we didn't want to sell for that price. Instead, we had five to eight men working on it all summer—five on the day shift and three on the night. As they say, we were taking out "good money."

Our cleanups brought a great deal of success. Throughout the summer we cleaned out the sluice boxes about every third day. One of our best was worth around four hundred dollars. The largest nugget found was 11.4 oz., valued[40] at a little less than $20 per ounce.

Originally, I got involved in gold mining as a means to make it through difficult economic times. Once I found success and got "gold fever" I didn't think about stopping until I achieved success in Sunrise, Alaska. I was even ready to return home at that time. Then the real rush started.

Once the excitement got to Lafe, Frank and me, we got caught up, especially knowing we had an advantage over the others. We'd already proven we had the skills and experience. It was during this past year that I'd set my mind on getting enough money for an education that would set me up in a different, long-term profession. I figured that if I acquired at least one-thousand-dollars-worth[41] of gold, that would more than pay for a college education.

---

40 **Value**: a $400 cleanout in 1898 is worth $12,973.25 in 2021. $20 in 1898 is worth $648.66 in 2021.
41 **One-thousand worth of gold** in 1898 would be worth $32,734.46 in 2021.

Did I achieve my goal?

We had enough success to make me want to stay, which I did through the summer of 1899. But by October, I was ready to go home. I did not want to go through another freezing winter. The smoke in the pits following a night's burning had given me constant headaches and with the freezing temperatures diseases were rampart in the big towns. I missed my family, and wanted to share with them my plans for the future. While I'd originally considered both civil engineering and medicine, I finally narrowed my choice to medicine. I was ready to move on.

I left for Nevada, Missouri in October, 1899.

Chapter 71: Moving On

Seven Months Later, 1900

IT WAS HEARTWARMING, BEING WITH FAMILY AGAIN. Once hugs and greetings were behind us, everyone had plenty they wanted to talk about. Following our initial talks that primarily revolved around my life up north and gold mining, discussions moved to the ups and downs that the family had experienced in my absence.

The farm had survived without me. I learned of the issues they had endured as a result of the letter I sent from Seattle before I returned up north. My family had recovered from the house fire. And I had the opportunity to meet my sister's husband and welcome him to the family.

Eventually, hearing of my fondness for Seattle, they wanted to learn more about this booming city. We had many long discussions about how they had thought about *moving on,* and my desire to attend the University of Washington. Eventually, John came up with a proposal that we all showed an interest in.

By the end of my seven-month stay at home, John joined me on the trip back to Seattle. He and I spent enough time there to establish a residence, while I looked into requirements for attending school. Then it was time for me to continue north to join Lafe and Frank at our Alaska claims.

I was now looking forward to working the claim and only intended to stay long enough to sell my share.

Stopping by Skagway, on my way back to Alaska, I visited Jefferson "Soapy" Smith's grave and discovered that it was marked by a modest slab, with no explanation of his death.[42] I also heard that four of Smith's top lieutenants[43] were sent to prison. Later, I found out that Frank Reid had died during the shootout with Smith. I felt sad for his loss. I had dealt with him when we staked our claims and even bought a couple of lots through him. He'd also been part of the secret vigilante "Committee of 101," a self-appointed group of citizens who wanted to bring law and order back to the town.

After a four-hour ride from Skagway on the White Pass Railroad, I arrived at Bennett City. This trip was a great contrast from the first one over the Chilkoot Pass two years earlier. I recalled trudging over the pass in high winds and low temperatures, when I wasn't hunkered down in one off our various cache sites along the snowy mountains.

Although I had some reluctance about returning to Alaska, I knew it was necessary. At least my family would be taken care of in my absence. They were excited about moving to Seattle. Even Eva and Ted, now Mr. and Mrs. Bohannon, joined us.

---

42 **Death of Jefferson "Soapy" Smith:** on the evening of July 8, 1898, the vigilance committee organized a meeting on the Juneau Wharf. With a Winchester rifle draped over his shoulder, Smith began an argument with Frank H. Reid, one of four guards blocking his way to the wharf. A gunfight, known as the "Shootout on Juneau Wharf," began unexpectedly, and both men were fatally wounded. Smith was shot in the heart and died shortly afterwards, and Reid died of his injuries 12 days later.

43 **Smith's Lieutenants:** John L. "Reverend" Bowers, W. E. "Slim Jim" Foster, Van B. "Old Man" Triplett and W.H. ('Turner') "Professor" Jackson were shipped out to Juneau, then to Seattle and served prison sentences that ranged from one to ten years. The rest (26 who were rounded up) were put aboard the Steamship Tartar, bound for Seattle and points south, and advised, under pain of death, to never show their faces in Skagway again. HISTORYNET Soapy Smith: Con Man's Empire https://www.historynet.com/soapy-smith-con-mans-empire.htm McNeil Island Penitentiary records on microfilm at the National Archives.

Chapter 72: Train West

One Year Later, 1901
Nevada, Missouri

B LACK SMOKE BILLOWED FROM THE ENGINE'S smoke stack. "ALL ABOARD!"

William, Ann and Sam Schooley settled into their seats, feeling both anxious and excited about the future.

Soon the cars began to move—out of Nevada, away from home. Mrs. Schooley dabbed her eyes with a handkerchief as her husband and son stared out the window. Familiar people and buildings slid by, faster and faster.

Once they were well underway, Sam asked, "Pa, I know we'll have to switch trains in Kansas City, but what about after that?"

"If I remember correctly, we head north after we make a stop in Denver, then we'll change to another railroad line. I think we also change again near Salt Lake City. Not sure after that."

"How long will that take us?"

"Best ask the conductor," William said. "I understand that if it all goes smoothly, it'll take less than a week to get to Seattle."

"If Bill or John were here, they'd be able to tell us," Ann said.

"I wonder how they're doing now?" Sam wondered aloud.

"I'm sure he's busy mining his claims,[44] but I know he's excited about joining us in Seattle," his father responded. "And I'm sure John is staying in contact with the railroad to see when we arrive."

"How about the Colemans, Pa? They've been close with Bill for so long. I was hoping they might settle there, too."

"The last I heard from Bill, he said the south sea islands seem to be drawing them. They said something about running a sheep farm in the Philippines."

With a heavy sigh, William settled into his seat for the long ride west. "We all seem to be ready for a change."

---

44 **On June 3, 1901,** Bill left Wade Creek for the last time, after selling his share to Lafe for $525. That, plus what he'd brought in over the last couple of years, at the Wade and Chicken Creek claims, would pay for the next stage of his life. He received his degree at the University of Washington and opened a pharmacy in Seattle (across from the location of the Olympic Hotel) and later in West Seattle. He also studied law on his own and passed the bar exam. (from Gladys A. Schooley Brady's notes in W.M. Schooley's diary).

Mace Brady taught writing and history at the secondary level where he developed a strong desire to personalize history and bring it to life. The book, *Caught in the Rush*, shows the events that his grandfather encountered while prospecting in the north. Using his grandfather's diary—one of the most prominently quoted diaries of the Klondike goldrush—Brady tells a story that helps the reader grasp the prospector's adventure.

After serving in the US Army, Brady published his first book, *Supreme Truth* (found on Amazon.com) that was based on real events, terrorist attacks in Japan. Throughout his military career, Colonel Brady held multiple positions, such as battalion commander, commandant of US Army Reserve Forces schools and Washington state's emergency preparedness liaison officer.

His interest and skill in writing stems from teaching in Washington state's public schools as well as the 6th US Army Area Intelligence School. He is twice retired after 32 years teaching and 30 years in the army reserves. Mace and his wife reside in Seattle's greater metropolitan area.

www.ingramcontent.com/pod-product-compliance
Lightning Source LLC
Chambersburg PA
CBHW010525100726
47903CB00011B/2895